The Ghostwriters

The Ghostwriters

MJ Maloney

Goldsmiths
Press

Goldsmiths
UNIVERSITY OF LONDON

For Andrew

PART ONE

Susan

The day had begun with the familiar warm drizzle. The Capital was swathed in its shroud of greenery. Lush mosses padded the buildings and gooey lichens ate and etched their way into the Portland stone of the canyons of the metropolis. In amongst the rambling vines that wrapped and festooned the street-lamps and trees, flocks of colourful finches harassed one another as the dawn broke. The acid chemical colours of the lamps flickered and died as daylight crept across the city.

In her basement residence, Susan Jenkins, aka Blythe Bellingham, aka Winston Sayers, crunched her spine into life as she woke on her old mattress. A subterranean home had its advantages. The cooler temperatures of the nights that settled over the city lingered for a little while in her bolt-hole. The humidity and heat did not reach her until well into the morning. Susan hated to sweat, so she rose early as often as she could to set about her few chores before discomfort set in. She moved a little slower these days.

Susan trickled some water from the old tap into her kettle and put it on the two-ringed hob to wheeze into life. She carefully wrapped some dried and re-used tea leaves, a mixed blend, into a square of muslin, ready to steep for her morning brew. She hummed a little tune as she scraped an animal bone of undetermined species of its last residue and put the shreds and sinew on a saucer. She placed the little offering on the floor beside her kitchenette for Ellery, a young and bristly ginger cat. He immediately mewed and pounced on it.

"Patience, patience," she stroked his head as he greedily devoured the shreds. Ellery had spent the night in his usual spot, curled up at Susan's feet. She made her bed and spread the old crocheted blanket across the thin cotton coverlet. It was almost time to venture out. She was down to her last two tins, marrow fat peas and peach slices in syrup, and for flour and sugar she only had dust. Out of her shuttered window she checked the stairs up to the street. Warm drizzle hovered in the air and all seemed quiet at street level. As usual. The Capital's traffic was very sparse these days and everything was overwhelmed with leafy abundance, thanks to the 're-wilding' of former days.

Susan kitted herself out with her necessities for the day ahead. She petted Ellery and carried her wheely shopping trolley up the steps. Out of habit, she checked up and down the street. All clear. Always all clear. She set off through the quiet neighbourhood. Around here it was always stale and subdued, and she was grateful for that. She passed by the steps up to the entrance of Gunnar's 'Second-Hand Emporium,' aka a junk-shop, and she smiled. A rare smile. These days Susan had a permanent crease in the middle of her brows. Events constantly worried her.

The buildings around her had once been West London mansions that had formed a Square, from a time when the Capital was still known as London before the break-up of the United Kingdom. It had been a smart, proud place, a global centre for trade and economics. Now, there was nothing angular or regular about the neighbourhood. Neatness and grandeur were replaced with dilapidation and nature. Each house was divided into multiple dwellings where children tripped and played up staircases and along hallways. Lives spilled out into the cracked and rutted streets. At the centre of this relative haven, full of middles and lower-middles, was the Wilderness. This was a riot of growth – trees, vines, and lush budding bushes, spreading outwards from what had once been, and she recalled this from her girlhood, something more regimented and cropped. She recollected traversing a park along tarmac paths, now long smothered with decades of leaf-litter and foliage. She thought she had owned a little green bicycle once and had a memory of her grazed knees as she peddled in the sunshine.

Susan paused at the corner of the Square. This was the perimeter of her safe neighbourhood and she had to be careful from here. The morning was growing warmer, and the finches tweeted noisily above as they swooped in vast numbers around the tree-canopy of the Wilderness. Insects hummed in the air. The humidity would be hard again today. She mopped her brow and the back of her neck. November heat was so oppressive in the Capital, and she longed for what she remembered of the coast further South. There was once a time when England had seasons. Summer into autumn, winter into spring. November, she remembered her older family members reminiscing when she was a child, had crackled with bonfires and the whoosh of fireworks breaking into a dark sky, above pitched rooftops. Why had people celebrated with explosions and flames? She could not recall the reasons they gave if they had ever known, but she did have a dim memory of seeing her own breath in the darkness. A puff of fog escaped as you blew out. People could exhale air into billowing clouds of miniscule ice crystals as they cradled mugs of hot liquids. What kind of life had that been?

Susan was jerked back to reality as a milk-float hummed past, the only vehicle out and about in this part of the city. It forced her to take a step back as it swerved out of the Square. As it passed her the slogan on the side stood out in chipped and scratched paint on an enamel sign, 'Drinka Pinta Milka Day'.

"Some hope," Susan muttered to herself. She had to follow the float, with the milkman encased in his secure cage as he drove. It soon outran her, though, as it turned into the High Road. She trudged in the same direction; her trolley trundled in her wake.

Into the High Road and Susan prepared for the long walk to the transport Hub. She had her wad of ration tickets in her pocket and forty-eight hours to use them at a Ration Distribution Truck, an RDT. She had received them only one day before, and if she did not hurry, they would be out of date. This was the fear, panic, and anxiety that bound everyone, and that middles and lower-middles fought with. Tickets were dispensed but it was a hit-and-miss affair, a bit like a lottery. You received your tickets, but they were only redeemable at certain Hubs and those Hubs might not host RDTs for days, and by then the tickets could be out-of-date. This time, Susan felt lucky and secure. She had an opening, and her tickets were in date, she had time. She turned a corner at a bend in the High Road.

Before her lay the milk-float, slewed over on one side. The milkman struggled out of his little caged cab. He whipped out a cricket bat as he clambered free. Susan on impulse took a step back into a doorway, in preparation for what she knew was to come. A little milk lake from shattered bottles had started to spread across the road. Next, Susan heard the noise. The jingle and clatter of spilled crates from the vehicle had awoken something in the High Road. Windows slid up, doors rattled open, and shouts arose. People spilled out from the tall buildings and shop fronts on either side of the wide thoroughfare.

"Bring a container, grab that bucket!" A hollow-eyed man shouted to his bare-footed son.

Individuals and groups started to circle the crashed vehicle. The milkman had to swipe at the air with the cricket bat, "Keep back, keep away!"

A woman darted out of the circling crowd and raced to the rear of the milk-float; she slopped in the growing puddles and made a grab for an intact bottle. She cut her fingers in the process as she reached through the broken glass. Another person, and another, followed. A child ripped at some carrots and tugged and tore at a loaf from the hopper that held the groceries.

Susan watched as the people grew bolder and started to swarm about, staying just out of range of the milkman's swinging bat.

"Keep off, keep off! Get the *fuck* away!" He grew increasingly desperate, but his efforts were more and more in vain.

The man and his barefoot son raced up and threaded their way through the crowd of now, perhaps, two or three dozen people. He confronted the milkman. A near-starving father with his shoeless child, each holding one handle of a tin bath.

"Get back," the milkman tried again and held the bat up.

"NO!" the man spoke hoarsely at him. "*You* get back!" The growling desperation in his voice caused the milkman to hesitate. Susan saw that he weighed things up in his head. He looked about at the increasing mass as they scrabbled around his vehicle. He placed the bat down as a demonstration and backed away. "All right, all right, mate," he held both hands up. "Screw this!" He turned and broke into a run. His route took him past Susan in the doorway. With barely a break in his stride he turned to her, "Better get out of her, love. They're all nuts!" And he was gone.

Susan cautiously looked out at the scene. Events were escalating fast. It could be called a riot, except that people were not loud, they were methodical and quiet. A swarm or a shoal circling a carcass, picking it clean. People scurried away, holding their spoils: a half full bottle, a handful of torn cabbage leaves, and a scooped-up potato. They tried to be careful but had to take risks. Blood mingled with the spilt milk. The bare-footed boy trod in glass to grab an unbroken bottle. He and his father stocked up their tin bath. The pooling milk was tinged a muddy pink. Susan noticed a skinny woman who slopped a rag into a puddle and sat on the kerb. In her lap a weak, wild-eyed baby hung. She wrung the rag into the infant's mouth.

The people dispersed as quickly as they had gathered. Susan realised that she had hardly breathed as the scene unfolded. She was about to step into the road when the blare of sirens stopped her. The milkman must have alerted the patrols. She ducked out of the way again, alert to the heightened danger. Two dark vans raced along the street and arrived at the remains of the milk-float just as the last of the scavengers chanced it for a few more scraps. The squad of patrol officers, from the Civil Order Federation, the COF, disembarked. Tooled up, they swarmed out of the vans' sliding doors. Whistles blew and boots scrunched on the ground. Faceless enforcers, behind smoked reinforced shields and visors, set about their business.

If the people on the High Road were not quick enough, a squad member of the COF collared them and dragged them to the ground, baton swinging. Thumped and swiped at, yelps and shouts escaped from these lowers and 'have-nots'. Susan winced as the mother with the dirty rag was dragged by the hair off the kerb. She managed to entangle her child in her arms to protect him. The baby began to scream as a black-gloved fist crashed into the mother's face, probably breaking her nose. More blood seeped into the cracks in the pavement.

Breathing hard, Susan did not stay to witness the aftermath. She turned away from the human and milk-float wreckage that littered the High Road. She scrunched her face up as she moved quickly, trying to block out the sight, and fighting back tears. She re-entered the Square and retraced her steps. No Hub or RDT today, she would have to manage, she thought. She took a tired, ragged breath and shuddered to a halt just by the steps to Gunnar's Emporium. The door opened with a jingle and Gunnar, statuesque and lean, beckoned her up.

"What's going on?" he craned to look towards the High Road.

"A double squadron to break up the looters. Scavenging the milk-float."

"Do you want to come inside?" He smiled, inviting and helpful.

Susan hesitated. The prospect of entering the inner sanctum of the Emporium was always tempting. She enjoyed Gunnar's uncomplicated, reassuring company. She wrestled, however, with the nagging need that she had to get to a Hub soon to redeem her tickets, or she would have no food supply for the next month. This would put her in a precarious position. As a lower-middle who still received ration tickets she could not afford to slip down the scale. Class mobility worked when it was in your favour and you rated an upgrade, but if you slipped thanks to lack of food, resources, desperation, or if you committed a crime, then it was easy to fall between the cracks and become a 'have-not'.

"Until it calms down," Susan looked up and down the Square, "I suppose." She felt rattled and uncertain, so a stop in Gunnar's shop was welcome, but the images of the injured and frantic lowers haunted her.

The cluttered interior of the Emporium was always something of a haven, especially when there was trouble on the streets. She edged past Gunnar's stock that filled the front of the shop: a pair of old sofas surrounded by stacks of chairs, a gambling machine, and some advertising signs. A black-and-white plastic bird with a huge hooked colourful bill perched next to a plastic pint of beer, also black with a white layer on top. In the back of the shop Gunnar had a little kitchen-office behind a partition of slatted wood and small glass panes. A large wooden table was surrounded by an eclectic mix of chairs, and shelves lined the room, stacked with tins and boxes. Hanging on the side wall above the table, visible to the whole room, the always-operational Sky-screen flickered away with its constant news feed and information. Gunnar, unlike Susan, had one on his premises because he was a businessman and a middle. Middles and above qualified for this access to media. Gunnar, Susan had noted, was also able to mute his Sky-screen.

"Look," Gunnar stood with his small fridge open, "it's real – not synthetic lactyl." He held up a small half-pint glass bottle. "Fancy a drop of the real stuff in a spot of tea?"

Gunnar, grey-haired, lean, and Swedish, had a charming way of mangling his sentences, making them ornate and florid but remaining perfectly understandable. If Susan did not know better, she could have found his affectations false or an act. His manner could be like medicine, however, as he brewed a pot of tea for the two of them and slid a mugful across to Susan. She did not add any of the milk. She could not get the images of the muddy milk puddles from the High Road out of her mind, tinged pink from the bloody cuts of the have-nots. She knew her neighbourhood. The Square was a little island, with the Wilderness at the centre, hemmed in on all sides by a sink district, populated by lowers of all kinds, have-nots, and 'pikeys'.

The two sat in silence for a little while until Gunnar began in his overly polite way, "To where were you headed, if I may ask?" he stirred his tea.

"RDTs at the Hub. Trying the one down by the Courts first of all. My stamps expire tomorrow, only arrived two days ago. I was going to queue there and if that didn't work then I was going to go over the Bridge before the end of today. I heard there was some supplies in this week – dried fish and meat and such, from Norway."

"The day will come when stamps are sent out only for us to find that they are already expired – what to do then?" and he laughed with a grim note.

"I'd better go," she pushed her mug away, "or there'll be nothing left."

"I'll escort you," Gunnar finished his last mouthful of tea. Always helpful, kind, and reliable. Gunnar could be trusted, Susan told herself.

CLARA

The canopy of trees surged and swelled in the darkness. Leaves rattled down to the woodland floor. Green Wood, one of the wildest places in London, where wild pigs and feral dog-packs roamed. It was a turbulent, enticing place for those who desired risk. Clara Stanley felt very much at home here. She needed to visit the woods to replenish her ingredients and she enjoyed foraging by night in the Capital's wild places. She edged along the old fence-line of the Wood, aware of where the surveillance cameras were. She reached a section of the perimeter barricade and paused. In a well-practised fashion, timed to perfection, one moment she was there and the next, gone.

The evening under the trees was a little cooler than the heated lanes, streets, and courtyards of the Capital, where even the buildings seemed to sweat. Clara took the chance to stop and breathe deeply, a soft breeze rustled the urban woodland. She opened her canvas bag and took out some scissors and knelt to cut some wild garlic leaves. Nuts and herbs abounded in the undergrowth if you knew where to look and Clara was an expert. This was yet another mast year, she mused, when nature's abundance increased many times over thanks to warmth and moisture. Her quick fingers sifted cobnuts, acorns, and beechnuts from the ground covering. The abundance in the woodlands no longer surprised her. Thanks to the rising temperatures every year for as long as she could remember this was nature's way.

She knew that a mast year used to come around maybe once every four or five years. A rarity that happened across the cycle of decades. Now, they were the norm.

Clara loaded her bag with the collection of fallen nuts. She would steep the acorns in cold water to remove the tannins. After that they could easily be ground into flour. Her brother, Edgar, loved the pancakes she made with the ground nuts. She stripped some white willow bark for its powerful painkilling properties and plucked chamomile leaves for soothing tea. She trudged a little further and came upon a red-leaved tree with clusters of small, hard berries. It was not much bigger than a shrub, but Clara knew what it was, and that it should not be there.

"The Balm of Gilead," she sighed.

The bitter-smelling fruit was firm to the touch, but Clara knew how useful it was once soaked in a small amount of olive oil. This tree did not belong here. It was the Turpentine tree, known as the Balm of Gilead, and a native of Turkey and Morocco. Now, its bright leaves blazed in the urban woodland on Clara's doorstep. The way things had changed. Clara could remember the warming; it had been happening her whole life. She had been told about the Break with Europe. It was in the anecdotal memories recalled by family to her grandmother, Cecilia, when she was a child. The decades-long wars had followed. Her own father, Harry, had fought in the Sixteen Years War and was with his battalion in the Third Battle of Waterloo. He was one of the glorious English warriors *but* called 'coloured' by many of his comrades and the public. After his return from combat, he faded, she remembered. Clara and Edgar were effectively war orphans even though Papa did not die in the fighting. When they appeared on the Sky-screen, filmed at the memorial services, they were, and she could quote, the 'picaninny' offspring of a hero, with their 'watermelon smiles'. Cecilia had cried for her son and become enraged for her grandchildren.

Clara edged out from behind the fence, carefully handling her bag of precious ingredients, and checked out the quiet street.

"Ouch," she muttered as one of her locks caught on a trailing bramble. She turned to try and gently release it when a noise, echoing from the end of the street, made her pause. She saw a flickering glow of light from around a corner, garish orange against the pale, crumbling facades of the buildings. She froze and listened to the gathering noise, alert to oncoming danger with a tendril of hair in her hand, and then she had to move quickly. Loud footsteps were running in the street. A dark mass appeared from around the corner. Faces and hoods were highlighted by the gaseous glow of the low-energy streetlamps. Clara tried to move and struggled with the brambles. She only succeeded in pricking her fingers and dragging some hair from her scalp. She dug into her pocket and grabbed her scissors as a petrol bomb exploded only yards from her. The fuel smeared the street and immediately ignited in a ripple of flames. With her sturdy shears Clara sliced through the strand of her hair, gathered up her things, and was gone.

The COF squad was on the scene just as she disappeared, and set about cracking heads and making arrests to break up the gathering.

A little sprig of one of her dark locks twisted on a hanging bramble.

SUSAN

"When you called the police squads they actually showed up."

"What, *police*?"

"When you needed supplies you just went to a supermarket or a shop and bought your own food. You could choose it yourself."

"We kept a pet when I was a child. A *dog*. A black-and-white patched animal. Walked it on a lead attached to a collar around its neck. But no one believes that now. Why would you feed an animal out of choice?"

"It used to be that illness was something that you got treated for. Nurses, even *doctors*, they say, would help you out. Then people began to get sick *everywhere*. It was out of control. Epidemics. *Pan*demics."

"It got warmer. And people got sicker."

"It was weird. At first, we didn't take it all that seriously."

Susan stood in line and heard the snippets of conversation from the elderly middles and lower-middles around her in the twilight at the RDT. The day had dragged on and the queue edged agonisingly slowly; her feet throbbed. She had steeled herself for a long wait and held onto the handle of her shopping trolley as an anchor. In it she kept lots of useful items, including some precious bags-for-life. Susan's trolley was a shield, a support, and a useful means of transporting contraband.

"We can move up," Gunnar indicated the progress made by the line up to the window of the RDT.

Gunnar and Susan had stood patiently at the Hub throughout the heat of the afternoon. They had opted for the closest one, near the Courts. He had agreed to escort her and, possessed of his reassuring presence, Susan appreciated his company.

Life at the Hub meant that groups of people milled around, looking sad, bored, or desperate. Electric trams clanged to a halt regularly on their clackety rails, with the recorded announcements coming in clipped tones.

"This stop, Law Courts. Next stop, Bridge 11."

"Old Cross, Newham, Bridge 4."

"Please mind the gap between the platform and the tram when travelling."

Informative, but not kindly.

A pile of mismatched shoes formed a slope against a wall near a tram stop. Women sifted through it in the advancing gloom and tried to match footwear to their ragged children. With no hope of an actual pair, they persevered to find a left and a right or two shoes that were not entirely worn out. Susan watched and thought how grey they looked with the dirt ingrained around their mouths and eyes, and embedded, immovable, around their fingernails. Grey and greyer as the evening humidity intensified and rivulets of sweat trickled through the grime on their skin.

Three Hubs were within reach for Susan and Gunnar. RDT visits were strictly regulated at all of them and it was almost a whole day's expedition to get out and collect your ration. There were about six people ahead of them in the queue by now and Susan looked up just as a small dark-haired woman with a characteristic rattish down-at-heel look reached the window. The woman nervously handed over her book of tickets and the clerk flicked it open. She chewed on her fingers that had a rust-coloured tinge as she watched the clerk's action. After some moments, he handed it back.

"Sorry, love. Out-of-date. Next!"

"No," she let out a plaintive wail, and Susan's heart began to pound in her chest. "Please," the woman looked up at the clerk, "just a couple, just this once. They only sent them through yesterday – what was I supposed to do? How could I get here?"

"There's nothing I can do about it – move on," the clerk had a strained look on his face.

"Please – just some scraps – something, anything! I can't help that they're out of date! Please, we haven't had any rations for two weeks. We've been living out of bins – scavenging – my children have nothing for tonight. We're slipping down the scale – if I get caught doing anything illegal, they'll make us lowers and then we can't claim any rations at all! We'll die if we're forced to be have-nots."

"There's nothing I can do," the clerk spoke through gritted teeth. "Please, move on."

Susan noticed, to her dismay, that nearby COF officers had detected trouble at the RDT. Two of them sauntered over, a burly, ruddy-looking, freckled woman and a man with a paunch, both black-clad and swinging their batons. Their eyes were shielded by black visors, their heads encased in matte, impersonal helmets. They reminded Susan of a pair of predatory insects, the way they gathered.

"What you doing – causing trouble?" the female officer, clearly the higher rank, stood hands-on-hips in front of the now sobbing woman. The two officers pushed her back against a wall that had on it a worn, streaked 'Keep Calm and Carry On,' poster in faded pink and cream.

"I didn't mean any –".

"Protesting about fairness over rations, are we?" the female officer prodded her in the chest with a condescending, sarcastic baton.

Announcements punctuated the air, the voice over the speaker system impersonal and bland: "All subjects must join the queue. Collect your rations and depart in an orderly and timely manner." Followed by: "Keep your distance and follow procedures." And: "Any disruption or disorder will be dealt with swiftly by authorities."

Susan, Gunnar, and the people in the queue and waiting at the tram stops watched furtively or averted their gaze as things unfolded. The skinny woman went from pleading to angry and then she lashed out. Susan winced at the sound of a baton thwacking the side of her head. The male squad member pinned the woman's arms behind her back as the ranking officer winded her with a blow to the abdomen. The woman wheezed and groaned, and then the officers dragged her away. The female COF officer announced, "Carry on, subjects, nothing to see here."

Susan, in that moment, made a move to step out of line. Gunnar grabbed her wrist and stopped her.

"Don't, stay back. Stay out of trouble."

"I've got to do *something*," she spoke through gritted teeth. "That poor woman. Enough is enough."

"Yes, but not this way. Not like this," Gunnar was close to her ear, discrete, in his reassuring way. "There are other ways to resist," he stooped in a little closer and his breath was warm against her skin. "I know some … people. We are trying to organise."

"Like what? How?" She watched, hopelessly, as the woman was carted off into the waiting COF van, whimpering and apologising from a bleeding mouth. "Everything has gone to hell. How can we stop this?"

"Not here," he whispered. "Later. We'll meet in the Emporium."

Jennifer

As the COF van containing the stricken, panicky woman drove away from the Hub, a conspicuous figure walked through the milling groups of lowers and have-nots.

Jennifer Sinclair was a 'have' by any definition, that was obvious, and she knew she stood out in this setting. Modestly but impeccably dressed, she walked along a little self-consciously. People stared as she passed, because she was so 'squeaky'. Her clothes were laundered and pressed, her hair washed and smooth. She held onto her bag, a shiny leather number, as she clipped along, picking her way around the litter and walking past the traders with their meagre goods laid out on blankets near the tram stops. Single tea-bags sat next to little wraps of laundry detergent in neat rows; little pieces of jewellery made from hammered and clipped metal tin cans, and even the occasional small jar of ancient baby food.

Jennifer checked her wristwatch and waited at the tram stop, to sideways glances from the lowers and have-nots around her. Middles and lower-middles queued at the RDTs or waited for their transport connections. She knew she stuck out as an upper-middle. Her vehicle had broken down and she was under intense pressure to get into work for that night's broadcast. Whilst Jennifer was nervous about being at a Hub, she was even more anxious about getting in late to the Sky-stream studios. She had seen the woman get hit and dragged away. The turbulent atmosphere affected her. It made moving around in public so irritating. People never seemed to learn. Jennifer did not think she was exaggerating when she compared herself as worse off than the have-nots around her. It might be very challenging for them, she thought, but they don't get it – they don't have my problems – try working for *my* boss!

Jennifer spent a short, cautious journey on board the tram. She chose to stand, in order to disembark as quickly as possible. In the fifteen-minute journey the geography of the city changed dramatically. She peered out of the window as the buildings lining the muggy, oppressive streets transformed from crumbling stone, overwhelmed by nature, to sleek polished glass and steel. The litter-strewn, cracked, overgrown streets gave way to glistening boulevards, well-kept and smart. Nature was under control at the Hub where Jennifer disembarked, but she barely glanced at the neat planters, tidy trees, and hanging baskets. In a nervous sweat, she trotted past the ornamental shrubs that decorated Media City Plaza and turned into Rothermere Square. As soon as she was within range on the tram her phone had begun to ping.

Evening Primrose, media star, presenter, influencer, and Jennifer's boss, was trying to track her down.

'Where are you?'

'I'm on my way. Breakdown.'

'I will break you – get here – now.'

'On a tram. Soon. V V soon. So sorry.'

'Really bitch? Sorry?' Evening punctuated her messages with angry, laughing, and threat-face emojis.

'I'm at the door.'

Jennifer attempted to placate her boss via message before the confrontation. If she could just mediate and explain before they were face to face, it would be fine. She approached the imposing Sky-stream HQ building entrance that dominated one side of Rothermere Square. It was flanked by rows of eminent figures, caught in characteristically strong poses. Important historical, wartime, political, and philanthropic figures: Harris, and Rhodes, Colston and Archer, Churchill, Murdoch, Savile, and Thatcher. Jennifer passed them and ran into the Sky-stream studios building, swiping her security card at the barrier without missing a beat.

In the middle of the sweeping, glimmering atrium of the broadcast HQ stood Evening Primrose, media mega-influencer and the most famous woman in England. She moved as if at the centre of a royal court with her glowing, contoured complexion, and was constantly surrounded by a cluster of nervous acolytes. Tension customarily crackled around her and followed in her wake. Evening Primrose, the beloved Sky-stream co-host of the 'Evening and Eliot' daily show was short in stature, but possessed a warm, approachable manner on camera. In person, she was always the most intimidating presence in the room. Dressed in her modest, neat style, her hair was beautifully coiffured.

Her image was constructed, Jennifer knew, to reflect what would have been the changing seasons if the climate had not warmed. So, as it was November, Evening was clad in a tweed ensemble, her hair a warm auburn with tawny lowlights. In a few months this look would give way to one that emphasised springtime freshness, with a brief stopover for a darker chestnut hue and some sumptuous red velvet for Christmas and the New Year festivities. Jennifer could not help but feel how odd Evening's outfit was when there was no chill in the air, no crisp freshness in the mornings, and just oppressive humidity at night. However, Evening lived round the clock in the air-conditioned Sky-stream HQ with its regulated temperatures. Jennifer's only experience of seasonal temperature fluctuations came from working there. She had heard about the warming, but it was not an approved topic of conversation, especially at Sky-stream. The output never referred to it. The regular forecasts that went out on the channel were in fact fabricated, everybody knew, and no one took them seriously. It was like an old, familiar tradition, long defunct, but something that no one wanted to drop. The word among the Sky-stream staff was that the forecasts were recycled from late twentieth-century weather forecasts drawn from the *Times*' newspaper archive.

Jennifer, flushed and sweating through her light-weight blouse, trotted up to the cluster of acolytes and braced herself for a tirade from her boss. She stood, hovering, as Evening spelt something out slowly and condescendingly to one cowering individual.

"So, get it right next time," she concluded and thrust a folder back at him, getting him in the chest.

"Yes, Ms Primrose, sorry."

Jennifer moved into Evening's eyeline as the staffer departed, and adopted the most suitable expression, a mixture of apologetic obsequiousness and willing preparedness.

Evening Primrose looked straight through her.

Jennifer felt an immediate sense of doom wash over her. If anything was worse than a dressing down from her boss over lateness it was this reaction. Evening swept past her and up the glass and wood spiral staircase to the artificially sunlit upper mezzanine where her office, private suite, and production facilities could be found. Evening's office was central on this upper level. Composed entirely of glass walls, with a wave of her hand over a sensor she could alter the opacity of these walls from complete transparency to complete privacy in a split second. This kept her team alert.

Jennifer sighed and bowed her head. She followed the team upstairs, perfectly prepared to clear out her desk. Employees had been fired for far less, with no notice. She reached the mezzanine as Evening was concluding yet another haranguing address to her people.

"And if we're going to resist the creeping, subversive, socialist activity we need to get tough. Now, what are you waiting for? Tell me what today and every day's motto is!"

They all chimed in, "To be truly patriotic is to be conservative."

"Better. Get the script together and stop dragging your feet. Useless," she muttered as she turned away. They dispersed at this.

Evening stood and scrolled slowly through her phone. Time passed. Finally, she directed her attention to Jennifer.

With a deep sigh, she addressed her assistant. "So good of you to grace us with your presence."

"Evening, I'm so sorry – I can explain."

"Shut up. Follow me."

Clara

"Grammere? You home?"

"In here, darlin.'"

Clara put on her slippers at the door to the apartment and walked along the narrow empty hallway. Sound, warmth, and amazing odours emanated from the kitchen at the end. A small room, occupied by a stove, two large cupboards, and a square table with a speckled melamine surface. Clean, a little worn, but well-kept like everything attached to Clara's grandmother, Cecilia 'Cece' Stanley.

"Grammere," Clara slipped into a little patois at home, "smells divine." She kissed the silver-grey closely trimmed hair on her grandmother's head as the old lady stood over the stove. "Hmmm, delicieux," she attempted to purloin a mouthful of sauce as it simmered temptingly in a crock pot.

"Ah-ah-ah," Cecilia smacked her hand playfully. "You wait!"

"Is little brother home?"

"On his way, I think. No word."

Clara sat at the table and started to unpack her bag of foraged stuff.

"Good pickings today?" her grandmother noted the cob nuts and wild herbs with approval.

Clara nodded and held some wild thyme carefully between her fingers, smoothing the soft leaves.

"Can I?" Cecilia held out her hand.

"Of course," and Clara gave the sprig to her.

The old lady bruised it in a pestle and mortar and scattered it into the casserole. "The fresh ones go in last, hmmm," and she wafted the smell from the pot up to her nostrils. Cecilia could work wonders with the most basic ingredients and conjure up memorable meals. "And your brother is to thank for this tonight. He brought some spice packets home from the factory the other day."

Clara suddenly looked concerned. "He must be careful. If he gets caught with contraband, Grammere …"

Cecilia looked at the array of herbs, nuts, and cut willowbark on the kitchen table and raised her eyebrows but said nothing.

"OK, OK," Clara nodded and began to clear the table, when there was a small tinkling sound from her phone.

"Who's that at this time?" Cecilia soaked some rice and stirred the pot.

Clara picked up a message from Gunnar Hansen, and her heart rose: 'Do you have the chance tonight for meeting up?' She loved his rather garbled way of trying to make sense. She tapped out a quick reply: 'Yes,' and looked up at the clock, but a wave of concern washed over her, so she began to compose a message to Edgar. As yet there was no sign of her brother.

'You OK, bruv? Home soon?'

"Clear some space." Cecilia put a stack of bowls on the table.

Clara looked up at her, "You expecting guests?"

Cecilia spoke quietly and discretely, "Mina – and her little brothers Adie and Aidan. I saw Jacinda today – she looked bad – before she went off to the Hub, and by late afternoon she hadn't come home. I've been minding her boys since then. Mina will be home from shift with Edgar."

The Sky-screen was on in the other room, as usual. Cecilia qualified for one because she was a retired Nurse Instructor, but she could not control her screen. Now, Clara could see that there were two dark-haired, scruffy, skinny boys on the worn sofa in the flickering light and shadows. Quiet and docile, their neighbour's twin sons sat together.

"So – Jacinda's gone?" Clara looked concerned.

"I'm very worried," Cecilia took out some cutlery. "I'll keep them fed and safe and mind them – and hope."

Jacinda, her teenaged daughter Mina, and her twin sons lived in the next-door apartment, but much of her children's time was spent in the warmth and security of Cecilia's tidy home. Mina and her brothers had for some years come home from school to relative chaos and disarray. Jacinda did her best, but the synth-dope, strong and numbing, was too easy to gulp back in order to obliterate reality and forget her worries. Many a time, Cecilia or Clara had helped her out of bed and tried to clean up her place; create a little bit of order. Thanks to Mina getting shifts at the food processing plant with Edgar they had a little money coming in now, and because Jacinda was a military widow they had a tiny allowance of ration tickets. But they were often out of date when she received them. Today, Jacinda Suresh had not come home.

Susan

"You need to make it work, kitty." Susan looked down at Ellery. "Go on."

The ginger cat, annoyed, sniffed at the insubstantial food on his saucer.

"There's the window, then," she gestured to the recessed casement that looked out onto the yard at the bottom of the basement stairs. "Go on, go out and hunt something."

The cat ignored her and hopped up onto her bed where he concentrated on washing his leg. Around Susan in her little below-ground-level world there stood two sets of bookshelves. These were her pride and joy, her whole reason for carrying on and going out into the world, their contents as vital as her rations. Each shelf unit housed a carefully catalogued collection of volumes. Colour-coordinated spines stood out to the world, a blend of paperback and hardback. Susan took them out for regular dusting.

"These were all commonplace once," she spoke out loud to Ellery, as she often did, while she used a soft cloth on the spine of an Agatha Christie novel, "everywhere. You could buy a book with your groceries, or when you took a trip on a train. Millions upon millions. This," she selected a copy of *Jaws* by Peter Benchley, "was printed in the hundreds of thousands and you could go into any shop – new or second-hand – and find a copy. When I was a student and didn't have any furniture, I built my bookshelves out of planks of wood and other books – I just stacked them up and laid them on top of each other."

Ellery moved on to one of his front paws and gnawed blissfully between his toes.

"*All* books are rarities now. So, we have to look after any that we find."

Her device sounded an alert.

"Oh, what does that thing want?"

It sat on the kitchen counter. Susan only used it when absolutely necessary. She loathed it. She called it 'the thing'. It was not like the phones and devices she remembered when she was younger. This one invaded her life constantly. Sky-screens might not contaminate everyone's home, she mused, but even she couldn't escape her device. It charged using built-in solar cells and kept the Sky-stream updates churning along. She looked at the screen. It displayed a message from Gunnar:

'Come tonight.'

Susan looked across at her bed, "I don't know. What do you think, cat?"

Mina

Damage. Hit back. Hold them off.

Mina's stomach growled.

The worst thing – no – *one* of the many terrible things about working at the food processing plant was the smell. Mina worked on packaging. Unlike Edgar, who was on the prep and processing line; and she envied him. No, Mina had to take the flat cardboard and slot the packaging crates together on a floor that was beneath the extractor fans that fed out from the main factory. All the outflow from the line came her way. If you wanted to take a young person who had not eaten any breakfast and was trying to last on the previous night's supper until they could eat again and try your best to kill their appetite with anything, then the smell of the main food processing line could do it. Sometimes the drench of odour that flooded from the fans made Mina gag. All the smells of different food and protein breakdown rolled into one. Sweet and savoury mingled to create a fog of sickly, salty, heavy scents. Unimaginable concoctions that together were the very opposite of appetising.

After their shift, Mina and Edgar met up to head home together to their neighbourhood. The two strolled out of the gates and halted for the standard search. The COF officers on the gates patted everyone down. The squad member assigned to Edgar did a swift, cursory job. Thanks

to this cooperation, Edgar could routinely smuggle packets of spices and seasoning out from the processing line.
The products from the line – the ration packs and tins –
contained a gloop with an umami or sweet flavouring and
were labelled accordingly. Nothing ever went stale. The
protein-carbohydrate rich paste and patties were designed
to last for years and relied on dried spice seasoning and
sweeteners to possess any kind of flavour. Deep frying
the synthetic carbo-protein, to give it a crispy outer shell
sprinkled with savoury seasoning was the best way of dealing with it. If you could get hold of enough oil. Anyone
who could lay their hands on savoury ingredients to boost
the bean and soy-based concoctions and pastes, well they
could name their price.

Tonight, however, Mina had a quick stop to make after
work and she could always compel Edgar to come with her.
She had passed this place on several occasions at closing
time, on the outskirts of a higher-up neighbourhood, and
noticed the lazy security measures. *Elegance – Epicure –
Duchesse Originals* … Words emblazoned on a banner over
the entrance to the store and on the signage at the end of
every aisle. It was a simple matter of prying open the doors,
so that Mina was in and could make her way stealthily
along the darkened avenues, with their wall-to-wall produce. This was a store for the haves and higher-ups, a ware-
house of wonders. Mina knew that Edgar awaited her out
in the alley, nervous and anxious. He did not want to enter
the store, he said, because he did not trust himself not to be
awkward and clumsy. He helped Mina, and took to covert

pilfering from the plant, but he drew the line at breaking and entering.

Mina's walkie-talkie crackled.

"Come on," Edgar's voice whispered to her. They had the use of a pair of old, salvaged short-range toy walkie talk-ies from Gunnar's Emporium. It was safer than using their phones when Mina was on the rob.

"Hang on," she whispered back. She enjoyed this, taking her time in a store. This must be what it felt like to be a higher-up – or something like it. She browsed the shelves in the half-light from her phone. What to get for Adie and Aidan, and for Mum?

Soups, fruit, tinned meat. The grocery stores outside the ration system were amazing places. Mina filled her backpack.

"Are you coming? What's the hold-up?"

"OK, OK," she came back.

Edgar was an excellent sidekick, she thought, he kept her alert and made sure she didn't spend too much time on the premises and make a mistake. Now her backpack was stuffed she felt it was time to leave. At the rear of the shop the door had slotted back onto its latch and a red light blinked on the lock. Fuck. Mina pulled a face. The alarm was live. She had to be decisive.

Damage. Hit back. Hold them off.

"Here goes," she said out loud and slammed the sole of her solid boot onto the latch.

"Go for it! Hurry!" Edgar's voice came over the radio. "Come *on*!"

Mina lunged and hammered at the lock, kicked and kicked. At last, she buckled it and it gave way. In the same moment she allowed herself to breathe out the door clicked open. An alarm ripped through the silence; its blood-curdling scream compensated for the flimsy security lock on the door.

"Oh shit," she heard Edgar's voice over the walkie-talkie.

Mina Suresh almost fell out of the door. She tumbled and rolled into the alley.

"Fuck's sake," Edgar was there and dragged her to her feet. "Come on, won't you?"

"I've got fruit – in tins. Soup. And some hotdogs!"

"OK – fantastic – now move it!"

Edgar and Mina, with Mina laughing triumphantly, exited the alley and darted down a side-street. COF vans could be heard in the distance, sirens wailing.

JENNIFER

The Sky-stream broadcast studio hummed around Jennifer.
She juggled everything. Her punishment for lateness that
was beyond her control was to manage the guests, the running order, and cue everything with the gallery for that
day's 'Evening and Eliot' show. Evening Primrose had given
almost the whole production office team the night off to
make her point to Jennifer. The cheery 'Evening and Eliot'
theme played over and over, threatening her with ominous
prospects, as the rehearsal took place. The crew wheeled
cameras into position, and she went to find the guests in
the hospitality suite. The Sky-stream HQ had everything
to support Evening Primrose's vision for her broadcast.
She lived on site, in her own luxurious accommodation,
and created a world for the public to follow. The sugges-
tion was that her co-host and husband, Eliot Charming,
and their twins, a son and daughter Plum and Peach, lived
there also. This was not entirely true, as Jennifer and the
team were aware, but they were sworn to secrecy. Eliot had
his own apartment on site and sometimes stayed over, and
the children were occasionally seen in their playroom for
publicity shots, cared for by a round of nannies and mind-
ers. Mostly, however, the perfect Sky-stream 'family' were
separate and accommodated in luxurious fashion, but well
away from each other.

Hospitality in the Green Room won everyone over, even
the most truculent or difficult guest. The suite had the

perfect balance of light and shade, cool and warmth. Delicious finger-food, hot and cold beverages on tap, exquisitely comfortable furniture. Every 'ordinary member of the public' who came on the show was stunned into silence by the luxury on display. Jennifer walked into the suite, balanced her phone, clipboard, and headset, to find the two guests for the day. In the middle of the large open-plan room a lower-middle middle-aged couple sat and stood. At an awkward angle on the large, sweeping sofa was the man. He had skinny legs and a paunch and wore a jumper full of holes. His jowly face was stubbly, and his droopy red eyes were watery and bewildered. A woman of about the same age, with grey hair, a faded summery dress and the tattiest shoes Jennifer had ever seen, stood beside the sofa. The woman looked ecstatically happy and beamed as she greeted Jennifer excitedly.

"Wow! It's beautiful in here!" She spoke in slightly hushed tones. "I've never been anywhere like this before. I've never seen such food!"

"Have you had something to eat and drink?" Jennifer looked along the table. Everything was still pristine, untouched.

"Oh no!" the woman looked aghast and shook her head. "Bradley wanted something," she indicated the tired-eyed man, "but I said no! I didn't dare touch anything."

"Please, help yourself," Jennifer gestured to the lavish table, "that's what it's here for." She looked them up and down. "And take some home with you. There's always lots left over."

The woman looked at her wide-eyed, and just breathed heavily. Jennifer watched them as she went through the brief and the running order. Bradley stayed put, but his wife – Jade, Jennifer's notes told her the name – edged cautiously towards the catering.

"You'll go along to hair and make-up in a little while."

"Gosh," Jade stopped by the table, mesmerised by the food as she listened, but touched nothing.

"We'll then take you down to the studio floor and you'll meet Evening and Eliot … Here, let me." Jennifer laid down her items and took up a plate. She had felt Jade's anxiety reaching her and decided to help. It struck Jennifer that the woman was intimidated to such a crippling degree because she had clearly never encountered this sort of thing before. It was a baffling mystery for Jade. She simply stared at the spread and the tea and coffee urns, the bottled water, and stacks of plates and napkins. Jade stood before the table as if it were an altar and she was not initiated in the ritual. She could only worship.

Jennifer picked out some food for them, a full plate each and dispensed each a cup of tea. The couple sat on the sofa and stared at her with a child-like wonder as she carried out these simple acts of hospitality. Once served, Jade picked reverently at her food. Bradley let his sit there for a few moments and then he pounced. He devoured two sausage rolls in what Jennifer realised was a matter of seconds. They were there and when she looked again, they were gone. She went through the order for the show. Jade raised a nervous hand to ask a question.

"And when we *do* get to meet, er – Eliot – can we, can we have some time to, you know, chat? For a bit?"

"That will depend on the timings for the show, if there isn't a delay, then perhaps."

"I *love* Eliot. I just *love* Eliot Charming," Jade gushed.

Jennifer escorted Bradley and Jade to the studio floor and took her position beside the camera. Fresh from make-up and wardrobe the couple appeared even more uncomfortable. Bradley was redder than before. The 'Evening and Eliot' theme interrupted her thoughts, and she could consider them no more. The studio darkened and lights swivelled and pulsed as Evening and Eliot strode onto set.

Evening was in her autumnal ensemble and Eliot with his greying hair at the temples wore an age-appropriate equally seasonal three-piece suit. Jennifer watched as Evening snapped into presenter mode when the studio went live. Eliot stood with her hand in his.

"My very own *Prince* Charming – Eliot!"

He kissed her hand gallantly and escorted her to the sofa. This was the nightly repeat ritual at the commencement of every live show. Jade looked up at them in awe as the couple seamlessly segued through their opening remarks and introduced the first segment. They cut to a live field reporter who was describing a patriotic achievement on the part of a war veteran. An amputee ex-serviceman from the Belgian Forests and Low Countries 'skirmish' had worked out how to do a sponsored walk with his walking frame and prosthetic leg. He was elderly and decked out in a shabby pinstripe suit jacket with medals weighing down a drooping lapel on one side. He had devised a way of tottering along his garden path. One end of the garden to another, repeatedly, until he built up the distance.

Evening wound up the segment with, "Indeed, look at that bravery and determination from a man with one leg and permanent injuries. So, what's *your* excuse?" she looked straight into camera. "No one can ever make an excuse for not doing your *all* after seeing that hero. Am I right, Eliot?" There was always a spiteful undertone to Evening's speech.

"Yes, you are, Evening. Conservatives are the true patriots."

"Yes," she reiterated, "Conservatives *are*, indeed, the true patriots. Which brings us to our next story." She switched to a more serious expression as she changed camera. "Something that comes as a warning to us all. How safe are we on our streets, or at the Hubs? Going about our lawful business and collecting our allocated rations?"

She turned to the couple on the sofa, "Bradley, Jade, welcome to 'Evening and Eliot.'"

Jade had a nervous, fixed, inappropriate smile. Evening's eyes microscopically narrowed, but still maintained a sympathetic expression. She took Jade's trembling hand and held it in hers.

"Tell us, what happened to you and your husband?"

"Well, Evening – Eliot," Jade gushed as she looked in his direction, "it was our worse nightmare. A form of hell. Bradley hasn't been the same since. He can't barely speak a word now – doesn't say a thing."

With feeling and concern, Eliot asked, "And what did he do before this shocking event?"

Jade looked at him slightly confused as if the question of her Bradley *doing* something had never occurred to her and simpered in reply, "Well, he didn't really have a job. He hadn't been working as it happens – but this has upset him terrible. It's his back, see?"

At this, Evening turned and threw a withering glance in Jennifer's direction. From that point on, the interview took an unfortunate turn.

Jade carried on, "It was the worse thing that has ever happened to us, Eliot. The people – they was like animals, and Bradley were caught up in it."

"They were after the food, is that right?" Eliot coughed nervously as he sensed a coldness emanating from Evening.

"The food, that's right. I knew you'd understand, Eliot."

Eliot tried to eke out a few more sympathetic nods and shrugs as the woman spoke in her weak, warbly voice about her troubles.

Evening was having none of it, however.

"Well, there you have it," she interjected suddenly, her warm tone abandoned. "We aren't safe on our own streets these days. We have to take a break now but stay with us and we'll be right back." She looked down the camera with a steely expression.

Eliot looked to Jennifer, bewildered, but Jennifer knew better what was going on and did not want to mess this up. She gave the wrap signal to the floor crew and spoke quickly to the gallery through her headset. The theme struck up and the lights changed.

"And … we're out," she announced to the studio.

Immediately, Evening was up off the sofa and strode across the studio.

"Evening, I …" Jennifer stammered.

"What. The. Fuck? Get *them*," Evening pointed at Jade and Bradley, "out of my studio. Who fucked up?"

"I don't know, Evening – honestly. You sent the production team home – and I didn't have the chance …"

"Are you blaming *me*?"

"No – I."

"Someone books the guests, and they don't check if the man's a bloody malingerer, and it's *my* fault? What do I even pay you for?" she spat at Jennifer.

"I'm so sorry, Evening."

"Get them out and we re-set. We'll go straight to the next segment. What's the order?"

"Er, …" Jennifer scanned her script. "It's cooking – with leftovers – and you're talking to guest Chef Cater Pilar."

"Tell me that you haven't fucked that one up. Please, tell me – the cook isn't a fucking smackhead?"

SUSAN

Hope is the thing with feathers –
That perches in the soul –
And sings the tune without the words –
And never stops – at all –

And sweetest – in the Gale – is heard –
And sore must be the storm –
That could abash the little Bird
That kept so many warm –

I've heard it in the chillest land –
And on the strangest Sea –
Yet – never – in Extremity,
It asked a crumb – of me.

The dour face of Emily Dickinson looked out from a faded monochrome picture on the back of the dust jacket of the slim volume that Susan held. The slight woman with the severely parted hair and pale face fixed her with dark eyes and a serious expression. A Victorian voice, from what Susan recalled. As a young woman, Susan remembered packing this very volume in one of a row of archive boxes lined up on the desk in her office. The day of clearing out and leaving her job. The day of departure from a job, a career, she had barely begun but loved. Her life was totally occupied by the college since she herself had graduated. Her promise was identified early. They had liked her and been impressed from the start. Susan's flair for language and her poetic sensibility had earned her a teaching post. She could inspire others. She was a great tutor, a natural teacher. When she was 'let go,' her students had even formed a delegation to protest to the college management. It was nothing personal, though, they said, she was simply another casualty of government policy.

Susan touched the cover of the poetry collection and smoothed the discoloured tape where she had made repairs to the spine. Emily Dickinson – A Collection. It had been a leaving gift from a student. A young woman who had cried at the injustice of it all. Susan was given half a day's notice to clear her office. She remembered the day like it was yesterday, when other memories were obscured and vague. At the end of the Belgian Forest campaign, when withdrawal for the English troops was inevitable, things took an unexpected turn. The Cabinet announced emergency and contingency measures. Another pandemic loomed, and that necessitated the closure of borders, the regulation of the economy, the introduction of the ration system, and the de-funding of non-essential programmes and professions. The teaching of poetry, theatre, literature and languages were determined non-essential. Why study books when they cannot fill stomachs or protect our borders? Why learn a foreign language when we can simply rely on our own English linguistic superiority?

The Prime Minister appeared on the last television broadcast before the Sky-screens were issued and the continuous Sky-stream broadcast began to beam out. He declared the shutdown and 'phasing out' of services and the immediate closure of institutions that dealt with leisure, culture, and the arts. War, disease – England was told 'she must re-group and re-boot' to 'protect our own' and restore her greatness. After this withdrawal – *not* a retreat – and preservation of our resources, we could come back better than ever. "I get it," the Premier said, "I hear you." Don't worry, everyone was told, we will one day restore our great cultural and educational institutions. Some did not close, however, but they were for the higher-ups and haves, because they needed to hold on to the knowledge, and enjoy the leisure of entertainment thanks to the hard work they did. They could not be denied a little pleasure, now and then. The responsibilities they shouldered sapped their strength, so they needed ways to recharge their batteries. Elementary schooling remained for the middles and lowers, but it was a lacklustre business. The separation of the Kingdom had been a costly exercise and coming after the Break from Europe – well – it only helped to reinforce the *English* national spirit.

"And we don't need to spend on unnecessaries now – time to tighten our belts, people!" the Prime Minister had waved a careless hand while the journalists fired questions at his back. That was the last ever press conference by a leader.

Susan had joined the trail of tutors, managers, and researchers as they filed out of the college buildings with boxes and desk accessories. Back then, she still owned a flat, and a little electric car, and had a living. The climate emergency of the twenty-first century had produced mixed results. The cheap, clean, easy-to-charge electric cars were one of the best. Re-wilding across the country was another thing altogether.

She placed the volume of poetry carefully back on the shelf and Ellery hopped up with a chirrupy purr and rubbed against her arm.

"All right, chap? Helping me put things in order?" She sighed heavily. She thought about the future, but there had never been a picture of a future since she had been forced out of her career. Day-to-day living, getting by, was the way life was organised. She felt old all of a sudden, beyond her years. She knew that she looked any age from fifty-five to seventy. Once she had possessed a sense of purpose, but all she had felt for years now was a sense of redundancy. Ambition, purpose, vision – all redundant. That word had a doom-laden, sonorous shape. Society told Susan it could not afford her and most importantly did not need her.

So, from being Susan Jenkins she had temporarily transformed into Blythe and Winston. Blythe Bellingham was a writer of stirring romances, some of which bordered on the risqué and erotic. Those titles had sold extremely well. Winston Sayers devoted his skills to thrillers and detective fiction. The flurry of activity in writing and publishing caused a book flood and a spike in sales for an industry that could hear its death knell. She and other redundant teachers busied themselves for a few seasons in the sun and made a little living, until the plug was pulled. The end of publishing. No tree-felling meant no pulping and no printing, no paper and no books. Re-wilding signalled the preservation of trees and the de-commissioning of all countryside management, parks, and gardens. Agriculture continued in a confined way but there was no exploitation of natural resources for an interest like publishing. E-books, regulated by the Sky-stream Media Group out of Rothermere Square, were all that were allowed.

Susan knew, however, that the dismantling of education, philosophy, printing, and publishing meant something other than preserving the earth's resources. It was clear to her that it meant control. The end of the spread of any free or unregulated thought. She stood and looked at the books on her shelves. Wherever she went she scoured for books. Any trader in the street, any stall or kiosk put up temporarily at a Hub, she was there. Gunnar's Emporium was a good source and she greedily bought them up with what little money she had. Books – any books – were her treasure. It was all she had now. It's all any of us have, she told herself. I must keep some of the knowledge alive, preserve it, and maybe – pass it on one day? No plan, just the sense that something must be done.

She locked up her basement flat and cautiously emerged into the Square. The night was warm, as usual, and birds on their way to roost chattered loudly as they swept around the Square, swooping and playing in the air before disappearing into the tall canopies of the trees in the Wilderness. She looked back towards her door and the little yard at the foot of the steps. Ellery sat in the window, a wary posture to his little body and his green eyes flickered from side to side as he tracked the flight of the birds across the Square. Susan saw a flash of emerald and gold as a lizard scurried around one of the limestone pillars at the front of the building.

Clara

Twilight had turned into night before Clara left her apartment. She had been able to talk to Edgar once he was safe at home.

"It weren't me, Sis," her brother spoke in an urgent whisper as they stood in the darkened hallway. Mina was in Cecilia's cosy sitting-room introducing her brothers to the tinned fruit and hotdogs from her backpack.

"I know, Eddie, cheri. She's a risk-taker. All we can do is watch out for her, help the little ones." She looked in at the two boys as they marvelled at the bright orange pictures of mandarin slices on the labels. "Grammere will have to break the news about their Mama."

"And no one has any idea where she might be?"

"Taken – that's all we know. At the Hub. You eat. I have a meeting with Gunnar. I will send out some feelers – try and find out what happened."

After this hushed exchange, Clara climbed down the iron fire escape at the side of the building. The main stairs were best avoided after dark. She went carefully as the damp and sultry weather had left the treads quite slick. She swung into a dark courtyard at the bottom of the fire escape and this brought her to the rear entrance of Gunnar's Emporium. There, she paused and listened, then tapped at the dark, recessed door and waited. When about to meet Gunnar, she always had a sense of excitement in the pit of her stomach. It felt dangerous to be around him; after all he was still something of an unknown quantity in the neighbourhood. She remembered when he had arrived and taken over the shop several years ago. He had stocked it out with so many wonders and rapidly made himself at home, as if he had always belonged there. He was very attractive and soon she grew close to him thanks to his support of the low-level dissidence in that part of the Capital. Clara and her foraging and illegal nursing services for the have-nots excited and intrigued him and he liked to help her out. She was grateful for his quiet confidence and had found herself well and truly smitten.

After about half a minute there was a muffled noise from behind the door and it clicked open a crack. Gunnar himself appeared in the dim light that came through the opening. He smiled, reassuringly, with that twinkle of mischief she liked so much.

"Good, good, she's already here," he spoke with his thick accent.

Clara entered the shop and edged past him into the storeroom. She threaded her way through Gunnar's eclectic mixed up stock. She squeezed past a pinball machine that had a dinosaur theme, long dark and covered with dust. She looked around at some of the other objects on shelves and in stacks. Magazines, comics, and old newspapers had a thick and musty smell. Bottles and old signage were ranged around, and some of them triggered nostalgia and memories for her. The brown beer bottles with peeling labels reminded her of Harry, her father. As a little girl, she could see the picture of a red triangle and her father's fingers holding his dark ale, resting on the arm of the sofa. One finger tapped the bottle in time to the bright rhythm of … Lord Shorty. The name came back to her. 'To unite people as one … Om Shanty Om …'. Harry would while away the evenings with his favourite twentieth-century Soca on the player, tunes filling the air. "The song you hear is an Indian prayer, from ancient times to soothe your mind …" Her father, after the army and the European wars, had sought only a life of peace and ale. As a little girl she had picked up a tasselled shawl that once belonged to her mother and danced to the Om Shanty chorus around the living-room. 'Sing the song as you go along.' Peace, Om Shanty, and dark ale.

"Let's all sit in here," Gunnar showed her into his little kitchen. At the table Clara saw a woman a little older than herself, probably. She was white with slightly wavy, grey hair. Kind eyes in a thin face. Her clothes were worn but well-cared for, patched and sewn, Clara noticed.

"Clara, this is Susan. Susan – Clara. I thought it was time you two met."

Mina

Mina Suresh looked on as Adie tried to decipher the label on a tin of 'Main Course Chicken Soup'. His little grubby finger pressed against the side of the tin, so it looked like a tree-frog's squishy toe pad. Mina loved the twins' cute little 'froggy-fingers'. She smoothed Aidan's shaggy dark hair out of his eyes. He sat, sadly, in the corner of Miss Cece's old saggy sofa. Adie was enthusiastic where Aidan was lethargic. The light from the Sky-screen flickered in his expressionless eyes. He held a grubby, blue, disintegrated fleece blanket up to his face and his crooked index finger sat in his mouth. He tugged softly on an earlobe with the hand that held the blanket up to his face. 'Wigging' he called it. Mina looked at him and smiled. Her brothers' little habits delighted her. They were, at least, protected enough to be able to sleep and watch, whilst she worked. Miss Cece was very patient, she let them hide out here whilst Mina was busy and whilst Mum was otherwise occupied – out, or not 'with it'. It was better for them here than anywhere else.

The boys had a place at the local school when it was open. It was an institution in the 'Cherish' academy chain that taught children up to the age of twelve. It was a chaotic, understaffed place at which children hung out in a large hall supervised by a shifting group of Mentors and an occasional visit from an Instructor. Adie spent his time racing from group to group, and Aidan sat in a corner, wigging and rocking. Mina preferred them to come to Cece's place.

At least she gave them some attention and food and told them stories.

"Come on, boys – mes petites – come get you some dinner."

At the sound of Miss Cece's voice Adie reacted quickly and was up to the table in a split second. Aidan gazed at the kitchen doorway for a few seconds, and registered Cece's silhouette framed in the light. He quietly and steadily slid off the sofa and ambled through to the welcome sight of the food in the warm kitchen, dragging his shredded blanket behind him. Mina watched Cece serve her brothers with fragrant bowls of vegetables, rice, and protein substitute, but she had no appetite. She felt too much anxiety in the air and returned to sit down in the semi-dark living-room. It did not surprise her that Cece came to sit beside her once she had finished in the kitchen. The old woman placed a bony and veined hand kindly on Mina's arm.

"So, where is she?" Mina knew there could be no satisfactory answer to this.

Cecilia shook her head slowly. "Clara's going to try and get some news and find out where they took her."

Mina paused and frowned, "They *took* her? Are you sure?"

Cecilia nodded sadly, "Yes, I'm afraid so. We think she was at the Hub. She was trying to get rations for you all with her book. Something must have happened."

Mina had not been expecting this news. She had become accustomed to her mother being absent for long periods.

Usually, she was on the scrounge for drugs, or if she was at home, she was out of it. She had the urge to burst into their flat next door, expecting to find Jacinda sprawled on her bed among a tangle of grubby sheets. She looked at the tin of soup in her hand and wished for her mother to be high, but home.

Mum. Fuck. Fuck! Taken? Mina scrunched up her face and felt her rage and tears boiling inside. She looked at the Skyscreen with blurred vision. Eliot Charming's handsome, insipid face beamed at her. The screen cut to celebrity chef Cater Pilar feeding a bite-size canape to Evening Primrose. The host dabbed each corner of her mouth with a crisp linen napkin, the whitest thing that Mina had ever seen through her tears. The audience in the studio applauded. Mina hefted the soup can in her hand and ached to lob it at the screen, right into the smug face of the presenter. The thought of the penalty Miss Cece would have to face for the destruction of state property was the only thing that prevented her.

Mum. Why do you have to be so careless? You just don't get it.

Susan

Susan felt a creeping sense of disappointment. She looked at the woman opposite her across Gunnar's tatty table. She appraised Clara. This was Gunnar's latest. She had seen her around the neighbourhood, walking across the Square, and going in and out of the Wilderness. She lived in one of the buildings a little way down from Susan, but there were so many people in and out she did not know anyone's name. A lower-middle of sorts, perhaps, and some kind of healer. Beautiful, with a thick collection of long locks only just beginning to turn grey at the roots. Relaxed and decorative clothing, a pierced nose, anklets, and Susan saw what looked like the edge of a tattoo peeping out at the shoulder and the wrist. She had the typical look of someone raised as an army brat. She was someone who had been brought up smart and with discipline but learned to express herself later on. Probably after her father came home from combat, maybe strung out with PTSD from the Belgian forests.

Clara was smiling at her. Beautiful and calm. Susan was disappointed because it was obvious to her that Gunnar and Clara were lovers. Gunnar's slim fingers had slid along her shoulder and lingered on her back where the skin was exposed, and she had looked up at him and smiled in an easy familiar fashion. Susan was not jealous. She had just hoped for better from him. When he mentioned the possibility of resistance, she had not thought it would have to coalesce around whomever he was currently sharing his bed.

Susan spoke, trying to keep the snark out of her voice, "So, why am I here?"

Gunnar beamed at her. She felt slightly disturbed by that look. Clara leaned in and spoke softly, "We need you." She looked back at Gunnar. "We have started a movement. We're trying to gather like-minded people together and make things happen." Clara's face was genuine and lovely. Susan noticed how earnest the expression was in her eyes. Could she be for real? A healer, an activist, a rebel? Susan was reminded of years ago and the voices of her students. Young, equally earnest, and sincere.

Clara continued, "We want to try to spread information, and education. I'm willing and so are others."

"What kind of information?"

Clara paused in thought. When she spoke, the question came out in a considered and serious way. Gunnar grinned proudly as she spoke.

"What matters, … today?" Clara looked directly as Susan.

Susan's response was a cagey, puzzled frown.

"And who matters? Who are the *people* in society that matter? These days."

Susan looked from her to Gunnar. "I'm not sure I follow."

"It's hard to put into words – I'm not a teacher or a writer like you -," Clara smiled.

"It's been a long time," Susan muttered.

"I feel – I imagine – that once, people mattered and cared. And that *ideas* mattered. I'm not sure what I mean. Oh, I'm sounding stupid and naïve."

"No," Susan sighed and with a fingertip traced a shape on Gunnar's worn tabletop as she spoke. "You're not stupid. You care. That's very, very rare these days. You're talking about education – the shape of education – that builds empathy and promotes criticism. It wasn't perfect – it wasn't always fair – but there used to be things we could do and anticipate, that we just can't imagine now."

She still felt a creeping irritation as she spoke but relished the opportunity to put into words some of her thoughts from way back, especially to someone so attentive and eager. Clara was so very beautiful, and Gunnar was clearly besotted. She had a way of speaking in a soft tone but with passion, and her gestures along with her words had a balletic calming effect. A therapist. Someone whose company alone could be soothing.

Susan found herself full of explanations for why Clara was right. She remembered the world as a complicated, unkind place but because of the feeling Clara imbued in her she wanted the past to seem golden.

"It was better. The weather was unpredictable, but cooler. Everybody got to go to a school or college. Food was better – some of it really, really good – *so* good. So much of it. I'm talking bakeries, supermarkets, and stalls for *everyone*. You could go out late at night and buy ice cream! Then take it home and keep it until you wanted to eat it because everyone had a little freezer unit to keep it cold." She was dredging some of what she knew first-hand but also what she remembered from the stories her parents' parents had told the family. Her voice ran on. Anecdote. Memoir.

"You see," Clara looked at Gunnar, "we need to hear about these things. That once we *could* have plentiful food and an education – a proper one – not just little ones corralled in a big room. Friendly, and kind."

"That's not all," Susan had warmed to her role. "There was an atmosphere and a culture in the country and in this city that was alive. It came from our language. There were so many people here from all over the world. People sang, recited, performed, and wrote in many languages. When I was a student, we had great books that taught us about our language. English wasn't a formal, stuffy Mother tongue. It was a messy, lively, teenager. It was a youthful, ever-changing, punk language. That's what we've lost. What we gave up on."

Clara looked intently at Susan as she spoke. Susan suddenly felt self-conscious. She stood up, "I'd better get going now. It's late." She pushed back her chair with a scrape and headed for the door.

"Susan," Clara called out to her and she turned. "Susan, this is *exactly* what we needed to hear and *you're* exactly what we need. You can tell people how it used to be with books and stories in abundance. Just think," and she moved closer to Susan who had paused at the shop door, "a world of warmth and full of plant life *and* a blossoming of the old ideas returning. We can have everything back – we *can*!"

Susan stood for a little longer and then turned and opened the door that let out into the alley behind the Emporium.

She spent a fitful night and awoke, still tired, to Ellery mashing her chest and purring close to her face with such intensity that she had to get up. She was annoyed with herself. Going through the motions of the early morning she pondered on how she had opened up the previous evening, and felt irritated at the memory. She thought about Clara's lovely, earnest face and scolded herself for being judgmental, immature, and too picky.

"You silly old woman," she said out loud. "This is exactly what's been on your mind for years. You're just peeved that someone else is *doing* something about it before you!"

She surveyed her bookshelf and reached down a dog-eared copy of 'Middlemarch'.

EVENING

Evening Primrose tapped her perfect manicure on the polished wooden rail of the mezzanine overlook. From this glass, wood, and metal stronghold she could survey her workforce at the Sky-stream HQ. Her very own panopticon. They knew she was there, and they were always wary, always on guard. Good, she thought, that's just as it should be. She was still ruminating on the shambles of a show the night before. When things went awry like that and the messaging got mixed up and problematic it made her very anxious. She awaited the fallout and very soon it arrived.

Her phone vibrated and the display on screen caused her heart to sink even further and her stomach to tie up in knots. She strode through the offices, decisively and purposefully to hide her anxiety, and made it into her sanctuary where she swiftly made the glass walls completely opaque with a wave of her hand and answered the call. With a deep breath she began as cheerily as she could, "Premier! What an honour – to what do I owe the pleasure?"

"Primrose, cut the shit."

The Premier, the Cabinet's highest minister and effectively England's authoritarian leader, was, in public, an affable and tousled-haired numpkin. A blundering, bowdlerising, blond bear of a man, protective of patriotic feeling, Englishness, tea and crumpets, and full of a 'Hail-fellow-well-met' manner. Evening knew his other side, however, one that was fickle, mercurial, and cruel, very, very cruel. She braced herself for the onslaught.

The Premier tore strips off her.

"On message – on *fucking* message, you feckless cunt! Why am I calling you? *Why* am I calling you? Why am *I* calling *you*?"

"To keep me on message, sir."

"And not *just* that – I am wasting my time, my *valuable* time – don't you think my time is valuable?"

"Yes, sir."

"Wasting my valuable *fucking* time – it's a waste of my time – don't you think that I have better things to do than *this*?"

"Yes, sir." Evening felt cowed and this only made her festering temper worse. She felt the stress building up in her head and her stomach.

"Why would I bother to contact you about a Sky-stream show? *Because* it matters – the *message* matters! You are the messenger, the mouthpiece – and you are on my *team* are you not, Primrose?"

"Yes, yes, I am, and I hoped the message would have been more clear – clearer. I didn't – …"

"Oh, so you aren't in control of your own media? Am I talking to the wrong person here? Should you put me through to whoever is *really* in charge?"

She felt his rage down the phone.

"I'm sorry," Evening muttered and breathed heavily, "I will personally see to it that such a thing does not happen again. Heads will roll."

"Yes, yes you will. Because any other slip-ups – such as getting some jobless malingerer on air – and I will *end* you at Sky-stream. I can replace you in minutes, so the only job you'll be able to get will be distributing rations at a Hub. The *only* reason you're still in your office is because of past loyalty. Repeat after me – I *will* stay on message!"

"I will stay on message," she took up a bland tone.

"Fuck, yes – you will!"

Evening slowed her breathing and opened a cabinet that was discretely camouflaged in the walnut and brass panelling. She poured herself a large Scotch over ice – something unknown to anyone but the highest of the haves and higher-ups. She downed a large gulp and hit the button on her intercom. She spoke abruptly into it: "Get in here, Jennifer."

Moments later, Jennifer Sinclair tapped and entered Evening's glass fortress.

"Yes, Miss Primrose. What can I do for you?"

Evening looked at her with smug satisfaction. She liked this woman performing servile acts for her. It was why she would never sack Jennifer – well not yet, at any rate.

It suited her to have her work in humiliating circumstances. Jennifer was an elegant – innately elegant – woman, from birth. She looked like a higher-up, as if born into that position. She was possessed of that long-boned natural poise that simply exuded grace. The cranium and the neck on which it sat sported a simple haircut that always behaved itself, whatever the atmosphere, as if she had just stepped out of a salon. Evening Primrose had always hated that type of woman. She was always forced to feel self-conscious about her short neck and mannish fingers, wide calves and hips. She hated the women who looked like they did not have to try. Surgery, strict diets, vigorous toning of face and body, and strategic tailoring of all her wardrobe had created Evening Primrose's TV-ready body. Although, the Sky-stream viewers were convinced that 'healthy eating, plenty of water, good bones from mother, and getting my steps in,' were what worked.

"Sit down," she spoke in a clipped fashion and instructed Jennifer, "take notes."

"Yes, of course."

"There has been a screw-up and now I have to firefight."

"I know," Jennifer broke in, "and I really didn't mean –".

"Ah-ah-ah – shut up," Evening interrupted with quiet glee, "this is instruction not discussion," and then she turned to Jennifer and spat out, "you stupid bitch." But she instantly regretted it. She should not let her feelings carry her away. Stay in control, Evening.

Jennifer looked down at her tablet and blanched.

Evening continued with a certain amount of sly triumph. She enjoyed bullying people and making this woman, in particular, feel sick and anxious for her job. She took pleasure in others' pain.

"We have a new policy – write this down," she prodded Jennifer's shoulder. "First, we vet everyone who comes into the building. Ramp up security. And then, she paused in her perambulation around the office and poured another Scotch, "we audition."

"Audition?"

"Anyone coming on air is an actor, or someone we can guarantee has no skeletons or flaws!" Evening cast a cruel look at her. "We initiate a system of auditions and recruitment for guests and interviewees. I'd prefer them to be actors – briefed with the correct *scripted* message. In fact, that will be an imperative. Find some writers to take it on – back stories, character biogs, and naturalistic speech and commentary. We invent a full scheme for each one, make it a major project from now. Wardrobe has to be briefed and – well you know the rest. Get on with it. Go."

Jennifer collected her things and just as she reached the door, Evening narrowed her eyes and followed up with, "And don't let me down."

Jennifer scurried out.

Evening sat in her office chair with her drink and sighed deeply. She massaged her temples. She felt choked up and anxious and wanted to take it out on someone else – but without making it too obvious. She looked around and considered un-masking her office but decided against it. She would leave the shields up for longer because she craved some privacy for now. Her staff had to live under regular scrutiny, but Evening wanted time. Time to think. She was angry. Angry at the Premier and Cabinet and angry at herself. The Prime Minister was good at many things and she believed in him, without doubt, but not without some personal conflict. She had been a loyal foot-soldier since the beginning of the Project, but now he and the others lashed out too quickly. She knew he would not be long for this world.

In the beginning, it had been fun almost all the time. Evening, or Patricia, as she was back then, had grown up in the post-war, post-UK-Split years. Those summers from her childhood, that grew warmer every year, when every-one could say: 'Who needs Europe?,' 'Who needs a house in France?,' 'We have our own great weather now'. Some people reflected on it with: 'If this is global warming, then we love it!' England had everything; beaches, vineyards, plantations, and cities, they did not need the rest of Britain. A right little, tight little nation. But then the seasonal storms grew worse and undermined the country's efforts to go it alone. Farming and food production suffered, and so rationing came in and the import of bulk food-stuffs for processing. It seemed to Patricia, growing up, that chaos and mayhem had steadily increased and were actively encouraged in all branches of the press and television, and especially the internet. She wanted to do something about it. She decided that a university education was the way to go. It would be meaningful. Evening sneered slightly at the memory of how naïve and idealistic Patricia had been.

What a joke! The plan to attend a good college at which she could learn critical thinking and argument was soon put off – permanently. She laughed at the recollection of the closure of her course and how she and fellow students had protested at the time. Such children, she sighed, and swilled the last of her drink in the tumbler as it combined with the melting ice-cube. Her life had taken a decided upturn after the phasing out of writing and literature studies.

At one of the protests that she had thought would be meaningful, she had encountered him for the first time. Derrick. Derrick Smallman. He was a determined, small-eyed man, already balding in his early thirties. He had approached her and asked, "Do you want to make a *real* difference?" And, if so, "What are you prepared to do about it?" This had been the call, and Patricia heeded it. So, she joined him and his newly formed 'think tank' made up of his circle. They also began a sexual affair, whilst he was engaged to the docile, loyal Charlotte. Patricia was groomed as part of Derrick's media revolution. She became Evening Primrose, a confrontational and radical radio and podcast host, and eventually the major Sky-stream presenter. She did not have to be accurate or consistent, in fact, better *not*, he told her. Be inflammatory and provocative. She was a 'voice of the people' and 'only saying what everyone is thinking'.

As Patricia she thought, for a little while at least, that she loved him, but as Evening she knew that she did not. Derrick paired her with Eliot, a veteran broadcaster, known for his sympathy to the Project and reactionary views. Eliot Chalmers became Eliot Charming in popular parlance and the name stuck. The 'Evening and Eliot' show was spawned.

Derrick had been quite hands-on at first. He helped her to chart the direction of the show and they even continued their affair for a little while after each married. Evening's wedding to Eliot was a glitzy, celebrity-laden event. Derrick and Charlotte had a low-key quickie morning ceremony at the Cheltsea Registry Office. Gradually, he had to pull away as he became more involved in the political side of the Project. And the politics took on a more and more authoritarian tone until it was as if it had always been that way. Derrick thrived in that environment and was a persuasive and passionate instigator with violent language and hefty amounts of prejudice. The Smallman Project became the foundation of the country's political direction of neo-Albion patriotism. Cabinet-controlled politics meant a Premier with increased personal power, and the Chairmanship of the government overwhelmed policy making. So, as Derrick had planned, he was able to put *his* man in the seat of power and reinvent Parliament's role as merely ceremonial. The regular jostling for power resulted in the current Premier, the bumbling, cruel idiot-in-charge. But his days (like all the others before and after him) were numbered.

Evening finished her drink. She had not seen Derrick in – what was it? – eight or even ten years. Hard to keep track of time these days. He had been ousted in a reshuffle. That benign-sounding operation masked, she knew, a much more sinister and sometimes brutal overthrow and action. Well, Derrick had known what might be in store. How the mighty have fallen, and she raised a glass under cover of the masked walls of her office and took a final dilute sip. Thanks to the Smallman Project, the existence of which was known only to a select few, she now wielded the kind of power and enjoyed the privileged lifestyle most in England could only dream about. Derrick had been made a casualty of his own success and what had become of him, she did not know.

Evening stood up and adjusted her beautifully tailored, flattering suit. Well, she told herself, remember dear Derrick's words: "Be extraordinary, be a weirdo, be a wild-card and a maven. Think outside the box!" She swiped the control to alter the opacity of the walls. Immediately, she could see her production team, their heads down hard at work. Evening walked out of her office and scanned the desks. Where was Jennifer? Skiving – again. She was a good producer, but she must always be made to feel she was hanging by a thread. Evening pursed her lips and frowned.

Mina

Twenty-four hours and counting. It was beyond a joke, now.

Mina wrestled another cardboard packing box into shape. Her hands, shielded in thick gloves, worked quickly. She kept an eye on the clock and the number of boxes she assembled. Everyone in the packing dock had to fill their quota. On your right was a flat trolley with slatted wooden sides. Every worker had to maintain a steady pace and keep the stack of flat boxes on their right as low as possible and the hopper of assembled boxes on their left as full as possible. Every half-hour or so a klaxon sounded, and the hopper was emptied into a trolley and the stack on the left side replenished. The workers must keep going and fill the quota. When a green light came on over your bay that signalled the end of your shift. You had to hope it came on at a reasonable time, to show you had met the day's allocation.

Mina was fast. She made sure of it. She never wanted to be the last out of the dock at the end of a shift. The loading dock foreman and the shift managers were a bunch of bastards. They liked to get the younger workers and the women alone, she knew, and by the look of them the next morning it was never fun. The factory and riverside area outside were grim places after dark. You had to be careful. Some of the older hands, grizzle-faced with gacky teeth, would often generously plod a little with their quota if a younger worker looked like they were flagging or had caught the eye of the foreman. You couldn't be obvious about it or you would get a thwack across the shoulder blades with a baton, or worse. They could deliberately limit your quota and so your wage would be even more pitiful.

Yeah, Mina thought, give them a little bit of privilege, let them into the upper-working-class with a promotion on shift and every one of them turns into a little tyrant. Fuck them.

Twenty-four hours and counting – beyond a joke – since Mum had left. She's really pissing me off now. Well, you can do one, Mum, as far as I'm concerned. This is the *last* time. I can take care of the boys. Unless, unless – Miss Cece is right, and you've been taken.

A cloud of new odour suddenly vented above her head. Mina had to momentarily pause as this mass of thick air moved past. Once the multi-savoury stench had abated, she could carry on. This belch of residue from the processing line meant that the filters had been changed and a new recipe batch was prepped for production. Mina wondered what it would be. The food plant sat on the banks of the river – 'The Old Father' – as its official name read. At the start of her shift, Mina had spotted some skiffs and a couple of wide barges at the mooring. Dockworkers unloaded a cargo of sacks on palettes. Probably soy or rice, she thought, so we can get ready for some new products. Useful to know.

She looked up at the clock. The red zone for the current shift ebbed away agonisingly slowly, but she kept up the pace. With soy and rice, she knew, that would mean more flavour packets. If they were already in stock, then Edgar might have some stashed away by now. Workers on the line had more chance to pilfer the foodstuffs and more notice of what was coming up. Mina's stomach rumbled, not at the malodorous fug around her in the dock, but at the possibility of new concoctions from Miss Cece's magical kitchen. This chain of thought, inevitably, brought her mind back to her mother.

Once her shift was done Mina joined the ranks of workers trailing along the factory corridors towards the locker rooms and security gates. The concrete and tile of the underpass along which they all walked caused every footfall and scuff to resonate. They peeled off in groups when they reached the lockers and the rattles and clangs sounded discordantly in the confined space. Drab grey rooms populated by dark-green-boiler-suited men and wine-dark-boiler-suited women. Mina emerged from the women's locker room and discretely scanned the wide underpass. Here, on leaving the dock or the factory floor, they were in the bowels of the factory, and the underpass was below the level of the river. You felt it too. There was damp in the air, and it was cooler here than in the upper sections of the plant. The harsh fluorescent lights gave no impression of what time of the day or night it might be outside, and moisture infiltrated everything causing the electrics to flicker. Mina walked purposefully into the corridor without looking up or to the side, conscious that the surveillance cameras had full coverage. She could be seen pausing and stooping to tie her bootlace.

A tall young man emerged from the opposite doorway of the men's locker room. He moved in her direction.

"Alright?" she spoke without looking at him.

Edgar Stanley paused a few feet from her, "Yeah, all good."

"Let's go, then," and still not looking in his direction she led the way towards the security gates.

This was the routine that Mina and Edgar maintained after each shift. They were careful not to follow a set pattern but mixed things up. Sometimes they met here, in the underpass, and sometimes just before the queues for security. They shifted and altered their tactics so that the factory surveillance could not track them and flag any suspicious activity. Mina had devised a system of signals and gestures for different days – odd or even dates – to let Edgar know where to rendezvous. They had to take these precautions because any extended communication between workers was always suspicious to the authorities and outside the gates there could be no loitering even for something as simple as to await friends. Socialising, overall, was discouraged. Expressions of friendship or affection in public were not exactly prohibited but were policed. Groups were broken up and simple association was highly risky. Nothing was enshrined in law, but it did not have to be. People understood, thanks to generations of discouragement and dissuasion with violence and threat. It was hard, though, to fight your human instincts.

Under the hard, chemical illumination of the security hall, Mina joined the end of the slow-moving march as, out of the corner of her eye, she noted Edgar slipping into place a couple of rows down. Each column of departing workers traipsed under the scanners, one by one. Mina, feeling alert, nonetheless kept a bland expression on her face. In public and work settings the English populace adopted a neutral look. You could identify their nationality in that way. Miss Cece called it 'bland-face'; a way of protecting yourself from suspicion – a mixture of agreeable compliance and vapid acquiescence. Mina aimed to be as innocuous as possible. She risked a glance in Edgar's direction. He was lucky, she thought, he didn't have to try. Her friend was tall and distinctive, but had a resting, innocent face. She quickly changed direction and looked ahead again. Focus.

Slowly, the line in front diminished. Mina reached the guards and raised her arms for the security sweep and pat-down. Once completed, they waved her through the scanner. She was free and clear for another day.

"Wait!"

Mina froze and felt as if her stomach had flipped over. She expected hands to be on her in an instant. Nothing. Instead, she heard loud scuffling to her right.

Edgar hit the ground, hard, with two guards on top of him. Mina heard the breath escape his body as they knocked the wind out of him. She had to clamp a hand over her mouth to stop from crying out. With the blood pounding in her ears, she watched Edgar being hoisted to his feet and dragged away. There was nothing she could do.

"Move along," one of the guards behind her barked.

She blundered her way out of the factory. People cast furtive looks over their shoulders to try and see where Edgar had been taken. But there was no sign of him. Mina was swept along in a wave of workers heading out to the Embankment pedways by the river.

Not Edgar. She ran this realisation through her mind. No – not Edgar, too. First, Mum. Now, Edgar.

Jennifer

Jennifer breathed deeply as another wave of nausea swept over her. Once across Rothermere Square, she used the coolness of the marble in the women's bathroom at the Sky-stream HQ to help it subside. She took a swig from her bottle of chilled cucumber water. Sickness, feeling faint. She wondered if she had caught a virus. Perhaps from travelling on the tram? That must be it.

Jennifer wiped her face and smoothed her hair then stepped out of the restroom, straight into the path of Eliot Charming.

"Darling!" his face creased into a broad smile. "How wonderful, just the person I was looking for!"

Before she knew what was happening, he had backed her into the bathroom again and the cold marble of the sink was this time pressed painfully against the backs of her thighs. He kissed her roughly and began to grope her breasts through her blouse. This hurt, they felt tender.

"No – Eliot – stop! I have to get back to work. Evening is waiting for me."

He pulled away from her with a smirk, "Really? Or is that a little bit of a fib?"

"Yes, she is. You know what she's like."

His handsome, craggy face was distorted again into a smug look, "I happen to know, little Missy, that my lovely wife is currently in with some big politicians about to have lunch. She told me, herself, to leave. In fact, her exact words were 'Fuck right off, now!'"

"You know that I have to leave, then. I have to be there."

His hands roamed aggressively over her torso once again, "I *know* that she's busy and I *know* that Big Daddy's missed you. Daddy wants his little girl. I want some num-nums!" he started to make smacking noises into her neck with his wide mouth and squeezed her buttocks with both hands. "Mmmm – mmmm – mmmm."

"No, Eliot," she tried to wriggle free. She hated it when he intoned this baby-talk as he accosted her. She could never get over how much worse it made their encounters. "I have work to do."

He pulled away again and looked her in the face, with a blank, cold expression. "Exactly, my happiness, my needs are your work. So, do your job." He turned her around to face the mirror and began to roughly hitch up her skirt.

Jennifer felt the tears welling in her eyes.

Later on, she retched into the toilet bowl as quietly as she could, then slumped onto the floor in the lavatory stall. Eliot had left her with the glib comment, "Your appraisal this quarter will read very well. I'm pleased," as he zipped up his fly.

She could just not get over the feeling of shaky sickness. Eliot's attentions at work were bad enough, and she only acquiesced to protect her job, but now she had to focus on Evening's demands whilst feeling miserable and nauseous. Between them, the famous married couple of the Sky-stream made her life almost unbearable. She remembered her mother's words to her as she smoothed her hair in the sunny room that overlooked the river at her old family home.

Elizabeth Sinclair-Webb used to slide a comb gently through Jennifer's fine fair hair as finches and hummingbirds flitted through the windows and around the awning of the conservatory. Orchids grew there, and blooms that her mother told her used to be rare and never to be found in England but now could be cultivated and planted out.

"You're like one of these flowers, my darling," Elizabeth kissed the top of her daughter's smooth, glossy hair.

She remembered looking up at her, "Why, Mother?"

"You are beautiful, delicate, and should be highly prized. You will make your mark on the world."

Jennifer looked out of the sun-room windows, framed by vines and flowers. The lawn of their lovely home sloped down to the Old Father whose dun-coloured waters lapped at the weed-wound supports of a wooden dock. Her father's elegant launch was moored down there. It was his transport down the river to his job at the West Minster, in the heart of the Capital. He had an office suite and a seat at the Palace of Justice in the Old West Minster Hall building. Simon Sinclair-Webb had family connections to government as far back as the early twentieth century.

"You have a bright future, Jennifer, in the halls of power."

"Why is that? I don't think I want to."

"*We* are patriots, my dear, and we have helped to restore this country's greatness for generations. The kingdom used to be controlled by the anti-democratic Europeans. They tried to take our power away, but *we* took it back, your grandfathers and great-grandfathers."

Jennifer felt bewildered by this. Taken back what, and from who? "But didn't we used to be a bigger kingdom – united with Scotland, and –?"

"Go and play, darling."

Elizabeth turned her daughter out of the hothouse.

Jennifer recalled the warmth and safety of her childhood home. The glinting glassware and outdoor meals on the wide terrace. She wiped the strong bile-tasting saliva from around her mouth and flushed the tissue down the toilet. She tidied herself up in the hard light around the mirror and contemplated her greyish complexion with despair before she exited the restroom. She joined the line of Skystream employees finishing their shift. With twenty-four-hour broadcast there was always a stream of people coming and going in and out of the HQ. They had to pass security checks for entry and exit. When Jennifer's turn arrived, the officer wafted the scanner perfunctorily over her body. She felt nauseous again. Eliot had only recently been sweating against her. Thank goodness there was not a DNA detector or geno-tracker on the scanner.

"Knocking off early today? Not like you." The officer spoke cheerily to her.

"Yes, yes I am not feeling very well."

"Not tip-top?" he continued with a grin. "Shame."

"Thank you," she picked up her bag and made her way hurriedly to the exit. She could feel his eyes still on her.

"Get well soon!" he called after her.

She knew it would get back to Evening *so* fast.

Still reliant upon the tram system, Jennifer decided to sit down this time. She was feeling wobbly and vulnerable. At the second stop, a Hub with RDTs, an elderly woman clambered on board. She immediately established herself on the curved plastic seat alongside Jennifer. The woman was swathed in an old cardigan, and a headscarf was wrapped around her matted grey hair. In the humidity of the central Capital, she stank of stale sweat. Jennifer's blue linen skirt was trapped underneath the woman. She cursed herself for not moving quickly enough before she had to share a cramped seat. She had to get off in two stops and she would have to interact with this woman if she did not move first.

"Maycourt – next stop." The prim recorded announcement sounded.

"This tram stops at Maycourt, Park View, Victory Parade, Churchill Square, St. James's-in-the-Woods, Old Father Embankment. Next stop – Maycourt."

The woman beside Jennifer did not look like she was about to move. She had settled in, a basket on her lap. It was full of what looked like old string and rubbish to Jennifer. The woman rummaged in it and retrieved some food – smelly – something pickled. Jennifer could not stay there. She did not want to risk vomiting on the tram.

"Excuse me," she managed to tap the woman's woollen arm. The smell of her stale body odour almost overpowered Jennifer.

"You alright, love?" the woman rasped to the pale washed-out face beside her. "Oh, I'm so sorry." She politely shifted a buttock cheek so Jennifer could edge her skirt out. She smiled at Jennifer as she rose. The woman's eyes, for an instant, reminded her of her mother, so she almost gasped in surprise. But, her teeth. Jennifer had to look away quickly. She had to get away. The rotten, withered mouth of the have-not woman repulsed her. She might have been in her fifties, but she looked eighty.

Jennifer strode along, breathing deeply, as she tried to shake off the smell and the taint of the tram. A brisk walk into her neighbourhood should help her sickness. The clear, clean, honey-coloured paving slabs revived her, and the attractive, tidy planters were surrounded by painted butterflies and multi-coloured bumblebees. She turned into Park View Mews, over which the balcony of her apartment hung with its river view. She was about to scan into the building when she paused and changed direction. Across the clean, well-aligned square a row of shops sat. A bakery, full of fine patisserie and rustic-looking loaves, and further along a wine-shop and bistro. But Jennifer headed for the Pharmacy, with its soothing exterior. Shelves were loaded with expensive jars and bottles of creams and lotions. Most valuable of all, however, and part of the neighbourhood's exclusive reputation was access to the dispensing counter at the far end of the shop past the wide, plentiful aisles. Jennifer approached the well-groomed, white-coated Pharmacist.

"I was wondering if you could help me?"

"Yes, Madam," the woman spoke in a gentle, reassuring tone.

Clara

"God is merciful!" Cecilia grasped Edgar's face and caused him to have to bend down so she could kiss her grandson on the forehead. She held on to him long enough for it to be uncomfortable as he stooped. "Thank you, Lord!"

"Let him go now, Grammere!" Clara said and transferred her affection onto him. "Petit!" She held her huge brother.

Once released, seated, and furnished with a cup of weak tea, Edgar was able to answer their questions. "The regular security was changed. Gil, who usually lets me through, had changed shift and couldn't warn me. I'm fine, I'm fine," he shrugged off their attentions.

Clara noticed, however, that her brother's hand trembled as he held his mug and sipped his tea.

Jacinda's boys, Adie and Aidan, stood in the doorway to the sitting-room, watching quietly and intently. After two more days of waiting and still no Jacinda, Cecilia had now taken the boys in proper. Mina had given her the key to their flat and the kind woman oversaw everything whilst she was on shift. The twins stayed close to Miss Cece now.

Clara decided to stop cross-examining her brother and let him rest. But there was a resounding interruption as Mina crashed in through the door.

"Fuck!" the young woman, Clara noted, always drew attention to her presence. "Bruv! Oh, my Christ!"

Clara watched as the teenagers were reunited.

"There was nothing I could do! Shit!"

"It's OK. I'm OK. They roughed me up a bit, that's all," he touched his side and winced slightly. "Then they let me off with a warning. I don't think they can afford to lose anyone else off the line." He looked around at the attentive group, concern on his young face. "Workers have been dropping off – a few here and there – for a while now. They can't keep pace with the hours, and they get sick." He looked at Mina, "They want to move workers from the dock onto the line."

"But that's great," Mina was celebratory, "because if you can't get supplies out, then I can!"

"No," Cecilia caught all their attention with her tone, "no more stealing. It's too risky. We can't be split up – anymore." She whispered to Mina, "You have to think of your brothers."

Clara saw Mina retreat a little and look cowed as the magnitude of the situation crept over her. Such a brave girl, Clara reflected, to the point of risky foolishness. She planted herself in the middle of things; she was outspoken and took things on her shoulders. She could give most of the COF a run for their money – but she gambled on her safety and that of others. Could she be taught some caution and discretion? Could she become useful?

Whilst the reunions were happening and her grandmother scolded the youngsters, Clara slid into the kitchen, passing the Suresh twins in the doorway. She sat down at the neat table and began to sort through her bag of foraged supplies. Whilst they had waited anxiously for Edgar, before his triumphant return, she had kept her phone close by for any word. Now, she noticed a pair of messages on her screen. The first was interesting and concerning; from PharmaGirl27:

'I have a case for you.'

Clara hit save to answer it later.

The next message caught her by surprise. The reluctant tone of it came through: 'I think – I suppose – we could talk, Susan.'

Unnoticed by the group in the sitting-room, once they were hypnotised by the Sky-screen and munching on some lentil snacks supplied by Cecilia's ingenuity, Clara took the chance to slip away.

PART TWO

CLARA & SUSAN

"He's a good cat, just a little mischievous."

"Well, I'm allergic to cats, so I'm biased."

Susan looked at Clara. She was slightly irritated by the woman. She still had to thaw towards her, but they had established a stable alliance over the past couple of weeks.

'She's a crazy cat-lady, that one,' Clara had thought to herself. 'How are we supposed to work together?'

The two women were chatting as they worked away with gardening tools: secateurs, clippers, rakes, and loppers. They were in the Wilderness in the middle of the Square. They had ventured in the night before to deposit these tools. Both had made their activities as unobtrusive as possible. Susan had discovered how good Clara was at covert actions. They had organised their equipment beside a one-storey building in the heart of the Wilderness, overgrown with foliage, vines, and ivy. It was a small cottage-like structure formed from thick black timbers, chunky and solid. Between the timbers concrete in-fill made up the walls, textured with many-coloured pebbles, most of which had been brushed and worn off with age but left their imprint in the cement. The roof was broad and steeply pitched, formed of grey slate tiles, now smothered with layers of damp mosses. Clusters of coloured finches hopped about and grazed on this rich food source.

'The Pavilion,' as the faded, peeling name above the door read, had once been a café in the park. Susan had sketchy memories of such places dating back to her early childhood. Probably from the same time as the green bicycle. Neat parks and gardens. Tea and cakes. Cold, brightly coloured ice-slush in clear plastic containers rotated by a corkscrew stirrer.

"We're in," with a crack Clara prised open the weathered, half-rotted door. By the look of it this barrier should disintegrate to the touch, but they noticed how thick it was once they had tackled the bolts. Loosened up with a crowbar it scraped, shuddered and protested as the two women applied more leverage. Susan retrieved a length of wood that lay to one side, choked with ivy, and used it as a tool. With leaf litter swept out of the way, great wodges of it that had accumulated in layers over years and years, they could free the door enough to get into the building.

Once inside, Susan and Clara could see that part of the roof in one corner had given way. Birds of all varieties had flown inside. There, they had roosted on the thick dark timbers that spanned the roof of the squat, low building. The bird-droppings were thickly crusted on the beams and in dense patches on the floor.

"Here," Clara handed Susan a hand-stitched cloth face mask, "put this on." She looped her own over her ears. Susan looked at hers. It was formed from pieces of bright print fabric, lined with a breathable cotton that had once formed part of a bed sheet by the look of it. "Don't worry, it's clean," Clara reassured her. "I use these when I go into houses where there's viral outbreaks, so I can still treat people." She surveyed the space with the eye of someone used to checking for contamination. "This is what I was afraid of. The particles from the bird-droppings and any spores that they carry could be very toxic. We'll have to be careful and clean everything in order to avoid lung damage and irritation."

"Because of the heat," Susan stated.

"Yes. Because of the heat."

Two weeks earlier the women had come together to talk, at Susan's instigation. Clara's words had lingered and impacted on her. Be a spectator, she had asked herself, or be a participant? She grappled with the idea of feeling that she ought to do something – something for education, justice, society, fairness, and other high-minded ideals. And then she paused in her ruminations on this. Why were these '*high* ideals'? Should they not just be *normal*, everyday features of life? Susan had sat on her bed in the basement and looked at the scrolling news on the Sky-stream feed on her phone:

> You **think** society owes you a living? But what do **you** owe society? **BIG SOCIETY** talking points on tonight's 'Evening and Eliot'.
> We can all do **more**. How to make your ration packs go further with celebrity Chef Cater Pilar.

*Our **community**. Our **Heroes**. Champion volun-*
*teers on receiving their **Platinum People's Choice***
***Homegrown Heroes** awards. What they can teach*
the rest of us.

Everything – all the content – targeted at people taking responsibility for every aspect of their lives, from how to eat, how to walk the streets, how to earn, how to spend. The constant feed of information reinforced to everyone that if *your* ration allocation was unsatisfactory then it was because *you* don't make it go far enough, probably because you are greedy and irresponsible. Never a word about the fact that the food is spoiled before it reaches you, or that the protein is so lacking you have no energy for anything other than getting to the RDT once a month and then making it back home, or that the portions are so meagre you eke it out as best you can for you and your children and then go hungry for a week trying to live off scraps out of the refuse, or you attempt to get some black market contraband and the Feds pick you up because *you* are the crook. If *your* neighbourhood is dilapidated, it's because *you* don't care enough and *you* need to mobilise a volunteer group to mend it and 'show some pride'. Never a word about how re-wilding means everything is choked with vegetation and the roots of trees have undermined pavements and foundations in all but the most privileged suburbs. If *your* children don't have a future, it's because *you* haven't worked hard enough to provide it. Never a word about how there are no schools like there used to be, Susan reflected, and that if education is something you have to provide at home you can't do it if you have no resources and no stability.

She considered the system they all lived under and how the Sky-stream perpetuated it and fed into it, reinforcing prejudices about haves and have-nots, highers and lowers. It told everyone that if you didn't have *things*, it wasn't up to society to provide them, and that extended to both nutrition and education. If you couldn't afford those things outside the home, you simply had to work harder to provide them and take action or start a social movement. The state would not be there for rescue or molly-coddling. 'Get out there and show some spunk and English pride! That's how we did things in the past, that's what made us Great!'

But, Susan knew, that if your doors and windows are regularly overgrown with vines and ivy and if the fabric of your building is dissolving under the advance of lichens and mosses, and you haven't eaten enough in days, then how are you meant to solve those problems with no tools? How do you form a home-school action group with no books or paper? Plenty of trees, but no paper. The more she thought about it, the more Susan saw the blindness and the bind under which they all lived. The need for help, support, training, or a new a start was not a personal weakness, *but* it was portrayed as such. Necessities were seen as limitations on ingenuity, and assistance as an obstruction to hard work. But people need calories to brighten their minds and complexions. She recalled the riot over the milk and vegetables. The desperation, the risk – and then she looked at the meagre rations on her own shelf. She was only a few tins or soy-lentil packs away from joining the next crazed scramble amongst the broken glass and blood for a couple of squashed cabbage leaves.

That is why she was in the old park Pavilion in the Wilderness with Clara, scraping bird shit off the floor. The two sat down on some rickety chairs for a rest.

"Let's have a breather before we carry on. Here," Clara offered Susan a piece of what looked like a little grey cake.

Susan took it. She sniffed it.

"Wild garlic and mushroom scone made with acorn flour. Try it," Clara smiled and pulled her mask down to take a bite.

Susan nibbled the crumbly, soft morsel. It had a dense texture reminiscent of baked goods, from what she could remember. Instantly, a delicious savoury taste filled her mouth, and she gobbled the rest in a few bites. Food for the body can also be food for the mind and soul. Scraps, bland ration packs, and spongy grey tinned food caused a humble snack to spark like a firework in comparison.

Clara looked around the Pavilion. "It has potential. You were right to suggest it. It's well-hidden but close by."

When the two had met up again, Susan had talked through her fears. Clara had listened. Without Gunnar standing over them, she felt able to open up. Clara had been a good listener. Susan grew passionate as they talked about their shared concerns. She learned about Clara's nursing experience, trained by her grandmother Cecilia. The Stanley family were typical – with a background of military and medical service behind them. Valuable skills, vital skills, which were no longer passed on and no longer valued.

"The things I know, and I've been taught," as she told Susan, "like your knowledge, should not be lost. If I let the knowledge of disinfectants and analgesic painkillers ebb away, then our future is doomed."

They had been sitting in Susan's clammy basement, and Clara had spoken at length about this legacy and sharing of knowledge. Susan had been gradually more and more charmed and enthused.

"You truly believe," she asked her, "that we – just a handful of people – can do something?"

"Yes, of course. And I don't mean start a revolution. We don't need any more blood on our hands – just dirt now. We can graft. We can spread knowledge."

"Yes, knowledge. I know I can do that. If we tried to agitate, we'd only get our heads bashed in! But we can educate."

Susan had recalled the little building, now lost in the Wilderness. It took them half the day to just find it, hidden amongst a riot of brambles, ivy, and clinging vines. The Pavilion teahouse, the faded sign reminded her.

"The Pivvy," Susan said to herself, as she remembered the words of one of her grandparents.

"The Pivvy? I like that. It would work as a good code. No one else will know what we're referring to," Clara approved.

This was to be their base. The clearance of the inside of the café signalled a new chapter for Clara and her activism, and for Susan an initiation into that activism.

"We're not after a revolution, but we will be at risk as radicals," Clara advised, speaking with the experienced voice of someone who had regular run-ins with authority. "The higher-ups and the COF won't differentiate over what we're doing. It's all or nothing. Are you in?"

"I'm in," Susan had agreed, with Ellery on her lap, placid but with his judgmental green eyes on Clara. Clara had eventually smiled at the cat and then looked around admiringly at Susan's shelves. Some of the titles were familiar to her, but most were strangers. She felt the gaps in her knowledge keenly when confronted with Susan's library. She took up a copy of a Shakespeare play, *Measure for Measure*. She also made a mental note of the fact that Susan did not have a Sky-screen playing out the continuous feed of propaganda, news, and entertainment. As a single, lower-middle woman she just qualified for rations but living in a one-room basement was not deemed important enough to be given a connection. She had her hand-held device with news-loops and text up-dates, but Susan had no family, no future, no usefulness. She moved under the radar; she was a middle-aged female – and that made her a ghost. This, Clara considered, was at the heart of her very usefulness.

Susan and Clara munched the last of the mushroom bread in the scruffy old Pivvy. Susan savoured each mouthful and looked around. The walls were streaked with discolouration from water damage; dust, leaves, and debris were everywhere, but she could tell that the fabric of the little building was mostly sound. They had some canvas tarpaulin to patch the hole in the roof and had cleared and fixed up some of the space after a few hours.

Susan sipped water from an old plastic bottle she carried, and returned her mask, before she spoke. Some words had come back to her, a recitation from bygone times:

"I will arise and go now, and go to Innisfree,

And a small cabin build there, of clay and wattles made."

"What's that?" Clara looked at her, breathless and sweating as she stretched from her work. Her eyes looked watery. "It sounds lovely."

"William, something – B – Yeats. Yes. Butler. Yes. William Butler Yeats. WB."

"Is there more? Can you remember it?"

"Let me see … Nine bean-rows will I have there, a hive for the honey-bee, And live alone in the bee-loud glade."

"A bee-loud glade," Clara repeated. "Plenty of those."

"And I shall have some peace there, for peace comes dropping slow, Dropping from the veils of the morning to where the cricket sings." She paused. "Err … what else?" After some slight hesitation, she resumed and the rest of the words came fluently, just as she had learned them at school, all those years ago.

"There midnight's all a-glimmer and noon a purple glow,

And evening full of linnet's wings.

I will arise and go now, for always night and day

I hear lake water lapping with low sounds by the shore;

While I stand on the roadway, or on the pavements grey,

I hear it in the deep heart's core."

"Linnet's wings and lake water, and the deep heart's core," Clara murmured.

Mina

It was not a good idea. Mina mused over their activity as a drizzle fell in the grey twilight over the city. She had ascended a tall block in a have-nots neighbourhood near the river. It was a greasy, ancient brick-built place with narrow makeshift stairwells rising through cut holes in plank floors. Once quite smart, now everything underfoot was covered in a thick layer of grey dust, with plenty of rat-droppings mixed in. A classic doss-house.

As she moved up through the building with Edgar, Mina felt more and more doubtful. They made their way cautiously. The inhabitants looked up from smoky electric hobs plugged into overloaded sockets or slept in corners packed with cardboard and old rags. Hollow, haunted eyes of children followed them as they trod the rickety staircases.

"I'm not sure about this," she whispered to Edgar. "It's a *real* dump. No one's gonna be here who can help us. Your sis got it wrong this time, man."

"It's right up at the top. She was positive. Let's keep going."

"Who is this Charlie guy, anyways, man?"

"Someone Clara knows, from way back. I think he served under my Dad in the wars."

"So, he's a vet, then? Well, isn't everyone? Don't mean he can help us."

"Here," Edgar emerged out of the final stairwell and into a narrow upper hallway. Before them were lathe and plaster and chipboard walls that looked old but had been repaired and maintained with a level of care and competence. A door at the end of the hall stood closed with its mottled and cracked panels bearing signs that read: 'No Entry' and 'Private'.

"Not very welcoming," Mina felt herself falling further into a sceptical and sarcastic mode.

Edgar tapped tentatively at the door. They heard a movement within.

A voice came quietly, "Can't you read?"

Edgar coughed discretely, "It's Edgar, Clara's brother. She said you could help us."

Silence from within.

The door opened a crack, a watery green eye looked at them from a pale, freckled face.

"Charlie?" Edgar asked.

The door opened a little more and Charlie stepped back to let them enter.

"This is Mina. Charlie, Mina."

Mina looked at the quiet man in front of her. Charlie was wiry with a shaved head, but evidently possessed of red hair. He was not much taller than Mina and only in his forties, she guessed, but like so many people he looked broken. She noticed he had a slight limp. His clothes were army surplus, combat trousers and a khaki shirt with a regimental insignia, and his tattoos also had a military theme. Mina noticed the words 'Lest we forget' and 'Sapper' inscribed on his lower arms. She took the chance to look around this little bolt-hole home up in the roof of a semi-derelict fortress. A setting for an army of have-nots, most of them ex-army. They were there in the evening, but the whole place felt like a perpetual twilight world.

Charlie's room was full of things, but very tidy. An ex-soldier's neatness. It gave Mina the sense that everything was kept straight at the risk of unleashing something dangerous. He wanted to keep things contained. The order was there to control the intrusion of memories and distress. More competent carpentry was visible with the shelving that held his possessions, pictures, and boxes. The metal-framed camp-bed was immaculately made up. Charlie's room was open to the sky. There was a large cavity in the roof, an opening where tiles and rafters had long since collapsed. Charlie had made it structurally sound and Mina saw that some ends of broom handle and dowel had been wedged into gaps and crevices. She understood the purpose of these within a few moments. The sunset could be seen through the opening, and a piece of canvas stretched over one section kept out most of the drizzle. As the light faded, a swirl of birds came in to roost. Each found its place on one of the perches. Charlie sprinkled some crumbs into little pot. A few nuts and seeds here and there offered up as a humble meal.

"I love what you've done with the place," Mina watched him as he held up a little tray of sunflower seeds to a collared dove in the roof space. Edgar shot her a look.

"Thanks for letting us in, Charlie."

"What does Clara need me for?"

"She said she can make use of your resources. She didn't say exactly what."

Charlie went over to an old table with a drawer. He pulled it open and took out a black plastic fob.

"She doesn't need to. I'd do anything for your sister. She saved my life." He went over to a corner and began to sort out a backpack.

"You've got a great view from up here," Mina tried to redeem herself with a change of tone as she peered out of the opening in the roof and breathed out as she looked over the city while the sun set.

Flocks of birds flew in and out of the woodlands and the forest on the horizon. Peeping out from amongst the trees were the buildings. The edges of the architecture were smothered and blurred by vegetation. Fuzzy swarms of midges were up at this height. No wonder Charlie had built his own perch here. The ghost of the city, shrouded in green, was visible in all its mystery and wonder. As she looked to the horizon Mina could see the brown, green, and grey blending together in the glow of the setting sun. It was quite quiet. Discernible were the hum of trams and the cries and chatter of birds. The sound of voices came up from below through the calm rustle and swell of the trees that lined the street. Human voices, yes, but mostly the cries and calls of small green birds. A type of parakeet – she had heard Miss Cece describe it to her brothers. Once, people kept them as pets, along with other 'exotic' animals and reptiles in their homes in cages and tanks apparently. Mina only knew the animals and birds in all their jewel-like brilliance as wild creatures that scuttled up the walls or swooped low around the wild parks and woodlands of the Capital. From Charlie's vantage point she could see out to the North and West and the wide expanse of Richmond Forest with the setting sun glinting off the Old Father, a sparkling ribbon in the dense greenery.

Cutting a swathe through the green was Airstrip Row. A hexagonal concrete pattern. Now, in the dimming light, yellow and green beacons blinked and floated into the evening sky as the Helioships taxied and jostled for take-off and landing. The transportation was silent and wafted gently into the sky. The hooting of the barges along the river interrupted every so often. The soft, quiet exchange of travellers and precious cargo, for the haves and higher-ups, in the clouds and along the waterways. Mina felt a pang of something that felt like loneliness, maybe envy, she was not sure what it meant. She did not know what it felt like to travel, to go anywhere. She knew she wanted to travel, though, as she looked at the lights in the sky and heard the haunting calls of the vessels.

"Come on, are you ready?" Charlie stood by the door backpack loaded. He led the way back through the passageways and down the stairwells, silent and careful. No one said a word. Out in the dark street the chemical lamplight flickered into life.

"This way," Charlie took the two youngsters into a side road. For a man with a limp, he moved fast, with a long, loping stride. In the darkness of a courtyard Charlie took out a flashlight from his pack and wound the coil. When it came on, he put it in place to illuminate a dark corner.

"Give me a hand with this," he gestured to Edgar who helped him remove a plastic cover off a small van parked in a gap between two buildings. The cover was old and faded. A good camouflage down this hidden by-road. The vehicle beneath was in good condition. It was well looked after and carefully maintained like everything connected with Charlie, Mina was learning. She noticed the cable from the side of the building, coupled to a further cable that syphoned electricity from the building's supply in order to charge the van.

The lights on the dashboard blinked. Mina was wedged in next to Edgar as Charlie turned the engine on. She watched as he operated the vehicle, fascinated. He had used the black fob to unlock it remotely. With the flick of a switch what looked like little buttons clicked upwards on the inside of each door and made her jump. Mina had never seen that, and now she was on her first ever vehicle ride – other than a tram. Charlie pulled slowly out of the narrow side road. Mina squeezed Edgar's hand involuntarily.

"You OK?" he whispered to her.

"Uh-huh," she nodded and breathed steadily and excitedly as the sensation of being close to the road and moving smoothly along took hold. Now, the real adventure, the true endeavour struck her for the first time, as they navigated the dark, quiet streets.

Susan

The first day of orientation. Susan had tried to gather up her things and be organised, but she dropped most of them. Her aluminium water bottle clattered and pinged down the stairs. Embarrassed, she sidled into the library foyer. The air conditioning made the crowded space just about bearable. In order to hear the Chief Librarian's address to the new students, she had to get closer. She prompted some tutting and an exasperated look from the Librarian when she tried to edge around the group, unsuccessfully. Her bag swayed against a metal post that was looped to another post, and another, with velvet rope. The row clattered over.

"Young lady!" the Librarian reprimanded her. "Please!"

"Sorry, sorry!" Susan had only wanted to meet people and be liked and do well at college. But she seemed to have made the worst impression wherever she went. It was a smart place. A venerable network of halls and courtyards in a leafy Borough of the Capital. Tiled corridors echoed with the sounds of the student population, ringing up to vaulted ceilings and stained-glass transoms.

Susan tried her best to rearrange the metal posts around the library display and for the first time looked up at what was featured.

"Moving on, this way," the Librarian ushered the group on to the carels.

Susan stayed put, looking at the imposing object in front of her. The sign read: 'An Original Heidelberg Windmill Printing Press (20th Century)'.

Clara

Clara congratulated herself. She watched as Susan deftly lifted the finished sheets off the delivery pile of the press. She knew it had been a good move to bring Susan into the activist circle, along with Charlie. The plan had moved ahead and blossomed – more than she could have hoped. Charlie had driven with Mina and Edgar across the city and brought the printing press from its old home at the college to their new base at the Pivvy. It had been a two-night project, with Gunnar also lending a hand. They followed a map drawn by Susan and broke into the college building. Despite Mina's infectious enthusiasm to get it done, they had to lie low during the day.

"This is fucking mint!" she had declared once they hid out at Gunnar's shop. It was there that Clara could introduce Susan to Edgar, Mina, and Charlie.

The six sat at Gunnar's table and appraised one another. A former soldier, a young factory worker, a teenage girl with a lust for robbery and passing stolen goods, a tall Swedish shopkeeper who never seemed to sell anything, a middle-aged writer and teacher, and an activist and largely self-taught healer. All have-nots, and some with a lot to lose, but others with nothing to lose. Clara smiled at Gunnar. She felt something change that night.

Once it was dark, Gunnar, Charlie, and Clara had wheeled the van from its hiding place and circled around to the

Square. When the printing press was unloaded, Charlie made himself scarce and the tedious chore of manoeuvring the printing press to the Pivvy had taken five of them working as a team most of the night. But with a sturdy trolley from the Emporium, some planks of wood, and clearance of the old paths through the Wilderness, they made it. Working together. They went back to cover the path they had cut through the undergrowth. As dawn broke over the city, they installed the Heidelberg Windmill in the Pavilion.

Clara's early attempts at direct action and activism had taken shape around painted signs, handwritten manifestoes, and graffiti. Until, that is, Susan had stepped in: "If we can source pigments, inks, and paper, then we can do even more."

She had pointed them in the direction of the printing press housed in her old college and after much sweat and effort, the Pivvy could be their base and studio. Susan had shown Clara how to operate it, and they got it working again with Charlie's help.

"It's a solid piece of machinery," he said, "with very little wear and tear." With it came all the accessories, including a precious case of type and rollers.

Clara inked up the plates and Susan showed Edgar how to set the type. He was dextrous and capable. Mina, on the other hand, could not sit still long enough, so Clara sent her off to scout possible locations where the products of their studio could be posted. With Susan providing content, she planned a poster campaign. They could draw images and reproduce material from Susan's library and the depths of her precious memory. The writer could compose slogans or offer up quotations and text. Clara planned some decorative borders with flourishes based on embroidery patterns she borrowed from her grandmother. Susan copied words and Clara took out her brushes and pens to reproduce them as prototype posters.

"Lord, what fools these mortals be!"

"All animals are created equal, but some are more equal than others."

"I declare after all there is no enjoyment like reading!"

These were good, Clara thought, and noticed how Susan could call upon some easy, snappy dialogue. Characters who spoke their minds. She remembered some of them. Shakespeare, Jane Austen.

"Who's Shakespeare? Weird." Mina had returned to the Pivvy and was sitting on a table swinging her legs and eating some toasted cob nuts. Susan explained, trying her best to recover the words and thoughts from her long-ago classes. She started to recall the state of mind of being a teacher, a sort of behaviour that she thought she had forgotten. What seemed to have been lost could be found again, under the right conditions.

"He was very descriptive, er, versatile with his language. He learned to write plays at a time when the English language was blossoming, growing, and books were being translated. He went to school when printed books were available, so his learning could thrive. You can't write without being able to read and read well, be an active reader."

"Eh?" Mina poked around in the little bag for the next nut.

"It's the opposite of watching a screen. When you read a book, you engage in an activity, a sort of deal with the writer. You write it, and I'll stay with you on the journey, thinking as I go."

Mina pulled an approving sort of expression and shrugged and nodded as she munched. Susan could tell she had her attention now.

"And in Shakespeare's time people had begun to read more than ever in the history of the country. It was still not a majority of people who *could* read, but many more than ever before. Ordinary people. And with printing there was more business, and of course theatres. Professional theatre for the first time. It was considered a Golden Age – a renaissance.

"That means, in the French, I know," Clara eagerly recalled, " – a re-birth – that's it!"

"I think so. They were rediscovering lost knowledge from past ages. Translated old texts. And travelling – from England and Spain to America. There was new technology, and creativity that came with it."

Clara contemplated the Windmill Printing Press as Edgar turned the wheel and operated the mechanism. Charlie had oiled it up and set things in motion. 'That's us,' she thought, 're-discovering, re-birthing, adventure, and drama.' She felt excited and turned to Susan.

"I could get into that," she smiled at her co-conspirator, "restoring and recovering something that was lost."

"I suppose," Susan replied and looked down at her scuffed shoes.

Jennifer

It was no longer bearable. Things had gone too far and moved too fast.

That was how Jennifer found herself on a worn sofa, encased in a patchwork blanket. She breathed as slowly and as calmly as she could. The pain was just about tolerable, and she preferred to lie still. The woman that the Pharmacist had put her in contact with sat beside her and rubbed her lower back – a welcome touch. She was a kindly black lady with long, to Jennifer's eye, woolly locks. She looked like the idea Jennifer had of some sort of tribal woman in 'ethnic' clothing. In the near darkness of this old room, she was a comforting presence. A tear escaped from the corner of Jennifer's eye and the woman hummed a delicate, quiet tune as she patted the area where the most intense pain flowed out in spasms from her abdomen. The backs of her legs also felt weak and ached.

"Down by the Sally Gardens,

My love and I did meet.

She passed the Sally Gardens with little snow-white feet.

She bid me to take love easy

As the leaves grow on the trees,

But I, being young and foolish

With her would not agree ..."

The woman crooned this in an absent, habitual fashion. Jennifer felt lost in her Nurse's song.

"What's that? What are you singing?" Jennifer murmured tearfully.

The woman moistened a cloth from the bowl of cool water beside her and smoothed it over Jennifer's forehead and cheeks. It was stuffy where she lay, and this soothed her tearful state and refreshed her skin.

"Was I singing?" the nurse asked. "I don't always know I'm doing it. It's a romantic lament, I think," she explained. "A little something a friend taught me."

"It's lovely, but it sounds very sad," Jennifer breathed deeply with a slight sob. She doubled over and started to moan intensely.

"All right, all right," the Nurse soothed her.

The worn sofa on which Jennifer lay was situated in the open-plan living-room of a bedsit. On one side of the room was a shadowy kitchenette. A table and chairs were stacked up against a wall. Cracked and peeling walls surrounded them, covered in the marks of penetrating damp. She had arrived at this little bolt-hole after following a set of careful, secretive instructions with cryptic names along the pedway route of the Capital. The anonymous Nurse met her and made her comfortable. She had not known what to expect twelve hours ago. Would there be an operating table? Some sort of clinic? It was drab and quiet, and very ordinary in a zone with faded signage reading 'The Barbican'.

The Nurse had donned a sterile apron and gloves and laid out a freshly laundered sheet on the sofa. This instilled some confidence into Jennifer, but she still felt fearful and shook slightly. She had received a packet with instructions a day earlier. It contained one tablet that she had to take straight away, as long as she could guarantee that she would be at the address the next day. One pill, and then the Nurse explained the rest of the process.

"We'll make every effort to keep things safe and get you through it. You're in good hands." She gave Jennifer a reassuring smile in response to her earnest, fearful expression.

Jennifer watched as her Nurse pounded some dried herbs and powders together.

"Make yourself comfortable," she said and gestured to the sofa. "It's going to take a little time."

Jennifer held onto the bag she had brought. It contained a change of clothes, as instructed, underwear, and some sanitary pads. The directions and the first pill had made it clear what she needed. Her Nurse blended the compound with some oil into a thick paste. She rolled it into a capsule form, using a wooden paddle and scoop.

"Here," she offered Jennifer two portions of this compound. "Take them with some water, they will help with the pain."

"OK," Jennifer sat down and looked at the dark green, rank capsules in the palm of her hand.

This had been hours ago, just before the second pill. The pain and cramping had taken hold after that, and she had to spend some time in the little bathroom cubicle off the living-room. The woman kept a careful watch and helped her through it. Jennifer was so grateful for the reassurance as her Nurse's tone told her that everything she experienced was expected and normal. She went into the living-room and prepared more pain relief by hand as Jennifer steadied herself against the side of the stained plastic bathtub. The Nurse had told Jennifer that they could not run the risk of using any more manu-factured, over-the-counter drugs than they had to. The Pharmacist near the riverside apartments was trustwor-thy and could covertly supply the abortifacient. Other than that, they needed to be as self-sufficient as possible. So, Jennifer swallowed the chunky, bitter, herby pills the nurse prepared.

The products of the termination once they appeared could not be flushed away, she learned. Jennifer had hoped it might be that easy, but she quickly learned that even flushed materials – the tissue and the foetus – could be traced. The Nurse showed her the bio-secure bag with its special lining.

"This will protect even from genetic-tagging tracers. And I'll take it away with me and bury it. Don't worry, they won't be able to detect it."

Following the first pains and show of blood and at her Nurse's instruction, Jennifer took the chance to grab a little sleep with the help of the painkillers. She roused a couple of hours later in a pain-riddled fog. The Nurse stood over her.

"This is it. It's going to be tough, but it will soon be over," she reassured Jennifer who felt sick.

"That's it, just breathe."

But Jennifer had to cry out in pain as the cramps took over. "I don't – I don't think I can!" She clenched her fists and sobbed.

"Yes, you can," the Nurse soothed her again. "It's a natural process. But you must try to be as quiet as you can."

Jennifer cried and sweated as the waves of pain washed through her, from her abdomen down her legs. She soon had to stumble to the bathroom with help from the Nurse.

A little while later, she was able to venture out and lie down on the fresh sheet. It was at this point that the Nurse went into action and busied herself in the cubicle to clean everything thoroughly and scrupulously. In the scruffy bedsit, the bathroom was spotlessly sterilised. She packaged up everything left of Jennifer's pregnancy, ready for a secret disposal. A baby, Jennifer thought, now no more. A baby, fathered by Eliot.

The Nurse came and sat with her again.

"It's worked," she rubbed Jennifer's lower back, "everything is accounted for. But there might still be some residue."

"I have some sanitary pads."

"Good, good. And you can stay here for a little longer. You have to rest as much as possible."

Jennifer lay still and looked around the bedsit that had been her haven for the past hours. She felt a wave of misery and self-loathing, and clenched her eyes tight, not with the pain of what was finally expelled from her womb, but at the shame and stupidity she felt. Eliot had pursued her with a relentless focus from the start. She spoke to colleagues about it and found out that she was one of many. That was just the way of things at Sky-stream HQ. She had walked in on him abusing staff more than once. He treated them exactly as he wished, but she blamed herself for being blind.

The first time had been only a few days into her job. Eliot had risen sharply from the wide leather sofa in his office. She had felt embarrassed as she saw the young woman lying on the sofa, rearranging her dishevelled clothing. Jennifer noticed that the garments – a blouse and pleated skirt – looked like a school uniform from one of the higher-up grammars, like the one she had attended. Just a girl, she realised. Flushed and distressed. Two glasses were on the side table, tumblers of whisky. Had she been tipsy? Or drugged? Now that she thought about it, lying in shame on a dingy bed-sit sofa, Jennifer thought how stupid she had been. She had said nothing as Eliot ushered the girl out, her eyes cast down towards her lace-up shoes.

"Dear me! Is that the time?" he had been breezy and quite smooth about it. He gestured at the teenager as she retreated. "Daughter of a friend of mine – wants to get into the business. I lose track when I'm giving advice and mentoring. She's very keen and I can't say no." He nonchalantly adjusted himself, flopped down on the sofa and downed the rest of his drink.

Similar episodes occurred. Anecdotes and rumours abounded, until one day as she leaned across his desk to plug in his phone and tablet, Eliot had slipped a hand into her blouse to cup one of her breasts. He had immediately teased her nipple through the fabric of her bra, and she recalled with disgust his husky breathing and the sound he had made.

"Totty," he called her. "My bit of posh totty."

Jennifer looked over at the kind face of the Nurse as she packed away her instruments and ingredients.

"Thank you," she murmured over to her.

The Nurse smiled, "You're welcome." She was very beautiful, with delicate facial piercings. Jennifer did not know any 'blacks' personally. She had always been told to avoid 'those people' by her father. They made good soldiers, 'loyal, not too bright' he explained, but she had never had to apply any of this information in real life because she never crossed paths with 'foreigners' in her world. Jennifer thought about this as the pain eased further.

"Why do you do this?" she asked her calm helper quietly. "Why do you do something so risky – so shameful, for complete strangers?"

"Risky? Yes, certainly. But shameful? No. It's not shameful. That's not it."

"But this is a crime – a crime against nature and against England. The law says it's wrong because the country needs new offspring …" Jennifer trailed off. She felt how incongruous her words sounded; they dropped with a hollow sound in this situation. The words of Evening Primrose from the pulpit of her Sky-stream broadcasts did not translate to the predicament in which Jennifer sat. Her boss liked to mount a regular tirade against the moral degeneration of English society. Abortion was a 'denial' of your female identity. Such a thing was the ultimate misogynistic act, she declared. To deliberately shed the child from your womb. Evening knew, Jennifer recalled, all about the pain and loss of trying to become a mother. She had bourn her twins, Peach and Plum, Eliot's children, with 'wonder, awe, and gratitude'. When she looked at her own struggle to be a Mother, she was astonished at how selfish a woman could be – to flush away a healthy pregnancy. What if the child turned out to have the cure for cancer?

Evening's words hung in Jennifer's head.

The Nurse interrupted her thoughts, "What would become of you, though? With a child, on your own. Unable to name the father." She looked at Jennifer with a sharp, penetrating gaze.

Jennifer just shook her head. She had no answer.

"Your work would disappear. Is your housing status related to it?"

Jennifer nodded.

"So, you'd lose your home, and you'd have to fall back on the help of family and friends, if they'd accept you. Or worse. Charity and the Homes."

Jennifer felt the weight of what the woman described. Her family would want nothing to do with her and from what she knew of the Homes, well, they were fearful places for have-nots. Better to go to a doss-house by the river.

"You would slip down the scale and lose everything," she continued, "and the world says that the shame should be yours. You would exist on the margins, rejected as a woman *and* a mother. But the shame, they say, should be yours?"

Jennifer's eyes filled with tears. "I might have been able to make it work."

The Nurse came and held her hand again. Her touch was cool and welcome.

"We are subordinate to so much, to so many people, aren't we?" she asked the question softly but firmly.

"Yes, I suppose."

"You, even as a higher-up, you have so many to answer to in authority – but this way, at least, you aren't subordinate to another person. One who isn't even yet born."

Evening

"Don't put that there. Idiot!"

The departure suite at the Airstrip was fully air-conditioned and almost empty, but Evening was sorely irritated and felt stuffy. She had a potted orchid with her and a luxury food hamper. The orderly who had seen her into the VIP lounge tried to put the delicate plant on a chair.

"On the table."

"Sorry, ma'am."

"Shut up. And fetch some fresh water."

She took off her silk scarf and threaded it into the handle of her leather bag. She looked out of the window at the early morning sunlight coming up from over the Flatlands to the East. The sea sparkled in the distance. It was closer to the Capital than it had been in her childhood. The Flatlands were threaded through with saltwater channels. Much of Norfolk was long gone, lost to the sea now. The Old Father was broad and wide and flooded regularly. From high ground, the derelict silver fin-shaped structures of the river's long-obsolete flood barrier could be seen when they emerged at low tide, peeping up from fast-flowing dark waters. Beyond the Eastern horizon, Evening knew, settlements constructed on stilts hugged the estuary shorelines of Essex and Kent.

Today, however, she was heading West in a softly humming Helioship. The vessel taxied from its long, low hangar on one of the spokes of the Airstrip's wheel-shaped layout. Evening settled into her lush seat in the ship's gondola. Thick carpet, fresh juices, percolated coffee, and crisp champagne took the edge off the early morning flight out to the Duchy from the Capital.

With only a small number of passengers on board, Evening looked forward to a quiet hour and a half. The Helioship lofted into the air, powered by its twin fusion-electro engines. The judder of propellers and the rapid rise into the air made her ears pop. She yawned to clear them, and that reminded her she had been up since three in the morning. An early start to make the flight to visit Mother. A frown wrinkled Evening's perfect brow under her velvet sleep mask at the prospect of seeing Aurora. The ship reached cruising altitude and motored serenely through the clouds on its helium-solar-powered journey. Below, the ship's shadow drifted across the brown and gold fields and ample swathes of dark woodland, its twin matching the journey in ripples across the countryside.

The Great Western Freightway was the route used to navigate. In the air, the haves and higher-ups could journey swiftly and smoothly, whilst freight, goods, and have-nots used the old rutted multi-lane highways, the marshy waterways, and two old railway lines. The strata of different beings passed by each other, over-taking, catching up, and wending through the Southern Wilds. The Duchy, spread out to the West, was a large and irregular region.

Soft, undulating hills led up to stretches of high moorland and finished in rugged coastline. It stretched from the Cutswold Hills to the Far West Reaches. Bristole serviced it with a great cluster of docks, and trade came and went with ease. The Duchy had its own supply chain.

Evening inhaled and exhaled a deep, calming, air-conditioned breath that contained notes of lavender and citrus. The carpets were so soft that the feet of the stewardesses made no sound. A soft, butterfly touch landed on Evening's arm where it lay on the soft leather rest and made her jump. She lifted her sleep-mask at the corner and the attendant in a chic pastel-blue outfit indicated the tray.

"Your champagne, Mizz Primrose." Her emphasis was obsequious.

"Leave it," Evening waved a hand. With her mask up she looked out of the tinted windows of the gondola. Below, the freightways and canals sparkled and flickered. The arteries of Southern England fed the Capital from the Duchy. Up ahead and to the West lay the landscape with its wooded hills and honey-coloured towns. Evening remembered how it had been the favourite province of an old monarch. He had kept a home there and when the re-wilding began the Duchy had embraced it with gusto. She thought, had that king been partly responsible for it – for the re-wilding? Maybe. Somewhere in history the answer lay buried. It remained a favoured district to this day, with only higher-ups allowed to call it home, of course. To the North were the Middle-lands, the Shires, and the Borders.

In the West, near the Taff-border, the Duchy was effectively an independent state.

The Duchy had everything. Education, crops, townships, and its own religion of Ancient Albionism. This was a mixture of Anglo-Catholic medievalism and a sort of nature worship, based upon homeopathy and a fixation on ley lines. To gain residence in the Duchy you had to prove your adherence to Albionism and your wealth. It was about membership of certain institutions, legacies, and clubs. Residence was therefore the attainment of ultimate higher-up status. The haves were in their element. That was why Evening had established her mother's care near Glowstar, in the heart of the Duchy. Rich, organised, well-catered, Evening knew that Aurora was looked after. It took any responsibility off Evening and maintained her public image of affording the best of care for her parent.

Evening disembarked, mid-morning, at the Hub on the outskirts of Glowstar.

"Mizz Primrose, allow me," an orderly brought a trolley for her bag, the hamper, and the potted orchid. "Your vehicle is awaiting." He led her through to the departure area and loaded her things into the boot of a conveyor-limo.

"Where to, ma'am?" the driver tipped his hat.

"Cheltnam," Evening informed him, "and I'll direct you from there …"

They cruised out of the Helioship Hub and around the lake at Great Witcombe, leaving Glowstar behind. Evening directed the driver Eastwards. Bentham, Coberley, Withington, the old names scrolled past on her phone as she tracked the route on her map to The Mill House. She sat in air-conditioned comfort in the back of the conveyor and looked at the chauffeur's closely barbered neck as he navigated the network of lanes and villages.

Honey-coloured stone, well-clipped hedges, pristine watered lawns, and lines of riders, clip-clopping along the lanes. Horses. Always interesting to see this phenomenon in the Duchy, she thought. Any four-legged hoofed mammal in the Capital had been hunted down and devoured by now. She looked on, unimpressed, at the booted and tweedy riders emerging from the side-roads. The Duchy, she reflected with irony, was a hateful place but she had battled to get her mother into one of the most exclusive residential homes in the region. Aurora Hegarty. Mother. She had been a burden, an unpredictable force of nature, but now she was their problem – at The Mill House – and Aurora got all the tolerance and patience that money could buy.

Evening paused on the steps of The Mill House Rest Home by the river in the village of Withington. She detected a photographer taking a series of pictures from a distance. She held the potted orchid with a thoughtful look on her face, one of concern and care, and raised a hand to ring the bell. All this so that she could be 'spotted' on a mission to the rest home. The shutter clicked numerous times to achieve the best, natural, unposed shot. This was destined to appear across the Web and on the Sky-stream bulletins.

Evening composed the captions: 'Sky-stream host snapped on one of her regular visits to ailing mother'; and, 'The mother-daughter bond is as strong as ever as Evening Primrose takes gorgeous blooms to bedside.' She pinged the message to Jennifer to have it posted on the updates within minutes.

As Evening entered the squeaky lobby, she thought about how one day the wording of the caption would sound when it came to the inevitability of Aurora's death. She speculated on 'Beloved Mother loses her fight against illness'. Illness was always a fight to be won or lost, but no, that tone did not offer enough of a focus. 'Evening Primrose at her Mother's side as beloved parent slips peacefully away'. Better. She would have to work on the balance and structure of that.

"Mizz Primrose, good morning," the receptionist stood up to greet her. "So very good to see you today."

Evening's hackles were immediately raised. She never trusted the obsequiousness shown her at The Mill House. She felt that despite her valued custom they were laughing at her behind their hands. Run by the Excalibur Corporation that handled illness and death in sterile ways, The Mill House was slick and refined. It was a facility constructed around an old stone building by the river. New, smooth, creamy marble butted up against the old stone; perfect timber panelling with a silky, waxed grain hugged the interior. Glass and metal, wood and stone – all very natural, thought Evening, but not very homey. Appropriate for Aurora, however, who had hardly been what you would call affectionate or domestic as a mother.

The receptionist addressed her politely and cautiously, "Your mother's care manager is in her office. She wanted to have a word with you when you arrived." The exquisitely groomed attendant took Evening's trappings, the hamper, and the orchid. "I'll see these go to your mother's room. It's this way," she indicated the direction to the office as she glided along the smooth floor.

Evening was shown into a neat, corporate office. From behind a glass and marble desk a woman rose, dressed in a crisp sky-blue nurse's uniform cinched at the waist with a navy blue wide elastic belt held with an intricately scrolled silver clasp. On her head, she wore a nursing sister's cap, formed of starched white linen. She was, Evening knew, no trained nurse, however. She was the care manager but costumed in order to give off an aura of professional ministration and a tradition of nursing.

"So pleased to meet you, Mizz Primrose, I'm Sister Jean Bold. She had a slight West Country accent to Evening's ear, probably fake though. "Thank you for agreeing to meet me, please take a seat."

Evening slid into the exquisite chair opposite her amongst the gleaming surroundings.

"I needed to talk to you about your mother."

"What's Aurora done now?" Evening sighed; she should have seen this coming.

"It's not that, Mizz Primrose, it's nothing – er – troublesome in that way."

Well, that's a relief, she thought, certainly makes a change from the other places I set her up. It would only take about six weeks and the phone call would come. Aurora had thrown her dinner at the staff, hoarded her pills, or deliberately run down the corridor, streaking and whooping and trailing her nightie in her wake.

"It's her diagnosis, I'm afraid to say. Her cancer is now terminal, she's incurable. We've done all we can. From now on, it's a matter of making her as comfortable as possible."

So, that was it, thought Evening, the end. She stood up.

"Thank you, Sister," and made her way out of the office.

"Oh, one more thing – it's rather important."

"Yes?"

'She doesn't know."

"What do you mean?"

"She doesn't know how ill she is."

"Why wouldn't you tell her?"

"We have a policy of not disclosing a terminal condition to our guests. We find it's less distressing for them that way."

Evening walked down the corridor to her mother's room. At first, a bleak look covered her face and then a smirk flickered there until she broke out into a raucous, derisory laugh. She had to pause and lean against a wall. A nurse pushing a trolley gave her a look of alarm.

"Non-disclosure is less distressing!" she addressed the woman, who passed on hurriedly. "That's rich! If only you knew."

Distress and open secrets had been characteristics of Evening's childhood in Aurora's slipshod care. She had known about her mother's sporadic, intense love affairs thanks to the shouts, thuds, and arguments heard through the thin partition wall between their bedrooms. How was that for disclosure, 'Sister' Bold? Now, Aurora could be treated with tenderness and delicacy of a sort that she had never shown as a parent. Thanks to me, Evening mused as she calmed down and turned the handle to enter her mother's room.

More a suite than a room, and the only resemblance to a hospital was the equipment by the adjustable bed that monitored Aurora's steady decline. Silence reigned, as Evening collected a chair to position it close to the bed. Without opening her eyes, Aurora spoke, "Is that you?" It was not a frail voice and her finger raised in the direction of the orchid told Evening what her mother referred to.

"Who else would it be? It's not as if you've got any fans."

Aurora Hegarty let out a crackled cackle, opened her eyes and pressed the button to raise her head.

"Unlike my daughter, the famous TV star with her many admirers," her yellow teeth were revealed in a broad grin. Aurora had impeccable hair and nails. She kept up her cosmetic regime in the rest home thanks to the beauty technicians in regular attendance. Blonde tresses and sunshine yellow nails. She also had some subtle shading on her lips and around her eyes beneath perfectly plucked and shaped brows. Evening looked at her withered body, breastbone prominent beneath an exquisite peach-silk nightdress. Aurora's neck and collar bones were gaunt, the skin stretched across the bones like translucent parchment.

"I don't want to get into anything with you. I'm here for an hour and that covers me."

"That was always you, wasn't it, Patricia?"

Evening flinched at the recognition of her given name on her mother's puckered lips.

"Just do what's expected for show."

"I learned from the best, clearly," as she focused again on her mother's sartorial choices for her deathbed. She tapped her phone and saw with satisfaction the updates were scrolling past on the Sky-stream. Jennifer was good for something at least.

Aurora blinked slowly and a smile creased her face, "You're looking well, Patricia, broadcasting suits you. How are the twins?"

"Well."

"When will I get to see my lovely grandchildren?"

Evening paused and then decided to be blunt. She looked up from her phone. "They aren't your grandchildren."

"You know what I mean, you silly girl."

"They have no biological connection with you – no resemblance, nothing! I made sure of that. I purchased the best DNA moulds and templates that money could buy. Their mothers were athletes and intellectuals, their fathers were scientists and artists."

"Didn't want to do it the old-fashioned way? Not that Eliot has it in him!" Aurora cackled again in a spiteful way. This was interrupted by a bout of cruel coughing. The living conditions throughout her life, from damp mildewed terraces in the Capital to tenements on the humid South Coast as a seasonal worker with the resorts and carnivals, had wrecked Aurora's lungs. The drinking and NicoTin-pens had not helped, Evening mused, as her mother hocked up some multi-coloured mucus and collapsed back onto her pillows. Aurora wheezed. Her sternum heaved up and down.

Evening checked the time. Not long to go now, she sighed, and walked over to the window. The subtle, sunlit gardens could be seen across the terrace. She just wanted to see out the clock. Any paparazzi or member of staff from the rest home could catch her out. Her mission of mercy to her ailing mother had to look convincing. The Cabinet's Chief Health and Wellness Minister told her to make sure of that. 'Trust no one. Family values, family values, Primrose.'

"Why do you hate it here?"

Evening turned and looked at her mother. "What?"

"You hate it here, in the Duchy – why?" Aurora squinted at her. "You squirreled me away here which means you have to come visit me, and I've always suspected you wanted to join the higher-ups proper. Get with the genuine elite!"

Evening walked around her mother's bed and laughed quietly to herself. "You've never got me," she looked at Aurora and shook her head, "you've never understood me."

"I never tried!"

"NO, you didn't. People dismissed me – including you. I worked hard for everything I have!"

"What about that Derrick?" Aurora smirked. "Didn't he give you a leg up – whilst getting his leg over?" She cackled again.

Evening felt the anger churning inside. Her visit to The Mill House was following the usual pattern.

"Face it, girlie, your attitude has always been shitty!"

Evening fumed. She met her mother's eyes with their thick black lashes heavy with mascara. Aurora blinked a spidery blink.

"Do you know what I've been doing since I got here? Aurora? Do you want to know?" She leaned in to the old woman. "I've been composing your obituary, Mother.

Planning what will be written on *my* Stream once you're dead and gone. Because you're dying."

Aurora looked away.

"Yes, the nurse told me – you're not long for this world."

Aurora looked back at her, tears welling in her jaundiced eyes. "That's not true, you little bitch. I'm getting better. I'll be out of here and I'll outlive you! If it was that serious, they'd have told me!" She began to wheeze again.

Evening laughed. "They lied, Aurora, they've been lying to you all along. You came here to die, and you didn't even realise! I find that *so* funny!" She turned to walk out of the suite, and then looked back, "And I'm the only person with any connection to you, so once you're gone, I will go *out* of my way to forget about you. Wipe you out of existence!"

The journey home, along the lanes of the Duchy and before the Helioship take-off, gave Evening the chance to reflect on her mother's words about how much she hated the Duchy and its people. Evening resisted. She had long since ruled out expending energy on hatred. Disdain, yes, as the squeaky and elegant homes and people rolled by.

When Evening disembarked at Airship Row, she felt relaxed. The knots in her stomach from talking to Aurora had gradually unravelled as she neared the Capital. Walking through the silent lounge she noticed the orderly, the incompetent orderly, at work. He was scraping at a rogue poster that had been glued to a window.

The strange typeface on it caught Evening's eye. It looked old-fashioned and reminded her of bulletin boards from her youth and college days, something home-made about it. She walked over to the orderly as he finished peeling the last of it off the glass.

"Give that to me," she commanded.

She smoothed out the dry shreds and read the words.

'*The Universe is made of Stories not of Atoms* (Muriel Rukeyser, *The Speed of Darkness*).'

Evening frowned and tutted. Vandals. There was always someone feeling disgruntled amongst the have-nots and lowers but this made no sense. God – when will they ever learn? She looked around. The orderly had moved on to another job. She pocketed the tatty poster.

At the open foyer of the Airstrip, Evening awaited her conveyor-limo impatiently. She hated to be held up because that forced her to think and consider events. She liked to kill her feelings, especially after a visit to Aurora. Now a dying Aurora. This remembrance made her smile. She walked up and down to distract her thoughts and then the sole of her expensive tan leather court shoe slid on something. On the ground was a piece of folded paper, thin and flattened, incongruous on the pristine paving. It must have blown in from somewhere. She picked it up. It was scuffed and soiled but the printing on it was perfectly distinct and legible. Like the poster in the lounge, it sported an old-fashioned legend that this time read: '*Books are the treasured wealth of the world and the fit inheritance of generations and nations* (Henry David Thoreau).'

"What the fuck is this?" Evening said out loud.

Clara

Clara held on to her bag, the one she had fashioned to make the disposal of bio-material possible. Geno-tagging was a reliable method of tracking the population's activity and whereabouts. Any trace of genetic material could be used against you as well as being planted for incrimination, or so the rumours suggested. Her method of disposal was with the use of an innocent-looking fabric bag, hand-sewn and patchwork. Her grip on it was firm but looked casual. To all external appearances she blended in with the other lowers and middles in the warm breeze of the afternoon, a woman going about her business near the riverside humbly dressed in salvaged garments and accessories. After a couple of changes on the tram she walked at a steady pace, not rushing but purposeful as she made her way out of the fug of the Capital and along the Old Father's banks to the upper waters.

In this stretch of the river there were more residences for middles, upper-middles, and then on into some higher-up neighbourhoods. The elegant old buildings, ivy-covered and crumbling at the edges, still housed an affluent community a little detached from the rest of the populace, up-river and aloof. Vendors were dotted along the banks and near the bridges. They sold little luxuries and trinkets from smart, quaint stalls. Quality stuff mostly, although Clara knew that the powdered sugar on the little cones of sweets was more chalk dust than sugar.

As she moved through the crowds there was a festive feel to the afternoon as the temperature rose. Punts hugged the banks as pleasure-seekers sought some cooler air. The central current of the Old Father flowed too fast for small, light craft. The waters were so high that the bridge at Richman was little more than a stone roadway. Crumbling balustrades lined it, and the old silver-grey of the stone was smirched and darkened by water stains and weeds. Richman and its neighbour Twicknam still bore the hall-marks of a once grand past life.

Clara had confided in Susan about where she was going today, but not the reason for her outing. She had not seen Gunnar for a few days and having always been her con-fidante their relationship had of late cooled a little. Since starting the press, she had grown closer to Susan but felt more distanced from the cautious shopkeeper. He seemed enthusiastic about their endeavours, and still attentive to her when they were together, but there was something a little cold about him recently. She did not want to say that she suspected him of anything, but he struck her as a little guarded, the light in his eyes was extinguished. Clara had, by contrast, felt herself growing more reckless. She had the urge to do more and more actions and move faster, impa-tient for change. But she knew she had to be careful.

Today, she had a vital job to do as she neared the gates of Richman Woods. She maintained a low profile, padding along in her soft quiet shoes holding the homemade bag. She knew she looked like a spiritual woman, a common healer or fortune-teller for the populace who could not afford healthcare. That was her best defence. She looked 'kooky' and 'ethnic' and harmless. No one would attribute her with intelligence or cunning enough to foil a geotracker or restore a printing press. She was a ghost woman, and like Susan with her shopping trolley, easily written off.

The locals milled around the gates with the huge swathe of woodland beyond and Clara bided her time amongst the stalls and musicians until the mid-winter sun began to dip and the shadows grew. She had picked the right day for a covert mission, darkness came early. Braziers were fired up and appeared along the riverside at intervals. People gathered around to toast bread and sup warm drinks. A strong breeze rippled the waters. Winter had finally arrived in the Capital.

Clara seized the chance to slip away, unnoticed, into the gloom of the woods. Beneath the trees the temperature dropped rapidly. The canopy above swayed and dry leaves rattled. Some subtle changes in the weather, from humid to a dry chill, signalled the arrival of the shift in seasons. The slight changes in the weather were sometimes interrupted by unpredictable, catastrophic systems and this was the time of year to watch out for them. The trees swelled and tussled. She looked up and reckoned she had to speed up as the conditions looked more threatening. She trudged across the crisp leaf litter on the woodland floor as inky clouds built up on the horizon to the East and obliterated the first of the stars.

Susan

In the Pivvy, Susan took refuge from the incoming weather and busied herself with laying out type. It needed to be cleaned. So much fluff and dust accumulated on the press, and it risked getting clogged up without regular maintenance. Charlie had done a good job of fixing up the interior and patching the roof. Susan could sit in the relative warmth and security and work by the light of a flickering lantern.

She was occupied at the sturdy table when the door creaked open. Mina stepped inside, shaking her head and brushing leaves and water from her shoulder.

"Man, it's minging out there. Dirty weather. Alright, Suzy?"

Susan felt her thin veil of sanctuary shredding. She was still not used to Mina and her bluntness and slang. She felt the gulf between her and the girl as a tangible distance. A yawning, widening, tectonic divide.

"Yes," Susan responded in a monotone. "I thought you were at the factory."

"Just come off shift. Miss Cece's cool with the boys, and I fancied popping round here. See what you're up to." She sat on a nearby bench and crossed her legs and then delved into a pocket and produced a protein snap, one of the snacks that were occasionally distributed at the factory to keep the workers upright. "Want one?" she offered it across to Susan.

"No, thank you," Susan replied without looking up from her task.

Mina munched on her snack. She sat for a little while, and then, "What 'cha doing?"

Susan sighed quietly and still did not look up. "Cleaning the type."

"Uh huh." Mina swung her legs off the bench. "Got any more posters for me to put up?"

"Not yet."

"I've enjoyed doing that – you know, going in, slapping them up, getting out before anyone sees us!! It's been brilliant so far."

Susan sighed again and looked up from her work, peering over her small spectacles. "It's not a game, you know. This is serious. And, well, might have deadly consequences for us."

"Whatever."

Susan looked at Mina, ready to launch into a critical tirade, and then she stopped and really scrutinised her for the first time. Guiltily, she realised that she had written the young woman off without knowing her. She had thought of her as streetwise and a pair of safe hands, safer than Edgar. Mina had confidence in abundance. Now, though, Susan saw her – shrugging and feigning bravery and indifference – for what she was. A girl. One of society's stragglers and a fighter, but so very young.

"Here," Susan jerked her head towards the type in front of her, "take this rag – like that. Dip it in the solution, that's it. And then you rub the dust off." She guided Mina in cleaning the metalwork. In only half an hour, a row of gleaming type was slotted into place. Mina's method was very efficient. She leaned over the table and rubbed the type energetically and thoroughly. Susan watched in awe as she seemed to generate friction with her rapid buffing.

"Well," when she had finished Susan decided to move on to the next stage, "you can start to work on this. It's a simple layout – no punctuation." She slid a piece of paper towards Mina. On it was written only a dozen or so short lines.

Mina looked at it thoughtfully, "Moonwise," she mused on the title. "OK."

CLARA

Clara knew that the trees know.

She looked up at the undulating branches of the stirring beech and oak. She knew they had a language and a network for communication. There was a subterranean web in the woodland – the mycelium growth. This organic support system saw to it that the trees could nurture their own and other species. Clara felt tears well up when she remembered how she discovered this knowledge. It was one quiet night, after sex and homemade wine and homegrown weed with Gunnar.

Gunnar had rolled over and begun to snore deeply, his lean, strong body satisfied, and his brain settled and spun out with pleasure and intoxicants. Clara lay beside him for a little while but then grew restless and left the futon bed that was situated behind the partition in his living space above the Emporium. Making her way down the rickety, winding, wooden stairs she came to the tatty but functional kitchen and filled the kettle. Gunnar liked a hot cup of tea when he woke up after sex. As she waited for it to boil, Clara browsed the stacks of old magazines and journals. She often did this when she stayed with Gunnar, much to Cece's disapproval. 'He ain't good for you,' her grandmother's words rang in her ears. But it was fun to forget and give in to pleasure from time to time. Plus, she got to read from the yellowing stacks of old paper that were a goldmine of knowledge.

This one night she made a discovery that filled her with wonder and awe, and a sense of the veil lifting – that this was a mighty, mighty world – with a hidden ecosystem just below the surface. The mycelium, she read, was the mucus-based fungus network within the woodland floor. She thumbed through a copy of the *New Scientist*, from decades – a century – ago, with faded photos of imposing trees and woodland canopies. So, she thought, if this network was noticed in the time before re-wilding, then what must the mycelium be like now? When the woodland is so vast, and the plants have taken over. The organic world has mechanisms to exchange information across species. She read in amazement about how trees sensed a damaged or felled comrade and directed food towards their injured 'fellow'.

Out in the midwinter night of Richman Woods, as the weather closed in, Clara moved stealthily through the landscape. She thanked the trees with a quiet internal voice for providing cover and safe haven. She knew she could place the protective bag somewhere it would never be found. She reached the glade – the Glade of the Ancestors of the Richman Woods. Around her, slender silver birches reached upwards, luminescent and flickering in the glow of the moon. The clouds blew across the darkening sky, billowing like black ink in water. The birches in the Glade surrounded her in a circle, and some of them had grown up through a set of chairs. Long ago, a circle of sculptures formed of dark, polished, hammered metal, had been placed in a ring in the park to commemorate – something or other. A long-forgotten drama. Now, the folk name for it was the Glade of the Ancestors, chosen for it by those, like Clara, who ventured into the wild spaces. The trees' irresistible growth over many, many decades had unrelentingly and progressively ruptured and warped these metal chairs. Now they hung in displaced, precarious suspension with the birch trunks' support.

Clara positioned the bag on the ground near one of the chairs and burrowed into the soft soil. As she performed this action, she murmured the 'Om shanti' chant.

At the edge of the Park, Clara made her way along the fence in the darkness, adopting her customary practice. The wind whipped at her hair and clothes as she felt the onset of the weather, but this felt more excessive than the familiar winter storm, as severe as these were. They were in for a freak weather event, again. Clara could sense the moisture and motion in the air. As she walked along the perimeter of the woodland, she noticed how the people had thinned out and left the braziers flickering. The coals guttered and gashed. Clara sensed the turmoil and started to run to the pathway that led to the bridge. The broiling waters of the Old Father stilled as she crossed.

Momentarily, she felt reassured and then the wind picked up as a rushing sound reached her ears. Before she could change direction, the grey shadow stretched across the river, coming at speed out of the darkness. The tidal bore appeared, consuming everything in its path. Even the high water of the Old Father could not contain the rogue wave. It came at the bridge and consumed the cracked and weathered stone at full force. A whirling, sucking, rushing action by the dull, muddy, fast water. Clara could not get away in time.

Susan

Susan carefully eked out the cat food for Ellery. Mina had supplied it from her pilfered contraband. 'Gourmet Pickins for Little Kittens' read the label. It did not smell very gourmet, but it did look and taste a lot better than most human food. 'It's all much of a muchness,' Susan summed it up as Ellery devoured it without pausing for breath.

"Steady on, fella," she smiled at her pet.

He purred and butted her thanks to the fishy, savoury odour and once he had eaten pounced on the bed for a wash and curled up on the crocheted blanket to sleep the sleep of the innocent. She closed the door to her basement quietly and set off to see Gunnar.

For once, Susan was glad that Gunnar had a Sky-screen at the Emporium. The Ghostwriters had gathered and stood in the back kitchen to watch. Mina swore silently as the screen displayed the aerial footage of the bore. It raced along the entire length of the Old Father.

"She must have been there, somewhere, and got caught up in it, but found a place to go." Edgar spoke earnestly, his face wore a strained expression, as he sat at the table his hands shaking, fingers tapping on it and stared at the screen.

The cloying, passionate commentary from Evening Primrose droned on: "An act of God! Something must have disturbed the equilibrium of the country and there had to be a re-balancing. We must look to ourselves and ask the hard questions. My suspicions are with the sodomites and the perverts! The ones who take our children and corrupt them!" The camera cut to her in the studio, and she changed angle to a close-up. "Albion must be cleansed. This is only the start."

Gunnar muted the sound. "It is enough to fret over Clara's whereabouts. We can do without that infection," he said in his deadpan tone, shook his head and turned away.

His reaction seemed to be one of genuine concern, but Susan was troubled. They all knew that Clara was his lover. Surely, he would be more distraught? Like Edgar. Gunnar's barriers were up, she surmised, perhaps to save himself the anguish?

The grey waters of the river washed between houses and along lanes, carrying litter and debris. The ticker tape across the bottom of the screen tried to account for the missing and the dead, but everyone knew that there would be no rescue mission, no outreach to the Capital dwellers affected by the flooding. The dingy waters, like a cup of dirty weak coffee, coursed their irresistible way into courtyards and through doorways.

"She's got to be OK, she has to be," Edgar spoke intensely with tears welling in his eyes. "What will I tell Grammere?"

Susan put a hand on his shoulder, "We'll find her, we're not completely helpless. Does your Grammere have a photograph of her?"

"I think so."

"Good, then we need to find Charlie."

Mina

Susan's next series of actions intrigued and bewildered Mina. Some of what she did took place in the dark of the Pivvy after nightfall.

First, Mina had to go and get Charlie, who when he heard that the project was to help find Clara, raced over to be with them. At the Pivvy, Susan showed them the collection of dusty art supplies. She had been on a scavenging run to the old college buildings, where they already had made many excursions to find paint and inks. Mina was mystified by some of the things she had brought, however.

Susan instructed Charlie in what she needed.

"A black line drawing, based on this photograph," she handed over the little snapshot that a weeping Cece had prised out of a family album.

"Keep it clear and clean. I need it to transfer."

"Got it."

Next, she took Mina through the process of using light sensitive paint on stretched silk. Being more and more handy, Mina could help rig this up. She had been paying attention to Charlie and Gunnar and learned some useful skills. She fixed a powerful LED lantern over the table for Susan, who shuttered the Pivvy so that it was almost blacked out. In the near darkness, she watched the process of exposing the screen to the light through a stencil cut from Charlie's drawing. Susan completed the task by washing the silkscreen, gently dissolving the paint away. What came through was a likeness of Clara. The words below the image read 'Have you seen her?'

Mina looked at Clara's kind eyes, rendered carefully by Charlie, her thick locks characteristically lying across one shoulder. Her nose ring and earrings and her delicate beauty on show.

"He definitely caught her likeness, didn't he?"

Mina nodded. "Do you think she's OK? Or, what if the Feds have picked her up and she's not drowned?"

"If she's alive, we'll find her. If she is anywhere, we'll get to her," Susan spoke bluntly and realistically as she squeezed Mina's arm with her sturdy hand.

Mina helped Susan prep the ink and paint that had to be suitably viscose. Then they laid out paper and Susan showed her how to use the screen to smooth the ink through onto the paper. They pegged up the posters to dry. Row upon row of Clara's kind face in a distinctive, eye-catching black-and-white graphic.

What if, thought Mina, we can't find her? What if *she's* gone too? She felt bad about her mother, but somehow worse about Clara. And this created more turmoil in her mind. Still angry at her mother but prepared to put up posters for her friend. What kind of a daughter did that make her? She turned to Susan.

"Can we ask Charlie to draw another picture?"

PART THREE

Clara

A drip-dripping was the first sound Clara heard when she woke up.

On a wall, close by her head, was a fresh-water condenser. Pure, clean, water dropped steadily into a container from a plastic pipe near to the bed where she lay. A little cup sat beside the condenser, and beside that a small chalkboard with the message, 'Please help yourself'. Clara raised herself, wincing in pain and feeling woozy. Her mouth was dry, but she did not take up the offer of the message on the board. She was wary, despite her remaining disorientation. Be careful, watchful, she told herself.

She had to drop back onto the pillows, a pain stabbing in her side. Her hand moved to her forehead, and she felt a dressing covering a wound that still throbbed. She drew in a shuddering breath and looked around. The space where she lay had a strange atmosphere, unfamiliar and disconcerting. The walls were old brick and white, rectangular ceramic tile, and felt contained. The condenser hung on a wooden wall, not much more than a partition, constructed from salvaged timber. Painted patterns brightened it up and Clara realised the source of the strangeness in the air. It felt fresh and cool. It was not muggy, and the temperature was constant. Clara recognised that she must be underground. But how?

"You're awake. How do you feel?" A curtain had parted at the end of the wooden partition and an elderly man stepped in and sat down on the end of the bed. "Hello, Clara. It's very good to meet you. They call me the Baron down here."

She tried to move.

"Steady," he laid a gentle hand on the cover. "You have a concussion from your head wound, and you seem to have cracked some ribs. You've got some bruises and you were covered in silt and leaves. We had to change your clothes."

Clara checked out her outfit for the first time. It was a denim smock dress of sorts. It seemed to be made of the same material as the Baron's functional garments.

When she was feeling a little steadier, Clara walked behind the Baron, or Samson as he informed her of his name. She looked around at the life of the subterranean community in which she found herself. Samson led her into a long, low space, a sort of narrow hall with a shallow waterway running parallel to it.

"Welcome to the Baron's Court," he waved a hand. He had long, grey hair and armfuls of tattoos. His old denim work clothes looked comfortable as he moved among the wooden planters that lined the hallway. Behind him, embedded in the black-and-white wall tiles was a red circle with a blue horizontal line and the name 'Warren Street' visible. Samson saw that Clara had noticed it.

"Yes," he said, "meet the Warreners," and he smiled at the workers, busy over the planters. They were dressed in what seemed to be the regulation garb of denim and canvas aprons, with their hair neatly trimmed or tied back. They cropped abundant varieties of mushroom in the half-light of the cool hallway.

Archways led off into further tunnels lined with white and green tiles and pale, chemical lights. People milled about, quietly, and smiled and greeted Clara with nods. No one spoke much above a whisper down here. She looked around at the water when she heard a distinct plip-plop sound.

"What was that?"

"Fish," Samson gave her a mischievous look. "Here, take my hand – climb aboard." He helped her into a little flat-bottomed open boat. "Careful now. You've been pretty banged up."

The receding flood waters, he told her, had washed her down river to the Kew Wilderness. Some Hollanders who were scouting for flood survivors picked her up and brought her into the Warreners. "It was the worst inundation for some years, but we were expecting it. The teams from Holland Park and Hammersmith were ready with ropes and floatation devices. They brought you overground at night and then into the tunnels. The Shepherds treated your wounds and brought you here on a skiff."

"Thank you," Clara steadied herself on the little seat in the middle of the boat as it rocked under her. "You were expecting the flood. How?"

"We know the signs. We can spread the word and activate the safety sluices and defences for all the Tube dwellers."

"No one ever warns us."

She looked down at the little boat, a sort of oilskin and canvas waterproof canoe. Samson stood behind her with a pole and gently pushed off from the platform edge.

"Is this the old Tube system, then? I've heard about it from my Grammere."

"Indeed it is. Ever since it kept flooding back in the early century they gave up on pumping out the rising waters. It was left alone after that, and people moved in.

"How long have you been down here?"

"My parents brought me here when I was a boy, but there were already many here with a thriving community. They found the crops and base-proteins to thrive."

As they entered the tunnel, Clara looked up and around. Her eyes quickly grew accustomed to the light as a luminous glow surrounded her. "Is that algae?"

"Yes, well spotted. We found a strain that was very durable and crossed it with some jelly-fish genes to create this bioluminescent hybrid. It's our main light source in the tunnels. And it doesn't disturb the breeding cycle of the fish."

Clara trailed her hand gingerly in the water and immediately saw it attracted a swarm of fry. They were a drab mottled grey and brown in colour and jostled around her fingers. She felt their little whiskers tickle her as a way of exploring the dark world. They had redundant nondescript eye pits. There was little sound as Samson punted the boat along.

Clara was greeted by more of the undergrounders, the Tube dwellers, in their simple overalls as they tended their crops of pale fungus and legumes. Once she was on a platform at Goode Street, with its moss-green tiles and smoke-stained ceiling, she saw a still. Jars of clear, strong alcohol were being packed in wooden crates.

"We have to be careful. There was a flair up here some years ago." He indicated the smoke-stained, fire-damaged ceiling tiles. "We take many more precautions now. The alcohol has many uses."

"What do you use for fermentation?"

"Vegetable scraps, anything we can find."

"And how is the air so clear down here?" She caught up with him after pausing to examine the jars. "It would have to be very difficult to keep it fresh."

"We have a system of vents and filtration, but we mostly rely on anaerobic bacteria and micro-organisms that consume the carbon dioxide. We have managed to create a good balance."

They walked across the Goode Street station and boarded another boat which took them as far as Leester Square. There, they walked across a much wider concourse where they wended their way among a busy cluster of stalls. Clara admired the produce, plentiful, succulent, and of good quality. Even below ground, in the half-light, food seemed less drab than on the surface. Samson stopped and chatted to a seller, and asked, "May I?"

"Of course," the neatly dressed woman clad in a russet canvas apron replied, "and here."

She passed a handful of yellow pea pods each to Samson and Clara.

"A lot of our foodstuffs are now enriched with vitamin D. We don't get as much direct sunlight as you, so this is how we compensate."

Onto another boat, and they made their way through more tunnels until they finally disembarked at their destination, Ho'bun.

"Here, we're at one of the deepest points of the system," Samson led her past the name picked out in bold, classic tiles with a green and black border.

Clara was feeling woozy again, and rather overwhelmed. The head injury, she thought, and stopped to lean against the cool wall.

"We're almost there, and then you can rest."

They rounded a corner onto the next platform where Samson showed her to a comfortable saggy armchair. She felt some relief.

Two young women, introduced as the Baron's daughters, were plucking translucent shrimp from a fine, hairlike net. A canopy sheltered an ample, homely camp with partitions for bedrooms and plenty of rough, worn tables for gutting and cleaning fish and shrimp.

"It's such a pleasure to meet you, Clara. We are so pleased the Hollanders found you," the elder of the two daughters spoke. She had pale, freckled skin, dark hair and nimble fingers that busily pulled the still moving shrimp creatures from the mist net that sparkled with water droplets. She was a bewitching, subterranean creature with a moon face framed by long, lank hair. Her younger sister looked ghostly and awestruck into silence, as with equal dexterity she plopped the wriggling creatures into a pot of boiling water. Once cooked, she extracted them with a sieve and laid them on cloths to drain. Then she set about shelling the cooled ones, sliding the flesh out with slippery, crackling sounds.

"Yes," Clara said curiously, "you all know my name. How is that? You know about me, but I know nothing about any of this, and no one who has ever heard of this underground place."

"Oh," the elder girl spoke softly, dreamily, "we've been watching you for some time, Clara, and we've looked forward to you coming down here to us."

Evening

Again and again, they came – the waves of irritation. Evening ignored the incoming calls. They would just tell her the same story: the Premier is not happy, and, come to the Cabinet Office. She was hounded by them as soon as she stepped into the Sky-stream HQ, and the intensity had only grown as the day wore on. She gave Jennifer instructions to filter and divert them because she needed to gather her thoughts and work something out. The timing could not have been worse. Evening had just returned from burying her mother.

The Christmas and New Year schedules at the studio were gruelling. Nowhere was more festive than Sky-stream, 'the Humble Home of Christmas', or more exhausting. Mostly because no one, except inhabitants of the higher-up neighbourhoods, could actually celebrate a holiday season. The calendar and the broadcasts might declare a state of national celebration but there was no sense of anticipation among the populace. The Hubs had strings of pale, washed-out lights but the rations were the same. The shopping districts and Media Quarter, some of the monuments – the Waterloo Frieze, the Tomb of the English Warrior, and the Thatcher Memorial, displayed rotating, automated sparkling orbs that could be seen from afar. At ground level, however, nothing much altered.

Once the season wound up, Evening typically took her vacation to the Caribbean, usually on the island of a close friend so that she could 'decompress' alone. Just as she was looking forward to her respite, Sister Bold rang her one night. Evening had posted on the socials about reading a bedtime story to the twins. As the nanny took the children into the next room, Evening took in the news of Aurora's passing. Things had been peaceful until this. Dammit. The cow should have hung on for a while longer, so she could take her scheduled trip. This would now be a headache to shoehorn into the week ahead. She had to postpone her trip and bump the human interest story from tomorrow's running order on the show to memorialise her bloody mother on air.

The send-off had been steady and sober, unlike Aurora, Evening quipped silently to herself. At the blustery, dull crematorium the coffin rolled through the curtains to the strains of 'I Am What I Am!' There's no one left to call me Patricia now, Evening smiled quietly on the inside, whilst keeping a suitably mournful expression on the outside. She only allowed quiet internal rejoicing, so nothing was betrayed to the ever-watchful cameras and socials. She returned to the Capital in a good mood that was soon shattered.

Those fucking Ghostwriters and their garbage causing trouble. They had amped up their activity in the last few weeks. It had started with that pamphlet she found at the Airstrip. Now in her office, spread out across her desk with its stylishly crackled glass top, were some intact examples of the Ghostwriters' output. Her eyes ranged across the leaflets and posters. They certainly kept busy and gave a good account of themselves.

Some of the materials were verses and pithy quotations. Evening mused on them and could not help but admire the neat typeface and the quality of the ink. Over time they had become more accomplished, until they were rather desirable objects. Almost artistic. She scrutinised a poster that bore the words:

> sometimes
> you know
> the moon
> is not such a perfect
> Circle
> and the master Painter
> makes a passing
> brush touch
> with a cloud
> don't worry
> we've passed
> the dark side
> all you children
> rest easy now
>
> we are born
> moonwise   *Jean Binta Breeze*

Black, strong text comprised of simple words with a magnetic clarity. This was dangerous, very dangerous. It could be read and understood by almost anyone, even just a tiny part of it. Understated acuity. Evening was annoyed by it. Sentimental dross.

She turned over another sheet and stopped. A coldness gripped her heart. No, it couldn't be. Could it? *She* couldn't be behind it. Was she even alive?

The words tumbled on the printed poster before her and caused a chill to roll across her from a years-old memory:

> Hope … Hope is the thing with feathers –
> That perches in the soul
> And sings the tune without the words
> And never stops – at all –

"More dross," Evening hissed. And never stops – at all. She felt clammy and peaky all at once. Swiftly pivoting on the cream carpet, she made it to the waste bin just in time to vomit.

Mina

"It's got her picture and my Mum's. They look like them. OK, right?"

Mina scrutinised Miss Cece's face, as the older woman looked at the drawing of her granddaughter.

Mina and her brothers had moved in with Cece and Edgar once it was clear that Jacinda was gone. And then Clara disappeared. They had come together as a unit. Mina had already noticed the change in her brothers. Adie had calmed down and Aidan had come out of his shell a little.

Cece's tapering fingertip traced the outline of Charlie's drawing and she looked at it sadly. Side by side the two 'Have You Seen Her?' pictures were haunting, beautiful, and heart-breaking. Mina had described her mother, and Charlie created the portrait, of large eyes in a thin face, a pointed nose and straight, sad mouth. A gentle, but tortured face. He had caught that about her. Mina's family had no photographs except for a single snapshot of her parents, young and hopeful. Her mother, in her best outfit, on the arm of her father in his uniform on their wedding day. This was just before he had shipped out for the first Ardennes conflict. Charlie's small portrait was more faithful to how life had treated her since. Mina had felt some creeping forgiveness for Jacinda for some time. She was also touched with guilt about her past feelings, so she determined to do something to find her mother. The young woman's raw energy and bravery was now channelled into this mission.

Edgar entered the kitchen, and his grandmother took his hand.

"Stay together, cheri, keep a good watch," Cece spoke in earnest.

"We will, Grammere."

"Let's see it, then," Mina turned to Edgar.

He reached into his trusty backpack and pulled out a set of stencils. The designs etched out of metal were of a droplet shape, that when viewed the right way up formed a little phantom. Underneath the words 'The Ghostwriters' were cut out.

"Spooky, man! These are fancy!" Mina looked at them, delightedly, and smiled for the first time in ages.

"These are for you," Edgar handed her a pair, and two cans of spray paint, one black, one white. "We can mix them up a bit – white for the logo and black for the lettering. But go easy with the paint, we don't have many cans left."

A short while later, Mina and Edgar left the building, quietly making use of the rickety metal fire escape and moving around behind the Emporium. They stayed in the shadows as they ventured out into the night-time streets. The acid lights of the lamps flickered and died, and they soon arrived at an elegant tree-lined avenue. Beech and plane trees, mature and solid, were growing new buds at this time of year. Their roots had entirely undermined the road, and Mina and Edgar had to pick their way carefully along what was once the pavement. Slabs of concrete, once even, were now torn up like teeth in the smashed mouth of a prize fighter. The surfaces and thoroughfares of the Capital had long since given way to the turbulence of subterranean root systems.

As they came to each tree-trunk the young urban guerrillas paused and stencilled the Ghostwriters logo onto the aged bark. They made a gentle rattle with the paint cans and a subdued 'ssshhhh' as they sprayed. Stark, white spooks positioned for maximum visibility and effect appeared on each tree on either side of the rutted, uneven road. Mina and Edgar moved on, silent and unseen, to the next target. They moved across the city as the night wore on, fixed on their goal, and punctuating their progress with the phantom graffiti.

The spring night was humid and alive when they reached the Media Quarter. Flying creatures droned and buzzed past and clustered for the rich nectar of the nocturnal flowering plants in Rothermere Square. Hummingbird moths, and some Eurasian species of hawkmoth that had found its way this far North daintily balanced on the blooms, supped and flew on. Tiny bats made swooping flights around their heads, tracing a figure of eight over the Plaza as they fed on the smaller insects. Wordless, Edgar nodded to the gates of the Sky-stream Centre. Mina gestured back and they each made their independent way around the perimeter of the Square, staying close to the buildings.

Mina kept low, out of any possible eyeline of guards that might be outside the Centre in the security lodge. She moved along the wall to the Eastern side of the gates. She paused and saw Edgar in position, her counterpart on the Western side. The two had rehearsed this action and planned it out to the last detail to avoid any unnecessary exchange and to stay out of the way of the security guard. Edgar deposited his backpack on the ground and extracted a large roll of fabric. Quickly and quietly, fingers working to thread sturdy rope through eyelet holes, the two unfurled the banner and draped it across the gates, securing it in place. The lights remained on in the Sky-stream building all night, but the night shift crew saw nothing outside. So effective was the operation. They sat at their desks, oblivious to the activities at the gate, lining up the fictitious weather forecasts and re-runs of old reality shows, so as not to over-excite the audience. It was the job of the morning news crew to amp up the viewers with sensational, breaking, overnight stories and get them shouting at their Sky-screens.

Mina knew that their banner would not cause much of an obstacle. She had wanted to try something more aggressive, some vandalism, but Susan had put a stop to that. According to her, Mina found out, this was what was called 'civil disobedience'. It sounded pretty tame to Mina. Disobedience was something a bit 'kiddie' in her eyes, however, she trusted Susan and she was unfailingly loyal to her – 'to the end' – as she said. Susan had helped her so much. Susan had opened her eyes, and if Susan thought that a banner across the Sky-stream gate would create even the tiniest fuss or inconvenience, then a banner she would have. Task completed, Edgar and Mina evaporated into the night.

Jennifer

Jennifer Sinclair felt renewed and ready to face any challenge. Her health had recovered over the past weeks. The Pharmacist near her apartment continued to be helpful in that capacity. She had been thankfully free of complications after she had expelled the birth matter – the foetus. Her helper and Nurse had reassured her that there was no risk for her future chances at motherhood. The procedure did not affect her fertility. This was not what she had been told growing up. If you denied your natural function as a woman, you would be punished with stillborn children. The kind, beautiful woman who had helped her out of her predicament with a soft voice and cool hands reassured her that nature did not work like that. Nature was not ruled by fickle, unkind, mercurial moralising. Nature was pragmatic and non-judgmental.

Jennifer had taken to using the tram system more and more these days. She drew some sneers and sideways looks from her Sky-stream colleagues who did not understand why she would do such a thing, but she ignored them. She felt more connected to others thanks to this daily commute. I'm no different to them, she realised, with the same fears and pitfalls. The kindness of the have-not Nurse, who risked her life to help me, she thought, showed me how wrong and mistaken I have been all these years. Her thoughts were interrupted. She had been looking along the benches of the tram from where she stood, when her eyes alighted on a poster. Small, black drawing on white, with the words 'Have You Seen Her?' The face was that of her Nurse.

This little portrait, so accurate that she immediately recognised her helper, had been rendered by a careful hand and taped to the inside of the tram window. There was no doubt it was the same woman who had administered the analgesics and sung to her, soothed her, as she endured the pain. The tram clacked across the Elgin Bridge and cornered sharply into Rothermere Square. Jennifer hardly noticed the lurch as she was transfixed by the pathetic poster and its simple message.

As she disembarked amid the jostle and odours of the lowers, she managed to pass by the poster and make a grab for it. She easily snatched it off the window and stuffed it into her bag. No one noticed. These passengers did not bother to register other's actions or catch anything in their peripheral vision. You did not get involved in their world. And there was another reason why they were currently distracted. There were some goings-on in the Square.

Jennifer's mind grappled with the risk she ran of having the poster in her bag and how she could keep it on her and get it past the security at the Sky-stream Centre. Something told her to keep it, and she felt comforted by the picture of her kind Nurse. She need not have worried, however. The studio gates were obstructed. People milled about, a little excited, and deeply unsure of what to do. Sky-stream workers were joined by onlookers, many of them lowers, on their way through the Media Quarter. A makeshift banner hung across the gates. Jennifer quickly assessed the situation. Clearly, Evening Primrose was not in residence, going by the inactivity and trepidation among the group at the gate. No one wanted to make a move.

Jennifer made her way past the gawping lower-middles and have-nots who had begun to gather in greater numbers. Laughter started to ring in the air.

"Woah – seen this? Someone's sticking it to the highers!"

"Fuck, yes. Tell them how it is. See if they like it!"

Jennifer peered around these figures in order to see the banner clearly. It was long, large, and made of canvas probably, and looped dramatically across the gates. Anyone looking at it could tell it had a homemade feel. Nothing about it was polished, like the advertising familiar from the Hubs and Centres. It was in clashing contrast to the slickness of the narrative on hoardings and billboards around the Quarter. Hand-done stitching and lettering finished it off, a concoction of paint, thread, and collage achieved with a lot of flair and imagination. Jennifer read the slogan it displayed: 'It is not possible for anyone to become rich without cheating other people'. And underneath this the name, Robert Tressell and 'The Ragged Trouser'd Philanthropists'.

She let the words sink in. Confusing, bewildering. How could a philanthropist be ragged? What did it mean? And she had no idea who this Robert was. But around her, as the people read and mused on the statement that did not matter. They nodded, many sniggered and some shrugged – and all had been forced to stop and wonder.

"True," said some, "totally."

"Fuck 'em, right."

Jennifer looked around for any official reaction. Where was Evening? No Sky-stream employees dared to assert authority in this vacuum. Jennifer could not help but smile at how impotent and indecisive the team were without their leader. She hung back to observe as across the gates the declaration of cheating drew more and more attention. People sized it up and more of a consensus was reached. The Sky-stream lot were rich – all of them 'haves' and 'higher-ups'. It did not matter who this 'Robert' was, the statement was clear enough. Cheating was going on.

Jennifer reached for the poster in her bag as the crowd around her stayed in a sort of limbo. She smoothed out the creases and pondered on who her Nurse might be – might *have* been? Could she have been something to do with this? Her actions were subversive and the words on the banner reminded Jennifer of her words.

The anxiety in the crowd grew. They were aware of their weakness and looked for leadership.

"Someone should do something."

"Yes, but what?"

"We can't get into work. I need to be at my desk for 9, otherwise I'm in trouble."

"We'll all be in trouble, but what can we do?"

She felt a simmering danger come into the situation as the have-nots around the Sky-stream workers moved closer and muttered about the 'cheating'. It was that word 'cheating' that had caused something to go off in the minds of the assembled. It was a trigger for them that indicated power *with* duplicity. They could accept circumstances; that was something you might be born into – but *cheating*?

"It's fucking right, is what it is, it's outrageous."

Everyone was meant to follow the rules of what it was to be English, but this went against that in every sense.

"It's bloody unfair."

The outrage grew, and the Sky-stream employees started to cower. Jennifer detected a creeping radicalisation infect the crowd. She stood to one side, not feeling a part of either group. She looked at the picture in her hand and considered the face of the woman who had saved her and started to change her view. Now, these have-nots were seeing the world a little differently too. Something had awakened. Jennifer recalled the Nurse's response to her guilt-ridden, self-punishing rant. She had told her that how a person is set up in the beginning will dictate how they see the world and what their path in life is likely to be. An irresistible social force pushes you in a preordained direction. If you acknowledge that, then what do you do about it?

Jennifer sensed a disturbance in the background. Two vans pulled into the Square. Black vans and the thud of sliding doors and boots crunched on the fine pale paving slabs. Someone had put in a call to the COF, and they duly turned up mob-handed to crack skulls and take names. Scurrying and scuttling ensued as the lowers immediately decided to flee, used as they were to the tactics of the Feds. Jennifer joined them. She reached one of the monuments at the edge of the Square and stood behind the plinth. The statuary around the Square reflected England's national values. Margaret Thatcher was flanked by Lord Baden-Powell and Sir Arthur 'Bomber' Harris. Jennifer sheltered beneath Rupert Murdoch's outstretched arm as screams and cries of fear and pain echoed around. The subjects who could not move fast enough were clobbered and brutalised by the COF troopers. Jennifer flinched at the sounds of shots. A man in a scruffy t-shirt fell heavily nearby, bleeding from his forehead. He scrambled shakily to his feet with a hand clutched to his injury. Plastic bullets ripped through the air. She decided to stay put.

Gradually, the disturbance subsided, and the shouts died down. Some further scuffling could be heard as the last stragglers were sent running in pain or dragged into the security vans. Jennifer peered out from her spot. Evening Primrose's spiked heels clicked and scraped as she strode across the Square from her parked limousine. She wore a dark suit with sharp shoulders. She was still in mourning for her mother. Jennifer stayed as discrete as possible because she was far enough away to stay out of her boss's eyeline. She watched as events unfolded at the Sky-stream Centre gates.

Evening slowly walked the length of the banner, deliberately and quietly. Jennifer recognised that as Evening's simmer. She knew the outburst would come soon, but when it did it was no less startling just because she expected it.

First there was a screech that sent a shiver up her spine and caused the troopers close to Evening to flinch.

"Fuck this! And fuck all of you!" She raved at the Sky-stream security guards and the troopers. This was very risky.

"Oh dear, Evening," Jennifer whispered to herself. "Temper, temper. The populace doesn't know you swear." Unwise and unguarded. Evening was clearly very disturbed by this.

"What do I pay you for? Who was on patrol last night?" She did not give them a chance to respond. "Well? What are you waiting for, you fucking idiots?" She shoved a trooper aggressively towards the banner. "Cut it down! Burn it! Get it out of my sight!"

Jennifer took this as her signal. Evening was preoccupied. She turned and bolted for the tram-stop. She hopped on board the first one that halted at the platform, regardless of where it was going, and peered cautiously out of the window as it pulled away. This was an exceptional situation.

Evening had to deal with activism and protest out in public. Her public façade showed cracks. The Ghostwriters were really getting to her. Jennifer decided to call in sick that day.

Evening

The smell of wood polish lingered in the air. It gave Evening the sense that the room had been prepared well in advance. The fallout from the past few days had come to a head and she could no longer ignore the multiple summons. This air-conditioned historical Cabinet Office chamber was the established venue for those receiving what the Premier called a 'dressing down'. Up in the Northlands and the Ridings the moors were burning. Over to the East the wetlands were suffering the most severe flooding of the century so far, more and more land was consumed by the elements – but, 'No,' thought Evening, 'I have to be dragged in her for a reprimand.'

The Premier stood. He was flanked at a central table by two men. They were all backlit. She realised that this Premier was not the fluffy-haired, shambling, buffoonish one. He had been replaced! Over the course of Evening's career, she had survived four Premiers – now this was number five. This current incarnation of the chief minister was a sly fellow and quick-tempered, but cautious. He seemed like a survivor. His hair greyed at the temples, and he had a full face, almost lipless. Evening sneered at their hackneyed methods of intimidation. It would take more than some lighting effects and power grabs to make her feel nervous. She could tell by the quality of the suits worn by the two men that they were mere functionaries, Civil Servants, padding, there for back-up. The Premier squeaked across the polished floor and round to the front of the imposing table where he leaned against it and folded his arms.

The English Premiership was a rotating post. No one man, and it was always a man, occupied it for very long. That was the way the Cabinet held on to control. They had achieved a delicate equilibrium for maintaining power among the higher-ups and upper-middles. Once the Kingdom had broken up this was the solution reached by the Old Schoolers party along with their advisory teams from the Oxbridge Dons and Beeb, and the former media heads out of whom the Sky-stream Corporation formed.

Scotland had their SNAPs – the Scottish National Ancestry Party. The restoration of the old noble titles North of the Borderlands was in line with many other European nations and Mother Russia. To the West, the Duchy and Wales had formed their own state, preserved and served by its own ports on the 'Lantic as a trading entity and playground for the rich. The Northlands and Ridings, the Wealdlands and Wetlands to the East and the Lower Shire to the South of the Capital came under the authority of the Cabinet. Evening knew, however, that the nation was in a state of chaos and riddled with feudal-style corruption. Disparate governance meant that England only had a shaky economy, and food supplies to the Capital were severely threatened. She knew that the result would be riots and unrest, again.

This supercilious Premier, she recalled his name might be David, or Percy, seemed not to have a grasp of these problems as he stood in front of her in the half-light of the panelled meeting chamber.

"It doesn't look good for you," David-Percy shook his head and pursed his almost non-existent lips. He wore an extraordinary, perfectly tailored pinstripe suit of grey with sky-blue accessories. Evening ensured she kept her eyes downcast to his handmade brogues. She scrutinised the hand-stitching and punched leather decoration as he spoke, and thought, 'Have your moment, David-Percy, and then I'll have mine'.

"I did not want to have to do this, genuinely, Mizz Primrose, this causes me real anguish."

She hated the unnecessary hyperbole and the waste of words. Was he trying to emotionally engage her, reach out to her? Some hope.

"But you left me with very little choice. The Cabinet are very concerned about these voices being raised. I've seen some of this propaganda from these Ghostwriters," and he emphasised the name with air-quote-fingers. Evening felt ill. "And I have to say," he continued, "it greatly disturbs me." He leaned forward and fixed her with a patronising stare, "So, what are we – or rather you – to do about it?"

"Excuse me, Mr Percival?" one of the flanking bureaucrats interrupted and held up a phone, "It's your wife, sir."

The Premier straightened up with a quiet cough. "I'll have to take this. Hello – Caro, dearest. … Yes, of course, it's

David – you got through to my aide … I know, I'm sorry, but it's work …"

Ah yes, thought Evening, he *is* David *and* Percy. This one is very forgettable, but he's still dangerous. What have we done to ourselves? Chaos and incompetence. She sighed as Premier Percival tried to finish his conversation quickly, without losing face in front of her or angering his wife. "What do you mean – *forgot* her? … No, no, I'm not criticising you … Look, I can't talk now. Later, when I get home." He hung up and turned to Evening. "Golly, family eh?" She met his look with a smirk on her face. She knew that he knew he had met his match.

"We must get this fixed, and so," he turned back to his pair of bureaucrats, "I – we – have decided to find a solution. I'm appointing a crack team – the absolute tip-top – of COF troopers to this. They will be under *your* control and take orders from you to track down these troublemakers."

Evening remained silent at this announcement. She betrayed no outward sign of emotion. On the inside, however, she rejoiced. Finally, something decisive! This was cause for her to celebrate. She felt vindicated. David Percival continued, now eager to wrap things up, "This action has become annoying and too attention-grabbing. It's made us all very concerned. Trying to publicise – material and such – poems and well, words," he moved behind the table and sat down, "it starts to encourage people to – think about things and develop feelings."

Premier Percival paused and finished with clasped hands. "Ah – um," he concluded, "well, there it is." He spoke in a more and more diminished half-hearted way, feigned seriousness and concern, with a furrowed brow. It was much like his performance in front of the Sky-stream cameras.

Oh Christ, she thought, this is the way he is *all* the time.

She rose to her feet. Now, it was her turn, she concluded, to stride the floor.

"You know, Premier," she folded her arms and looked him dead in the eye, "that's the most sense you've made in ages."

Percival looked chagrined, and his aides were offended on his behalf.

"Please," she continued, "don't get your knickers in a twist, as my recently departed mother used to say."

"My sympathies," Percival murmured.

"It starts to encourage people to think and *feel* things. Your words."

"Well, feelings aren't necessarily something we want to discourage, but …" he stammered.

"Yes, yes we do," she confronted him abruptly. "We *want* to discourage people and forbid them from accessing anything we don't control. And, if they get in the mood to rebel – then we let them – but we let them do it *our* way.

We filter it to them – drip, drip, drip, – with the scapegoats and the shifting of blame, and off they go. But, on the road we paved."

Percival and his men were attentive, but increasingly impatient.

"Mizz Primrose," the right-hand aide tried to interrupt, "the Premier is an astute man. He gets this."

"Really? He gets it? Well, does he get that one of the perpetrators who is probably behind this action is one of the most dangerous people in the Capital?"

"Dangerous? Pamphlets and home-made banners? It's an annoyance, that's all. We want to put a stop to the kind of disruption we saw in Rothermere Square this morning."

"Silly, silly men," Evening laughed derisively. "The woman behind this is a subtle, clever person in a clumsy, stupid world. She can run intellectual rings around all of us and she knows how to manipulate and drive emotions."

"You have your troopers now – bring her in if you know who she is."

"No," Evening shook her head slowly, "I need to do more than that." It was as if she was talking to herself now, pondering a plan and keeping her own counsel. "I know what she's like. She'll have a gang of acolytes and disciples working for her. I want to bring them *all* down."

"Er, this sounds rather over the top – very messy."

"Oh, it will get a lot messier before we're finished." She rounded on the Premier. "I know his name is a dirty word around here, but Smallman was right."

"What? No!" One of the bureaucrats was on his feet.

"Oh, shut up," Evening held up a hand and silenced him with a bored voice. "I was there, at the very beginning of the Smallman Project." She looked at Percival. "You know, the Cabinet knows, he was right about the English public. He foresaw most of it and he might be in disgrace now –".

"Well, that *barely* covers it," Percival huffed.

"BUT – that doesn't mean he wasn't spot on! The Project was something different – unique. He dedicated his life to it and was a maverick, a one-off – and you all know it!"

"But what's that got to do with us now? He's no use to us – he's long gone."

"*He* might be gone, but his ideas are still with us – his legacy lives on. He was right about how the English want to pursue the path of least resistance. They want a managed world of convenience with little responsibility."

"Smallman is gone, put away. No one knows if he's even still alive. So, we need to work with the knowledge we have. No arguments," Percival held up a hand. "No more. Just work with what we've offered you. Use the troopers to put a stop to the Ghostwriters and leave Smallman out of it."

Evening made her way out of the Cabinet Office and onto the wide Whitehall streets. Things were moving in the right direction, and she felt confident. Finally, after a long, long wait and biding her time, she had some power. Some troops at her disposal and authority to exert control. Thanks to Derrick Smallman, she was partially prepared for this new calling. She had a plant, someone deep inside the lowers' and have-nots' neighbourhood. Smallman's advice had always been about preparedness and being at least two steps ahead. So, she had recruited someone several years ago from within the ranks of the COF – a reliable, resourceful individual. He maintained a presence amongst the lowers and when he sensed dissidence his brief was to encourage the behaviour, draw them in, and implicate as many of them as possible. Now she had more bodies to do her bidding, it was time to bring him in and to devise a final solution.

Excited and pumped, Evening was ready for this. It was her calling, her wheelhouse. She knew she would succeed in tracking them all down.

CLARA

Clara was getting used to life with the 'Lunders,' as the London Undergrounders called their race. She daily sat with the Baron's daughters on the platform at Goode Street. Her head wound was healing, and her cracked ribs no longer hurt when she breathed. She watched as Florence's deft fingers plucked the glittering, translucent shrimp from the mist net. She sat beside Philomel as the younger daughter plopped the creatures on to boil. The girl showed her how to shell them, and Clara was a fast learner. She picked up the technique in a speedy fashion. You had to hold the legs first and split the segments of the shell along the back. When she started, "Is that right?" she asked her guide as she tried the first few.

Philomel just looked at her from beneath her heavy, dark fringe.

Her sister spoke on her behalf. "Phil don't talk. She never say nothink."

Phil and Flo, the Baron's daughters, with their pale skin and chilly hands were an intriguing and curious pair. Clara enjoyed getting to know them. They showed her the way to punt with the pole and how to pin out the nets. These were fine and wispy and sat wafting in the currents along the tunnels. The larvae and immature shrimp drifted through, so that the fully grown ones could be gathered up for the pot.

"Dad says, Phil got too much on her mind. So, she don't talk."

Clara's ear was gradually becoming attuned to the accents down here. They had a direct, blunt, simplistic way of speaking. Somewhat charmless, she thought, but that did not mean they were not expressive.

"Ululululuuuuuu," came the customary call from the tunnel to the West. Phil responded, with the only sound that ever emanated from her, a guttural clicking in her throat. She stepped down to greet her father's punt as it pulled in and tied it at the mooring. As the Baron alighted onto the platform, he deposited a large box of colourful fungi.

"The Gardeners were generous today," he announced. He dipped into a deep pocket in his tunic and withdrew some paper packets that he handed to Clara. "They sent them for you."

She took them gratefully, "Wonderful."

"Said sumthink about you want them for medsin." He sounded a little wary.

The Lunders spoke with careful enunciation that veered from enthusiastic to faltering. She found it easy to communicate with them, except for Philomel of course, the closed-off, cold girl.

"You done awright," Samson looked around approvingly at the raw and cooked catch and helped himself to a few.

"What you want them for?" Flo looked at the packets in Clara's hand.

"These? They are dry ingredients for compounds."

Flo looked puzzled.

"Well, you know how the Shepherds helped me with their treatments?"

"Uh-huh."

"I thought I would make some medicines that you can use – that your healers can share and store for when people need pain relief." Clara smiled encouragingly as she spoke. "It's the least I can offer after everyone has helped me and you've all been so kind. I'm almost better now and soon I can go back up to the surface – to my home."

Samson clattered some pots behind her. The noise made her jump.

"I've learned so much here from the Gardeners, and the Bakers, and the Shepherds of course. All about the medicinal properties of the fungi you grow. I'd like to take some back with me."

Wide-eyed, Philomel looked to her father and sister.

Flo said, with some hesitation and a warning note in her voice, "You gotta be careful of some of them. They's poisonous if you don't take them proper."

"Yes, thank you. It's important I learn the right balance. It's risky, I know, and that's why I want to ask your healers some more questions before I go. The benefits they bring, as food and medicine, are worth it."

After a pause, during which Clara noticed Philomel's eyes flickering from her father to her sister, Samson spoke with a chuckle.

"Questions, questions! There'll be time for that sort of stuff." He scooped up some more shrimp. "First flings first – we've got a celebration to go to."

JENNIFER

The Sky-screen in Jennifer's flat scrolled through the news bulletin, the same things every hour. She watched the sun sink to the horizon in the West, glittering over the waters of the Old Father. She sipped a glass of wine as she tried to tune out the reportage, but she did not have the power to mute her screen. Everything, according to Evening Primrose, had to be '*on*, at all times'.

"The wild-fires on the Northern Moors light up the night sky over the Shires and Ridings. This is more evidence of how drastic and treasonous the activists are. Their dissident sabotage betrays their determination to undermine our strong and stable government." Evening's commentary punctuated the footage in an emotional and provocative way.

Jennifer heard shots in the distance from over the river, and then more – closer to home. Unrest moved across the bridges. Emotions were running high in the Capital that night.

"Why do you do this, Evening? You have everything. It just hurts people!" She spoke angrily at her boss's face as it appeared on the screen.

Evening enforced, on a regular basis, the 'principles of governance,' and settled 'unrest,' but tonight was different. The sounds of the disturbance and the sudden reports of gunfire grew more frequent. Jennifer stood in the lounge of her apartment, on the linen rug on blond wood floors and watched her Sky-screen. A bright light illuminated the room and she rushed onto her balcony overlooking the river. Flares lit the sky and the echoing crack of troopers' weapons resonated around the neighbourhood. They were getting closer.

Jennifer felt useless and guilty. She had stood by and watched as troopers laid into people on Rothermere Square. They had been observing, not even protesting, and still they had their faces forced into the paving slabs. Eliot appeared on the screen, seated next to Evening, wearing his tight, tanned face with its dumb expression. They expressed their grave concerns and Evening even managed to look weepy. Jennifer knew it was eye-drops applied off camera; she was convinced Evening Primrose had no tear ducts. She put this down to the surgery, or genetics.

Do something, do *something*. Jennifer fretted as the tension from the broadcast and around the city ratcheted up.

"The Ghostwriters," Evening announced, "are the biggest threat to social order. They are the most disruptive, diabolical, vice-loving dissidents and socialists," she spat out the words, "that we have ever known."

Jennifer needed to tune out her boss's hate speech and hysteria, and the nauseating smarm of Eliot. She put her jacket on and swigged the rest of her wine. Instead of her usual pumps or slip-ons, she zipped up some sturdy boots and headed out of her building. She moved quickly in a business-like way across the courtyard to the Pharmacy. She felt determined to do something and she only had one point of contact.

The store was open late. The subtle lighting from the window displays spilled out to illuminate the softly coloured paving. With the clamour of the city's anger in the background, she shut the door and entered to the soothing sounds of the piped muzak. She did not delay and walked right up to the counter. The Pharmacist gave her a flicker of recognition with slight panic in her eyes. She looked from side to side as if she wanted to run away at the sight of Jennifer's blatant behaviour.

"I want in," she looked the Pharmacist directly in the eye.

"What? I don't know what you're talking about," she replied in a hoarse whisper with a frantic scan of the shop.

"I want in. Give me a name."

Evening

Evening inspected the line of troopers, up and down. They were a mixture. All shapes and sizes. The COF did not have a recruitment requirement for fitness or physical type, height, or weight. All you needed to show was a willingness to use force on the Capital's population and get through basic, very basic, training. She looked along the line. Pot-bellied, broad shouldered, some more muscular, others skinny – but all mean. None of them compared to her man on the inside down amongst the natives, but she liked the look of a female trooper with short red hair and equally ruddy cheeks and a stocky build.

"Last night's patrols were well-coordinated. You," she looked at the female trooper, "step forward. What's your name?"

"Shaw, Ma'am."

"Shaw. How would you like a command, Shaw?"

"Ma'am," Shaw's shoulders and chest swelled and lowered, and a proud smirk played around her lips, "me, Ma'am? Thank you!"

"You proved to be a great asset last night, I was impressed."

Evening was on the parade ground at the COF Barracks in Cheltsea. This was once a stylish, modern complex of buildings, now a little worn about the edges, and re-commissioned from residential property for use by the security forces. Once, long ago, it had been a crowded site of historic buildings with open yards for exercising cavalry horses and training the mounted troops. Partly demolished and then restored and re-built after the break-up of the Kingdom it was commandeered into service but retained much of its finery. Marble and limestone cladding, open spaces and careful lighting around the restored old brick, the Cheltsea Barracks stood for something enduring and provided a smart home for the COF militia. It was located next to the site of the old Loyal Hospital and the Victory Pier along The Reach, a stretch of the Old Father full of inlets and canals. A large complex in the heart of the Capital, almost completely surrounded by water, the Barracks and Hospital sat on their own marshy isthmus jutting into the river and could only be accessed via the Victory and Justice bridges.

"Shaw, I want you to form a troop. Pick your people and report back to me."

"Yes, Ma'am," Shaw stepped back into line.

Evening walked back to her office beside the Barrack block. A guard dutifully opened a large wooden door for her as she reached the top of a gently sloping pathway. Her office was housed in the old brick-built Garrison Chapel. It was well laid out, if not as high-tech as her place in the Sky-stream studios. She liked the age of it and the all-white interior with vaulted ceiling and fine tiled and flagged floors. In the entrance hallway, underneath the chapel porch's pitched roof, a trio of bronze busts stood on plinths. Elegantly modelled and cast they showed a heavy-featured, dour set of people. Two were of bald men with large ears and prominent noses, clearly father and son. The third was of a stern-looking woman. Her small, fine, unhappy features were only hardened by the solid cast bronze curls of her severe hair-do. Picked out in icy white enamel on the old patinated surface were a low, lace dress collar, and a cold set of jewellery made up of drop earrings, a pearl and diamond necklace and a spiked pearl tiara. A worn plaque suggested some information about the 'House of Windsor'. Uninterested in their provenance, Evening kept them there because she liked the texture of the metal busts and the tone of misery and disapproval they promoted as soon as anyone entered the building.

Since the Premier's directive aimed at her, Evening had embraced her new role and typically set about undermining those around her from the start. She reached out directly to the rank-and-file troopers, equipped them with rubber and plastic bullets, and then let them loose in a new campaign of patrols and crack-downs. Now, she had decided on the recruitment of a new leadership from among their numbers, to reward loyalty and brutality. This was a tried and tested tactic from the Smallman playbook. It instilled faithful service and dedication from the grassroots level. Bypass the leadership and promote from below.

Evening buzzed her assistant, "Send for Dr Crooke."

"Yes, Ma'am."

She enjoyed the protocols and deference in place at Cheltsea. The COF staff loved formality and severity and treated her with deep respect. I missed my calling, she thought. I should have joined the Feds long ago.

An underground tunnel, part of a network, ran from the Barracks to the Loyal Hospital next door. The Loyal had once been a veterans' home. Now, though, in the aftermath of so many European Wars, there were too many old soldiers to house in this way. They had to make do with vouchers and charity. The tunnel was the favoured route employed by Dr Helkiah Crooke from his billet at the Loyal to his meetings with Evening in the Barracks. The panelled door of the office clicked open, and Evening's diligent assistant ushered in the Doctor. He shuffled across the thick rug with the help of an ebony and silver cane and came to a rest in one of the deep, chestnut, buttoned leather armchairs.

Evening walked around her desk to join him in the lounge area. She poured herself a drink and offered one to him.

"No," he held up a wrinkled hand in a neat cuff, "never in the daytime. But I will take some of your usual beautifully catered refreshments."

"They're on their way," and she sat down. "We need to finalise the plan. When the Ghostwriters are rounded up and brought in will you have the cells ready?"

"The accommodation will be in place."

"I must be able to find out what goes on from the moment they are detained. And we keep them separate."

"Every room is wired for sound and monitored."

A tap at the door.

"Enter," Evening really was relishing her new security role. Her assistant sidled in with a tray.

"The Doctor's delicacies."

"Thank you, my dear," Helkiah tapped the tabletop, "just here."

The uniformed woman deposited some small dishes of whipped cream desserts, dotted with fruit, a metal beaker of frothy posset dusted with powdered cinnamon, and a plate of crisp macaroons and ginger snaps. Dr Crooke watched her leave. He took a delicate, lacy biscuit in his tremulous, bony fingers and scooped up some of the creamy dessert then snaffled it down. He munched and moaned with delight. Evening felt quite queasy. Helkiah Crooke reminded her of her mother. Possessed of the same shameless, slathering, messy greed of the aged. She never wanted to get old. She determined not to age, whatever it took. She took a deep, settling breath.

"We need to ensure complete discretion and I want a stream-lined operation."

"Well," Helkiah wiped his fingers on a damask napkin and sucked his dentures, "we can access the accommodation through the tunnels. They can be brought through the Barracks, or by boat from the river, The Victory Pier allows for that."

Evening nodded slowly. "That sounds good, very good, yes. A skiff – silent – no engine. And then up through the Hospital to the cells."

"To the *accommodation*," he corrected her. "And no one will ever know they've arrived."

"Except you and I, and *my* COF troopers." She smiled again. "This will work out very well."

Evening looked across at Helkiah and instantly regretted it. He had picked up the warm, creamy posset. He sucked it down, his lips pursed over the rim of the beaker. He looked just like Aurora with his crimped, greedy mouth. She steeled herself. Dr Helkiah Crooke had an impeccable reputation and track record with the Cabinet and various Ministries. She needed his skills for information extraction. Once a couple of the Ghostwriters were brought in, then she could almost guarantee that the ringleaders would soon follow. They would crack under interrogation and give everyone up. Even though she did not strictly need this to happen. She had another secret weapon that no one else knew about, not even Crooke, her inside man. But in order for the confessions to stand and for the public to witness the downfall of the Ghostwriters, she had to make it look like a legitimate break-up of a criminal operation. Her undercover agent had to be protected. He was far too valuable to be sacrificed.

"And you're sure your methods will work?"

"Of course," Helkiah cackled and shrugged carelessly, "never been known to fail."

"Good, because it will be soon. I have an insider who can help me round them up – quickly. Once we move in, I need to be able to place them and keep things very quiet."

"Discretion is my watch word," Helkiah picked up his ebony cane, and tapped it on the table. "Have the rest boxed up for me," he waved it over the dishes. "I love the superior products of your kitchens."

"No problem," Evening rose and sighed as she returned to her desk and buzzed the intercom.

CLARA

"I can help you if you help me. I can get you out of here too." Clara spoke to Philomel intensely and urgently.

Noise surrounded them at a large, clamorous gathering in the vaulted central hall of Circus Piccadillus. The mixed voices of the Lunders echoed around the impressive space. The acoustics in the tunnels and around the whole system gave musicians a natural performance space. Wonderful melodies filled the air from every quarter as Clara made her way cautiously with Philomel around the Circus. They kept away from the centre where the statue of a little winged warrior balanced atop a construction of salvaged metal and timber. The statue held a bow, frozen in the act of firing an arrow. Its silver-grey, lithe form was athletic and dynamic as it perched on one leg, its wings tall and sweeping behind. Surrounding this totem, the Lunders thronged in their groups, sharing food and mingling. Some exchanges erupted into conflict, voices rose and subsided. They were gathered for a celebration and some entertainment, so peace-making prevailed. Barbecue fires smoked in corners below inefficient vents, so the air was thick and sooty in places. And the music – the music surrounded them from all corners and from the tunnels leading off the wide, vaulted hall. Groups of Lunders clapped along to the echoing acoustics and although the melodies and the instruments were different, they did not clash. Instead of discord there was a strange kind of harmony that Clara had never heard before. Different groups, in their little tribal huddles, danced to their anthems as the smell of roasting and grilling food filled the air.

Clara had been looking for a way out for some time. She was well and fully healed, but she was never alone. Samson made sure of that. Ever since she expressed the desire to leave, she had been watched and escorted, by Samson, Flo or one of the Warreners. They did not say outright that she must stay but in every other way Clara was conscious of the suspicion and the threat surrounding her. She knew that her only opportunity was at one of the regular Circus gatherings. Either Oxfud or Piccadillus in the large central halls. The Lunders dropped their guard to eat, drink, dance, and watch the combats. There were enough distractions, she realised, to make a break for it.

When it became clear to her that she was hemmed in and under careful watch, Clara looked around for an ally. Samson and Flo were vigilant, and they trusted Philomel as one of them. Mute, thoughtful, and tough, Clara had been able to gain the favour of Samson's younger daughter. With her gestures and written symbols, Philomel communicated in her own clear fashion. She did not want Clara to be unhappy or a prisoner, so she agreed to help her out of the Lunderworld.

Amidst the gathering, Clara could lean in close to Phil and talk undisturbed. The girl nodded and gestured in reply. Tonight was the night as Clara had learned that there would be a big, popular combat. Everyone, especially

Samson, would be preoccupied. They stood against one of the walls, just beyond the crowds. So much was going on and there were so many distractions, Clara began to feel a little disoriented. She caught Philomel's eye. The girl smiled and patted her chest with a fluttering motion. Clara had learned that meant 'breathe' and 'relax'.

Samson was centre stage that night. He climbed onto the structure and stood just beneath the winged statue. He raised his arms for silence to address the gathered Lunders.

"My people," he looked around proudly at the population in their motley and homespun garments amongst their world of salvage, let's celebrate us Lunderworld! Who's here? The Victorians? The Bakers? The Gardeners? The Shepherds?" a shout went up as he named each tribe. "Let's prepare. Contenders – step forward!"

From opposite sides of the Circus the fighters entered. Whoops and cheers rose from the crowd. Clara dreaded this aspect of the Lunders' pastimes. They were obsessed with combat and pitting fighters against one another. She knew that was a reason why Samson wanted her, needed her, to stay. Healers were in short supply amongst the Warreners and they knew of her skills. They had been watching her before she happened on the doorstep of the Shepherds, and Samson had traded with them to bring her into his tribe. She had found the Lunders both admirable and sinister. They were resilient and cunning, ingenious and childish. A world of opposites and contradictions. The music and the beautiful voices that filled the natural acoustics of the tunnels, these she loved. The Lunders' culture of growing food and fishing had shown her so many possibilities, as well as their ability with fungi, hybrid plants, mosses, and aquatic life. She knew she could use this knowledge on the surface and put the properties of the flora and fungi to good use – nutritious, medicinal, and toxic. Now that she had to get back up there the true test had arrived.

The first bout of combat for the evening began. It exploded with cheering and roaring as an armoured woman, young and dogged, stepped forward with a net and a spear. She had a dead look in her eyes. A little man who only came up as high as her waist confronted her wielding a shorter spear and a small blade. They circled each other in the makeshift arena, whilst Samson stood in place to comment on the action using a loudhailer. From around the Circus and bouncing off the ceiling the chant came up, "Ba-RON, Ba-RON, Ba-RON!"

The warriors lunged forwards.

Clara could shield her exchange with Philomel whilst the excitement mounted.

'Be careful,' Philomel signed to her as they stood against a grimy tiled wall. They made sure to avoid eye contact with anyone. 'Wait,' the girl gestured and looked out into the crowd, judging carefully when to make a move. The action in the arena began to build and the Lunders surged forwards. Phil placed a cautious hand on Clara's arm.

"OK, whenever you're ready," Clara nodded and whispered underneath the din.

The female warrior parried blows from the smaller fighter as the Lunders bayed and urged them on. Clara moved a little way and crouched behind some of the spectators. She looked to Philomel beside her with a questioning glance. The other nodded and patted her shoulder. She put a finger to her lips. Clara readied herself. The woman had the man in a neck hold to the cheers of her people. Clara looked up and saw this. She could feel herself becoming mesmerised by the action, and felt choked up too, almost crying at the sight of the combat.

In the middle of the fight frenzy, as the man tried to wrestle free from the spear shaft pressed against his neck, Clara felt a tug on her sleeve. Philomel gestured towards one of the tunnels, urgently. This was it. They kept low and scampered into the darkness as the noise dissolved behind them. Philomel, in her rough fisher-smock and leg bindings, heavy hair and pale face, proceeded quickly and lightly. The passageway lay before them, curved and tiled, and leading downwards, darkening as it went. Down and down they went, until they reached a platform where a flat-bottomed skiff sat in the water. They clambered on board, steadying it as they got into position and Philomel clutched the pole.

"I'm ready," Clara whispered to her guide as she found the right balance point on the seat, and they pushed off into the silence of the tunnels.

Clara recalled and noted the names as they progressed, Leester Square, the Garden, and Ho'bun – the names partly obscured and half-remembered. They moved quietly on their way back towards Russell Square. At the platform, Philomel moored the vessel and helped Clara disembark. She looked back to her rescuer, "Thank you, I know what it's taken for you to help me."

Philomel smiled and shrugged. Clara got the distinct feeling that the young woman would cope if she was challenged. Clara made sure she had her pouch of supplies, the dried fungi and other seeds and ingredients she had collected before she left the boat. She had put together this little stash to bring the knowledge of the Lunders to the surface. With a final gesture of thanks to Phil, she headed into the deep tunnels of Russell Square.

Samson had taken the time to tell Clara how valuable she was to the Warreners as a way of persuading her to stay before he used more forceful tactics. She recalled his hand on her shoulder, friendly but heavy, and how uncomfortable it made her. As things closed in around her and she realised how inward-looking the Lunders were as a people, she discovered Philomel as an ally. The people fought and traded amongst themselves and remained in their drowned and buried world.

Making her way through the passages she allowed herself to stop and get her bearings. 'Beware, beware of Russell Square'. The young Lunders had chanted this, and Clara asked Flo what it meant.

"It's them Russellers – they's weird. They does terrible things," she had shaken her head grimly. "Not normal. They takes people and does terrible things and we dun't see them again."

Clara steadied her breathing and looked around. She held onto the railing as she climbed up the stairwell from the platform. It was different here, unlike the other parts of the Lunderworld. It lacked the cool comfort and just felt clammy and dank. There was no chemical lighting, just some vestigial illumination from the bioluminescent fungi, and root growth snaking down from above choked everything, winding down blackened walls, and clogging the low vaulted spaces of the station. Clara looked around to try and locate one of the landmarks Philomel had drawn on the little map for the escape. The girl had been so helpful, with her thumbnail sketches and gestured language, that Clara knew what she had to do. And the Russellers, the many warnings about the Russellers. She must take care.

She rounded a corner and spotted the two openings she recognised from the map. Between them stood a huge square tiled pillar. These were where the lifts had once sat, but now the shafts were empty. The lift cars had long since rotted and plummeted to the depths. Clara knew that the stairway to the surface must be close by, round to the right if Philomel's directions were to be trusted. She stopped beside a sign on the wall. Cracked, dingy plastic over dirty, peeling paper. She could make out the few words, 'staircase … 175 st … emergency'. Bands of turquoise and black tiles bordered the cream tiles on the sides of the stairwell, murky and chipped. Layers of leaf litter, years of it, blocked the foot of the stairs, as Clara started to scramble upwards. The desiccated vegetation and old hanging vines crackled and crumbled at her touch. The brittle noise made her heart thump. She was only a few metres up the spiral stairs when she had to pause and catch her breath. In the silence she heard it, the scratching noise. As she listened it grew louder. A flickering, scuttering, skittering, moving upwards behind her. She looked up to where the stairs curved away above her into the darkness, clogged with vegetation. The scratching continued. She had to move. Another sound reached her – this time panting and rasping. Harsh. Something made the vines around her tremble.

Heart pounding, she tried to speed up. The dried, twisted roots impeded her on the stairs and the hanging vines caught in her hair and clothes. Whatever it was moving up behind her grew louder, in the dark. She could still just find the handrail, or parts of it, wrapped with the old foliage. The stairs went on and on. 175 had not seemed like such a huge number when she was at the bottom. Clara skidded and slipped and banged her chin. She felt a wave of pain and dizziness. Her head hummed, and she had to sit in the darkness to try and recover. The seconds flurried past with the blood pounding in her ears, and she tried to shake off the pain. From behind the scuffling continued. It – they – whatever it was – the Russellers were there – still moving. No, no, no, she thought, the words swam around her head. Move!

"Beware, beware of Russell Square." She began to chant this in a whisper with her breathing as she started to climb again. She took a beat for each step pushing herself on and as she rose so did the humidity. Exhaustion started to creep over her. The stairs went on forever and the sweat made her clothes stick to her body, her lungs were bursting. It was not just the number of stairs, they were steep too and she was scratched and torn as she scrabbled upwards, ever upwards. Her legs were heavy and burning with pain. Still, she had to carry on with no sign of when she would reach the top.

Finally, lungs screaming for air, Clara reached the top – a hard floor on which she collapsed. Signs of light came from somewhere. She lay, sweating and dry-heaving until she almost vomited. She looked up and around a corner – more stairs! But this time a straight flight of a dozen or so into an open space. With relief she tried to lunge forward but something stopped her. She was jerked backwards off her feet. She twisted around as she was dragged across the floor. Thrashing out with her feet panic overwhelmed her and her insides froze when she saw what it was that had hold of her. She tried to wriggle and wrench herself away from it in horror. Struggling and kicking, her efforts were futile against a pair of strong, claw-like hands that had hold of her.

A hard thump from behind her, then another, and another. She crawled away and turned around in time to see Philomel panting hard and standing over the creature, its dark blood sprayed across her face. In her hand she held a long weapon, part sledgehammer, part spike. In shock, Clara staggered to her feet. Wide-eyed, she stammered, "You – you came for me? Th-thank you."

Philomel spat on the floor, wiped some of the dark slime off her cheek, and nodded. Clara looked down at the creature that twitched and pumped viscose blood onto the grime and dead leaves. It was a pale, small creature, scrawny and lean but incredibly powerful. Its large hands and head on a hairless body had translucent skin. Blood vessels and sinew could be seen poking through the surface in places. Whilst it seemed very dead, she approached it cautiously, and looked up at Philomel. She could not see it surviving the wounds that the girl had delivered, but she remained wary, nonetheless. Up close it was repulsive and pathetic. The Russeller wore an intriguing armour over most of its fleshy, pale body. She saw that it was formed from pieces of broken ceramic tile, metal, and other salvage, held together with wire and cord. The soft, delicate skin had to use this as an exoskeleton, and in places it had partly fused to its flesh. This creature had even embellished its armour with some pieces of patterned plastic and trinkets it had found. Philomel's heavy hammer and spike combination had smashed the outer shell and then stabbed the flesh inside, like one of the pale shrimp she harvested. Clara was not worried for the girl. She knew she could look after herself.

Once more she waved to Philomel and turned to conquer just one last flight of stairs to the upper hallway. But then she back-tracked. She held out a hand to her comrade.

"Come with me, you can join us – on the surface."

Philomel's stern young face looked back at her, and her eyes flickered towards the exit. She paused, and then shook her head, smiled a sly smile, raised a hand and was gone – back down the spiral staircase and into the darkness. She had, Clara realised, come just far enough to save her, and then headed back down to her world. She got the distinct impression that Philomel rather enjoyed the chance to take out a Russeller. She looked down at the maimed, twitching body and felt ill. She wiped her bloody chin and gathered herself to make it to the exit. A wave of warm air gushed towards her from the surface for the first time in forever and she leaned against the archway at the entrance. Dehydrated, nauseous, and bleeding, she keeled over and hit the ground.

PART FOUR

Jennifer

Jennifer still felt like an outsider.

She had worked amongst the Ghostwriters for some time and tried to make her mark, find her place, prove her usefulness. Susan and Clara, Edgar, Gunnar, and Charlie were all fine. She was lickety-split with them. They encouraged her and made her welcome.

Mina, on the other hand, was hostile and difficult.

Jennifer sat in the Pivvy with Mina and Edgar, trying to set type.

"You getting on with that, Milady?" Mina looked across at her. "Is it too much for you? We don't have any refreshments or hospitality suite here – I hope that's OK for you? Or is it too hard without a massage or a manicure?"

Edgar intervened, "Just leave it, Mina. Let her alone."

Mina looked at him with a stiff, cynical expression.

"You're on her side now?"

"There's no *sides*," he was emphatic.

Mina looked him squarely in the face, "You believe what you want to believe."

Jennifer sat quietly and persevered with the task given her by Susan. She had decided to weather Mina's criticism and complaints without retaliation. Mina strolled casually across the Pivvy and came around behind Jennifer. She looked at her work and sighed and tutted.

"Mina!" Edgar protested. He looked at Jennifer with an apologetic smile.

"What? What? I ain't doing nothing!" but she was able to give Jennifer an awkward nudge before she moved on. "Oops, clumsy."

Jennifer remained mute. Her days with the Ghostwriters had been fulfilling and revealing so far so she let this slide past.

"If you give me a chance," she had said to Susan and Clara, "I can be of use."

She had sat in Gunnar's Emporium after following the channels to arrive there. She learned their secrecy mechanisms and made it into the inner circle.

"Ask me anything," she reassured them, "I'm committed."

Clara was still recovering from her ordeal with the Lunders. She had been dehydrated and injured, but mostly exhausted. But she was, Jennifer looked at her with wonder, the same kind Nurse that she remembered. Her joy and relief to find her and know she was back and safe, it was a glimmer of hope in a bleak world.

Susan took the lead and initiated Jennifer into the Ghostwriters' practices. Everyone had a role and she learned how to contribute to the type-setting and maintenance of the press. Edgar was especially kind. Mina's sceptical attitude persisted.

"Don't think you can come on in here and make like you *know*!"

She tried not to annoy the girl.

Instead, she learned as much as she could from Susan. She began to enjoy the esoteric and philosophic content of the texts that were to be found in the basement library. Poetry especially. She thought she had understood books and poetry as objects and possessions. Higher-ups typically displayed their books alongside pieces of art and expensive alcohol.

Jennifer sat quietly at the table in the Pivvy, once Mina and Edgar departed, reading a recommended book from Susan. There was something strange and symbolic about the landscape of language she was being introduced to by her guide.

'My name is Ozymandias, King of Kings. Look on my works ye mighty and despair.'

This was a slogan she had helped to print as one of her first jobs with the Ghostwriters. A departed king, a shattered visage, an old, old tale of vanity and failure. Powerful leaders do not last forever. Humanity can't be carved from stone.

"Smart people," Susan told her, "*can* be fooled."

Jennifer recalled these words and thought about the Sky-stream studios and the employees. Clever people but ones who scurried about and lived with fear and aggression every day.

Susan told Jennifer stories of table-rapping and table-tipping. She listened in curious bewilderment about how famous and brilliant men and women were persuaded to believe in the presence of spirits and ghouls. Michael Faraday – a scientist and sceptic – wrote: 'We do these things with rigour and learning – is it spirits or something else?' Susan showed her how evidence can con people or assist them into realisation. She re-read Faraday's paragraph:

'It is with me a clear point that the table moves when the parties, though they strongly wish it, do not intend, and do not believe that they move it by ordinary mechanical power. They say, the table draws their hands; that it moves first; and they have to follow it; – that sometimes it even moved from under their hands.' With a 'quasi-involuntary action'; this phrase made her think very hard about the ways in which Evening had encouraged the Sky-stream crew to promote material that caused viewers to respond and get riled up.

"What's the button we want to push today?" was one of her boss's mottoes. Hot button topics and emotive language. "I'm speaking to you – the English public – are you going to tolerate this?" "Take action!! Make your voices heard!"

Well, Evening, that's what I'm trying to do.

Mina

"Give me the crowbar," Mina held a hand out to Edgar. "Come on, come on!"

They were outside her favourite higher-up grocery store, where she staged regular raids, in the neighbourhood by the river.

"We shouldn't be doing this again," he complained.

"Stop moanin'! You want some of them noodles you like, don't you?" Mina grunted and twisted the crowbar in the security chains.

Edgar winced as the metal crunched apart. They both tugged the double doors open. On one of her previous visits, Mina had managed to sabotage the alarms and so, confidently, she now barged her way in. She felt sure in the knowledge that they would not have been fixed. She strutted down the well-stocked aisles and stuffed products in her backpack as if on a regular shop. Soups, dried goods, spices, flavourings. She took more and more – chocolate, cookies, muffins, alcohol.

Edgar put a hand on her arm, "Stop. That's enough. We can't get too greedy and reckless. We've already hit this place a few times."

But Mina was not listening to him tonight. She ploughed ahead. Her irritation turning into anger. As soon as that higher-up, that snooty, posh slag Jennifer had shown up then Susan and Clara were all over her. Typical. It doesn't matter what anyone says, they all want to crawl to the haves. We were supposed to be a team. We were supposed to stick together. The haves get everything from everyone all the time, even us rebels. She sounded off in her head as she ransacked the shelves.

"What's eating you?" Edgar asked in a scolding whisper.

"Fuckin' higher-ups. They get everything."

"Is that it? Is that what this is about? You're *jealous* of Jen?"

"Oh – you too? Fuckin' *Jen*, is it?"

"Get a grip. Stop acting like a silly little girl! This isn't about you or her. We have to stick together. You want to take stupid risks? Do it on your own!"

He turned to leave, and Mina grabbed his arm.

"Hey! Where are you going?"

"Out of here. Listen, if you got any sense, you will too."

"Go then," she walked away down the frozen food aisle.

A few yards down, she turned around and looked for him. Edgar was gone. Fuck that! Mina fumed at the idea that Edgar of all people would let her down. He always had her back. But not now. She decided not to care and swung around. A dark, solid mass knocked her off her feet.

The breath left her body and she struggled on the floor of the grocery shop like an overturned beetle.

The next thing she knew a trooper's solid baton pressed against her neck and her arms were pinned from behind.

"No – I – can't breathe!"

Her legs flailed and peddled uselessly against the floor. There was no way to break from the grip.

The ruddy, grim face of a burly female trooper thrust itself into hers.

"Hello, little Miss Suresh, you've been a very naughty girl, haven't you?"

The smell of bubble-gum vape juice hit Mina's nose. Before she could take another breath, a musty black hood obliterated everything. Tight plastic zip-ties secured her wrists, and she was marched off.

Her first thoughts in this blackened world were: 'Where's Edgar? Have they got him too?' The urge to call out his name was powerful in her desperation. She did not want to be dragged off to face the inevitable ordeal alone. Then her instincts kicked in and she kept silent. 'Leave his name – and anyone else's – out of it for as long as possible,' she advised herself as the realisation of her predicament sunk in. 'This is it,' she thought, 'it's my turn now. I'm one of the disappeared.'

Mina's own harsh breathing filled the hood and she felt queasy as the van barrelled along. She had sensed the hands with the tight grip loading her in through the rear doors. With her very limited experience of travelling in vehicles, she could nonetheless recognise the movement and the sensation of being driven. Wedged on a bench seat she bounced along and was aware of others around her – prisoners or Feds – she could not tell. She ventured to speak.

"Where are you taking me?" her own muffled voice was loud in her ears.

No response. Mina's defiance and built-in, reckless bravery asserted themselves. She tried to be reasonable.

"Listen, I won't cause any trouble. I've been stupid, I get that – but there's no reason for this. You don't have to take me away. Let me go and I won't try anything like that again. It was my first time."

No response. After another pause, she tried again.

"You mentioned a name earlier – Suresh? That makes me think you've got the wrong person. My name is – Jennifer – Jennifer Johnson. There's been a misunderstanding."

This time, over the rumble of the engine, a harsh reply, "Shut up, no talking."

"Can't you understand?" she persevered. "It's all been a big –," but she was halted abruptly by a thump to her solar plexus.

Wheezing, nauseous, and completely disabled, Mina had to finish the journey on the floor of the van. Once it stopped, she was jerked up so hard she thought her shoulder would pop out of the socket.

"Please, please," she appealed to the hands and boots and around her, "I think I'm going to be sick." In all of this, in that moment, the thing she dreaded most was throwing up inside the hood. It was wrenched from off her head, and she felt a welcome surge of fresh air before she fell painfully to her knees on a worn brick courtyard. Her stomach heaved and she retched hot, bile-filled liquid that made her throat burn. Dragged up once again, she was marched into a tiled corridor from where she was shuffled into a windowless room and deposited on a hard chair in front of a rigid table. The door slammed shut in a dead concrete wall.

Mina swallowed the acid-tasting saliva and mucus that lingered in her mouth. She sucked some air into her lungs as deeply as possible and took a look around. Grey concrete walls dampened any sounds and a strip light flickered above. The table and chair were bolted to the floor. She waited.

Now, the mind games will begin, she thought. They want to terrorise me and break me. Why did I get angry? She scolded herself. How could I have got angry at Edgar? Not Edgar.

"I was mad because of Jennifer," she muttered quietly.

"Because of Jennifer," a loud voice came out of nowhere and resonated around the cell.

Susan

Clara had been back for a while, but Susan was still concerned. She watched her friend closely, looking for signs in her behaviour and how she could read her. A secretive sort of person, anyway, Clara had been busy with some projects since her return. She did not explain any of it to the others. Instead, she regularly departed the Pivvy for the deeper Wilderness and gave no explanation other than, "I'll be back soon".

Clara, thought Susan, Clara who had been the heart and soul and energy of the Ghostwriters, now seemed distant and lonely. Susan decided to try and draw her out of it, and asked herself: If Clara saw *me* like that, what would *she* do?

Susan had saved some ration tickets and did her best, based on one of Clara's own recipes, to bake. She sprinkled some dry ingredients – flour, powdered egg, coffee flavouring, and sugar – into a bowl and added some synth-lactyl and a scrape or two of some wild honey. She had to keep adding water as the mixture got drier and drier. It was probably the chalk in the flour, she figured, soaking up all the liquid. After much mixing she had a lump of grey dough. She looked down at Ellery. The cat had that slight tilt to his head that made him look both coquettish and a bit dim.

"Hmmm, I don't think I'm cut out for baking," she mused to him.

Ellery responded by climbing onto the bed where he began to lick his anus.

"Now you're just showing off."

Once the biscuits were baked in her tiny, rusty oven with its single heating element, they resembled small, hard nuts, but Susan thought, with some weak tea they could be appetising. She tested one and it had quite a good crunch. These might work as an ice-breaker to begin a conversation with Clara.

Later that evening, at the Pivvy, she hijacked Clara. She had asked her to help, and Clara with the expectation that she was needed stepped up as usual and arrived promptly.

"Am I early?" she looked around the twilit space. The finches chirruped rhythmically up in the roof.

"It's just us. I hope you don't mind."

"What's going on?" Clara was wary. She had become noticeably jumpier and more suspicious since her return.

"Nothing, look – I made biscuits."

Clara looked at the dirty-grey pallid blobs that Susan proffered. She took one and nibbled it cautiously. "It's good. A nice crumb," she said kindly. A glimmer of the old Clara.

Susan took a bite and pulled a face. "That's disgusting – you don't have to eat it!" she laughed.

Clara looked relieved.

"What I really wanted to do," she said, conquering her self-consciousness as she spoke, "was check in with you – see how you are. And maybe, find out what happened to you?"

Clara sat down and scratched at a portion of her locks, a nervous habit Susan knew, when she was thinking.

"Don't get me wrong," said the gentle woman, "I'm so grateful that you're asking – but I don't know if I can talk about it. Perhaps, I can … with you, eventually."

"Don't think, just tell me what you're feeling. That's something I learned from you. Don't think – just say!"

"Upset," said Clara, embracing it. "Lonely. Nervous."

"Upset, about what? What happened to you?"

"Not about me, but for the people there."

"You haven't told us who you met."

Clara paused and looked tearful again. "It's not about me, or my time there, but them – and how they tried to help me. It's difficult."

She looked so sad that Susan felt herself choke up.

Clara looked as though she wanted to punish herself. She knitted her fingers together and turned to Susan in anguish. "They were so kind, but *so* troubled. They had found so many answers, but more questions."

Susan listened intently and grew more aghast, as Clara took her through the journey with the Lunders in detail.

When she got to the encounter with the Russeller, Susan's blood ran cold. After she had finished, Clara said, "So, you can see how much I discovered and learned from them – how useful it is to know about them. But it's all so, so disturbing. They are kind and sinister, and vital and cruel."

Susan processed this bombshell information about the subterranean civilisation and all its tribes, as Clara gathered her things. She opened a little pouch and handed Susan a small cookie. "I want to show you something. Eat this on the way."

Susan was glad of some of Clara's superior baking skills.

They scrunched their way through the leaf litter, moving deeper and deeper into the Wilderness in the Square, to where it stretched out to connect to some even wilder parklands. Susan went far beyond the Pivvy, further than ever before, following Clara's lead. The sun set and the chatter of birds grew to a crescendo as they wheeled and swooped to their overnight roosts. The humidity rose as they walked, but Susan trudged on, accustomed to it and tonight she felt like she could handle almost anything. She sensed a different mood approaching and welcomed it. Springtime in the Capital was nearing, and she remembered how, almost a year ago, she had come up with the idea of the Ghostwriters.

A ghost woman walks behind a ghost woman. We vanish and we reappear. We diminish and we materialise. Clara had disappeared and left only a few people concerned for her whereabouts. But we were enough, we were genuine, Susan focused on that fact. She knew that Clara, Mina, Cece, Edgar, all of them, mattered.

It was a moonless night and so Susan was startled to find she was aware of some light as blue, flickering auras. Around the trees it played, like St Elmo's fire. From behind, Clara's head wore a halo.

"Here we are," she stopped in a clearing beside some dead, fallen trunks, turned to Susan, and held out her arms. The darkness had crept up on them but all around there was illumination. A glow permeated everything, so that Susan could make out shapes and forms in what should have been pitch black.

"What's this?" she scanned the mossy woodland.

"It's amazing, isn't it?" Clara looked at her with eager wide eyes that Susan found a little disturbing. She drifted past trees and logs, not seeming to touch the ground, and brushed her fingers gently over them. The glow they possessed grew stronger as she passed. Clara turned to Susan. Her face and hair were touched by an ethereal light. The halo form that had appeared and sat on her head was larger now and more prominent. From a woodland fey she had transformed into a tragic martyr – St Lucy or St Agnes – fated to perish but with a terrifying strength. Susan could only stand and stare, transfixed by her friend. Clara was so, so beautiful, standing between the trees, becoming like them but ruling over them. Her hair moved in living snake-like tendrils and the silver birch and beech trees rustled and bowed as if at her command.

"Who are you? What's going on?"

"Just enjoy it, Susan. It's wonderful, isn't it? A whole new way of seeing the world. There's bioluminescent fungi and lichen all around us. So much beauty that we still don't understand."

Susan was hearing her friend's voice as if it came from far away, and almost drowned out by the tinkling of her necklaces and beads as she moved delicately among the fallen logs and leaves. She felt tremors through her whole body and a feeling of euphoria wash over her. Blue and purple trails of light travelled from the treetops and entered at her fingertips. Voices echoed around her, speaking words she could not understand at first, until they formed into sentences:

"Watch and learn."

"And I, I took the one less travelled by."

"A life less ordinary."

"A room of one's own."

The flurry of sound subsided, and Susan felt herself grow weak and drained and heavy. She looked for Clara, who was built of light and birdsong now. As she watched her, she felt herself plop down into a crook in a log. She sat there and noticed something textured and strange with the same odd chemical light. She reached out a hand to touch it – whatever it was – on a nearby stump.

"No, don't do that!" Clara raced over and grabbed her wrist. "Don't touch that."

Susan looked blearily at the growth on the log; small, rippling light brown scales clustered on the dead wood. And then everything went completely dark.

The stillness of total night was around her when she awoke. She heard a crackling and managed to sit up. The smell of a fire. Clara sat near her, poking at the embers with a stick. She threw another piece of dry kindling on the fire, and it flared up as she turned to Susan.

"How are you feeling?"

"Confused." Susan smacked her dry lips. "And thirsty."

"That's the toxins, I'm afraid. An inevitable side-effect is dehydration. It's a little bit like the effects of alcohol." She passed her a flask of tepid water.

"I wouldn't know," Susan said warily, and took a swig, "I don't drink. What did you do to me?"

"An experiment. Sorry. If I had asked you, you would probably have said no."

"What did you do to me??" she stood up abruptly.

"You're OK, I just used a very mild concoction of some of those," she indicated some more fungi nestled in among the leaves around a tree root. They had thin stems and deep, dusky caps. "The Lunders call them Magik Mushroos. They liked to make a tea out of them for their gatherings. They had all sorts of other uses for the fungi they grew down there. I discovered a lot. See that one?" she pointed to the one that Susan had almost touched earlier. "That's the Autumn Skullcap. It's so poisonous that just touching it might kill you."

Susan pulled her hands into her body and sat down next to Clara, carefully checking the ground for any growth.

"Don't worry," Clara smiled, "I've cleared this ground and now I propagate them in dead wood. I got some of the dried samples and spores for growing from the Lunders. They showed me how to impregnate dead logs with them." She indicated another set of rippling, dark shell-like fungi, "Those are Alcohol Inky. They are harmless unless you eat them after drinking alcohol. Their poison reacts with the booze and your organs start to shut down. It's a really painful way to go, apparently."

They walked back to the Pivvy, quietly through the brush and trees, to the sound of birdsong the next morning. Susan felt something had changed. She had a new perspective. She put it down to the after-effects of her Magik Mushroo trip.

CLARA

"Slow down," Clara held her brother in a tight embrace, "and tell me what happened."

Edgar shook and wept against her. Struggling, he tried to speak but almost wailed, "I left her. I didn't mean to – we argued."

"Tell us, tell us what you saw."

Clara and Susan had left the Wilderness in the early hours and dropped into the Stanleys' flat where Cece had welcomed them, worried. Clara had been ready to sit down and talk about the mycelium network with Susan and tell her all about her theories of nature and how the forests and plants in the Wilderness were communicating as they grew but instead Edgar had tumbled in the doorway, distraught.

"They took Mina, they took her," he described in breathless terms.

Clara slowly extracted some details from him.

"They must have been lying in wait for us. But we had a fight and I left. I was so angry with her. I told her how selfish she was," and he sobbed again, "but I didn't mean it. I was scared. So, they took her." His face strained and his breathing fast and shuddering, his hands jittered on the table.

Clara transferred him to his grandmother, and Cece took him in her arms. "It's OK, it's OK, baby boy," she soothed him. The four of them locked together in the tiny kitchen.

"Will they let her go? Like they did Edgar? It could just be a slap on the wrist because she's so young?" Susan looked earnestly at Clara.

"That would be the best outcome, but the question is do we wait, or do we act now?" Clara pondered the problem, calm and with focus.

Edgar looked up at his sister, "It was different from the time they took me. That was security at the plant. This was the Feds, with a van and everything. I saw them drag her out, hooded."

Clara had to think quickly. What were they to do? Her fears were for Mina and how much pressure they would use to make her crack. They would want her to give way and reveal the identities of the Ghostwriters. She noticed Susan's furrowed brows and Cece's face full of pain and fear as she held her grandson.

Clara felt her mood shift as the situation crashed in on her. Everything was at risk, now. All their lives. She grew more fraught, until she looked up and was relieved to see Gunnar's face at the tiny kitchen window. He had climbed up the fire escape to the flat. She opened the side door for him.

"Is there any word?" Clara looked to him for information.

"Nothing definite, but my sources have hinted at a few things."

'What? Please, what's happening?" Clara's anguish built.

"That poor girl – and her brothers," Cece's thoughts inevitably went to the heart of the situation. "First their mother, now their sister."

"There is one thing, perhaps, one hope. Jennifer might be able to assist. These Feds are a new breed and take a new harder line, with Evening Primrose herself calling the shots," Gunnar told her. "Evening's mark is all over this. There's something new about it. The Cabinet has put a media influencer in charge of part of the security forces."

"That's something we should be disturbed about?" Clara questioned him. He spoke in such a familiar way about Evening Primrose. He knew about media; that was useful. She could not shake the feeling that she and the others were being cripplingly naïve about something, some important piece of this puzzle. The priority now, however, must be to spring Mina.

"Yes, we should be disturbed, very disturbed."

Later that night, Clara gathered with Jennifer, Susan, and a still shaken Edgar in the quiet of the Emporium, with Gunnar at the helm of the conversation. Behind his shoulder the Sky-screen played on mute. Evening Primrose could be seen passionately expounding on something. The tension was ramping up.

"There's more to this," Gunnar said folding his arms in thought, "our most difficult challenge. What do we know? The location of the store from where she was taken, the numbers of troopers, and that it was a sting at a known focus of Mina's past activities. So, their surveillance is effective, they know some of our movements *and* our names." He looked from Clara to Susan.

"How could they have done this? Got to know so much?" Clara said in bewilderment. "I thought we had all been so careful." After a period of thought, "They might have – could they – have infiltrated the group? But," she looked around at the familiar, hurting faces, "I can't believe that any one of *us* would do that. I don't believe that there's a traitor among us."

Susan and Edgar, however, both turned their eyes to Jennifer. Clara watched the young woman blanch. She got to her feet. "Wait, no! You can't think that I would do that. You can't suspect me of betraying you! I wouldn't, I wouldn't."

Edgar retorted, passionately, "This has all happened since you came along. We had our group, and we were keeping it secret. Now, they've taken one of us. What have you got to say about that?"

"It's nothing to do with me!" Jennifer looked around, desperately appealing to Clara and Gunnar. She spoke urgently as she fixed on Clara, her Nurse, "You know what I've got to lose."

Clara certainly did know Jennifer's situation. It was precarious. She had not disclosed to the others how she knew Jennifer or what the Sky-stream employee risked by helping them.

"I'll prove it to you. I'll go back into the HQ and I'll find her. I'll find Evening Primrose. No one suspects me yet, and I can get the information we need. I'll get her to tell me what happened to Mina." She got up to leave.

"It's the least you can do," Edgar snapped hurtfully.

"You'll see," as she left the Emporium, "you'll see that I can come through and you can trust me." Flushed and angry, Jennifer departed.

Clara shook her head.

"What's wrong?" Susan asked Clara. "You don't agree?"

"I'm not comfortable with this. Her safety is at stake now, and I'm not confident she can do this. They're too cunning."

Edgar made a noise, "Let her. Mina didn't trust her and neither do I."

"Mina wasn't exactly careful about her activities," his sister replied.

"Oh, so it's her fault she got taken now, is it?"

"I didn't say that." Clara's anxiety grew. "Petit frère, please – let's not do this."

"Yes, let's not fight among ourselves, it's getting us nowhere," Susan chipped in. "Let's split up now and not meet for a few days. We need to disperse and let things blow over. We'll lay low for a while. We have to protect ourselves."

Clara could not dispute her friend's wisdom on this point. Better to be cautious and protective of who was left.

Clara stood at the darkened doorway of the Emporium and watched Susan leave. She walked across the street, pulling her trolley, until she trundled out of sight. Gunnar came to stand behind Clara and put his hands on her shoulders. He kissed the back of her neck tenderly. Gently and slowly, he brushed his fingers down her arms. She shivered with delight.

"Come inside, my sweet girl."

She turned and they kissed.

"I'm so happy and overjoyed to have you back. I was so concerned. I missed your warmth and your exquisite body," he spoke in his deep voice and over-elaborate English.

Clara felt tempted to stay with him that night. She thought how she could relax with him into a blissful fog of forgetfulness. Perhaps, she could introduce him to her Magick Mushroos mixture? But she resisted in the next moment and stepped away from him.

"Please, forgive me. I think I need to go and be with my brother. He needs me."

"Of course," Gunnar kissed her again, tenderly. "You are bravery itself, my gracious warrior woman." He kissed both of her hands gallantly.

Susan

Susan's trolley made its familiar rumbly sound as it trundled behind her. She had left the Emporium and popped downstairs to her basement. She had a couple of things to do. One of which was the inevitable – Ellery. He needed to be fed and petted before she set off for what she had to do. Because what she had to do was now decided after the scene in the Emporium. She collected what she needed and departed up the steps from her basement. She walked and planned. The first thing was to follow Jennifer. If she was, as Susan suspected, going to try and confront Evening at the Sky-stream HQ, then she had to take the tram from the transport Hub. So, she could take her time. Susan knew the timetable, and knew she had a half hour before the next tram arrived.

She walked along the High Road on this warm evening, past the decayed housing, out of which the populace had spilled on the day of the riot over the crashed milk-float. The blood had stained the milk a sickly pink that day. At the tram stop she spotted Jennifer. She was, Susan saw, anxious and strained. She looked more down-at-heel these days, ever since joining the Ghostwriters. Jennifer had changed her outlook and her style. From a well-groomed higher-up, she now blended in a little better with the middles and lower-middles on the tram.

"Take me with you," Susan approached her, "take me with you to the Sky-stream studios."

"What?" Jennifer turned to her, shocked. "Why – what are you doing here? We mustn't be seen together."

"We can travel together, and I will go in and give myself up."

Jennifer

The tram pulled up and before Jennifer could protest, Susan was on board. She stayed close to Jennifer and spoke quietly as the journey progressed. The evening light illuminated the carriage as she listened intently to Susan who unfolded the events from her past.

"It was many, many years ago, in my past and hers. We were both young."

The tram clacked across the bridge, and they sat in a near-empty carriage.

"She went by Patricia, then, of course."

"Patricia. That adds up. She has reinvented herself."

"Indeed. But when I first knew her, she was quite shy and mousy. The thing that struck me, however, was how very earnest she was. Passionate, sincere, and hard-working. Her heart was easily broken."

"Hard-working and driven, I can see ... What changed her, do you think?"

"As far as I know, the closure of the college, the end of her education, it triggered something. It certainly affected her as we all cleared out. I hadn't thought about Patricia in years and then I saw her on the Sky-stream the first time I was at Gunnar's. I began to remember. She looks very different now, of course, but there was still some of the young Patricia there."

"She's had a lot of plastic surgery."

Jennifer looked out of the window, a knot in her stomach. She started to speculate about how things would unfold. How were they to secure Mina? If Evening wants Susan, how do we know she'll let Mina go once she has her? Jennifer's mind raced as she considered every possible permutation. She had to make a decision, even if it meant she was exposed. She had one piece of information that could prove to have some leverage over Evening. It was a huge risk, but she felt she had to play that card.

When they disembarked off the tram the expanse of Rothermere Square lay before them. Jennifer walked with Susan, slowly, across the well-lit route. People mingled in sparse, small groups at the late hour. Stretching off into the distance the decorative trees in tubs were ringed by statues. Nobility, royalty, and notoriety of past ages watched over the diminutive figures of the two women. One, quite smart and modestly dressed, the other scruffy with her shopping trolley rolling behind.

Jennifer walked up to a security guard at the Sky-stream HQ gate. There were more guards on duty than she had been accustomed to, and in addition to their numbers some COF troopers patrolled the area. The regular in-and-out and bustle of the studio were subdued in the weeks since the incident with the banner protest. Broadcasts were still beamed out, but staffing had been pared down to skeleton crews under the eyes of the Feds.

"What do you want?" the guard leaned on the barricade.

Jennifer displayed her ID badge. "I need to come in and I need you to contact Evening Primrose. We want her to come out and meet us."

The guard sneered and looked at her, and then at Susan standing a little way off, her trolley parked behind her. "What's her story?"

"I'm on Evening's staff. You can let us both through – please," she played it carefully.

The guard gave her ID badge a perfunctory glance. "OK. I suppose. But there's no use hanging around here. Evening doesn't come her anymore."

"Where is she?"

The guard shrugged. "She's got bigger fish to fry these days. You'll probably find her over at the Loyal – on the Island."

Jennifer retreated to join Susan.

"Are you still determined to do this? We'll have to go over to Cheltsea."

"Of course. I'm sure."

Susan even smiled. Jennifer felt sick to her stomach, for herself, and for the leader of the Ghostwriters, and the imprisoned girl who hated her. They walked to the nearest bridge and down the river along an embankment path to the next transport Hub. There, they took the next tram to the Justice Bridge crossing. Jennifer got a sense that Susan wanted to take her time with this journey. She sat by the window of the tram and looked out at the river.

The two women arrived at the imposing red brick front of the Loyal Hospital. Ground-based floodlights pointed upwards. At the top of the stone staircase, the large double doors opened slowly. Evening Primrose appeared. She was dressed in a chic, purple suit, cinched tightly at the waist, and her arms were folded. Her voice echoed across the great courtyard of the Loyal Hospital.

"Susan, how good to see you."

Susan stepped forward, "You too, Patricia."

Jennifer saw her boss react, minutely, to this. Evening then strutted down the steps towards them. "You're here. Impressive."

"Let Mina Suresh go. You don't need to torment that girl anymore, Patricia."

"You don't know what needs to be done, Susan. You couldn't survive thirty years ago, and you can't survive now."

"We just want Mina back. You can release her, and then we can talk. You want the Ghostwriters, so you want *me*."

Evening Primrose strode up and down in front of the Loyal steps. "Let me think, now. NO."

She turned to face them both, staying on a higher level. "What's in it for me? You want your person, but there's nothing in it for me. I'll keep her and have you two arrested." She pointed at both women, and Jennifer noticed two figures, burly troopers, standing in the doorway behind her. Both armed with batons.

Jennifer stepped forward and steeled herself in front of Evening and in sight of the troopers. "It's not what you get in return from us – it's what I *won't* reveal. That's your payback."

In the silence of the courtyard, the heat throbbed around the three women. Evening looked back at Jennifer with a penetrating gaze.

"What?" she approached her assistant. "Speak."

Jennifer moved in closer. The troopers stepped into the light, but Evening held up a hand to them. "It's alright."

Jennifer spoke quietly, close to her boss's ear, "You're a clever, careful woman, Evening. And I know that you like to be in control. I wish I didn't have to make this deal with you, but Susan is as brave as you are cunning."

Evening smirked and looked them both up and down, "Go on."

"I have it in my power to make life very difficult for you. There was a lot of stuff that went down when I worked for you that you wouldn't want to come out."

"Such as?"

After a pause, Jennifer responded with her own question, "How much of a family man is Eliot, would you say?"

Evening's eyes narrowed.

"He was a very hands-on employer, wasn't he?" she continued, astonished at her own audacity. "He used to pay me and many, *many* other women – and *girls* – a lot of attention. He had that mentoring programme, for example."

Evening tutted and rolled her eyes. "Well, that's not exactly a surprise to me, but who would believe you, a disgruntled ex-employee?"

"What would convince you? Ah, I know," Jennifer smiled sweetly, "physical evidence."

She saw the blood drain from Evening's face.

"Yes, he did – and yes, I did. And if anything happens to me, and if this exchange – Mina for Susan – doesn't happen, then it becomes public knowledge."

Evening seethed. "I'm going to kill that prick!" she fumed quietly as she turned around to the figures in the doorway.

Impressively, Jennifer had not flinched, although she felt as if her knees would buckle at any second. She had made the famous media influencer who had made every day of her working life a misery cower in the face of the leverage she could use.

Evening gave an order to the large female trooper on duty at the door. She departed and in a short time reappeared roughly escorting a struggling, hooded figure, who she pushed, almost head-first, down the stone steps. Her wrists were bound in front. Jennifer pounced forwards to help Mina, now released from the grip of the trooper. She had to break her fall and removed the hood. Mina looked around, desperately, only to meet Jennifer's face. She looked shocked and curious, and then angry, "You?"

"Shaw," Evening ordered, "you can undo the restraints."

The trooper cut the zip-ties that held Mina's wrists. She immediately resisted Jennifer's help and headed over to Susan. Jennifer thought how young and small Mina looked. She also noticed her bruises and injuries.

Mina turned on Jennifer, "What are *you* doing here?" She spoke confusedly and turned to Susan. But there was no chance to explain.

"She's all yours," Evening dismissed Mina and gestured to the troopers. "Take her," she indicated Susan. They grabbed her.

Mina shouted, "No, no – you can't do that! You can't take her!"

Jennifer held onto Mina, but the girl wrestled free to lunge at the troopers.

"No, don't!" Susan held up a hand. "Go back – go back with Jennifer."

Jennifer held the distraught, protesting girl and tried to quiet her, as Susan was led up the steps of the Loyal. The wooden doors shut heavily behind her.

Clara

In the Emporium, Clara comforted Mina and applied a salve to her wrists where the bindings had cut into her skin. She treated her other injuries with the same gentleness.

She tried to soothe more than just Mina's wounds.

The girl's temper was still directed at Jennifer, who stood in the corner – quietly taking the brunt of her outbursts.

"Get that bitch out of here! Why is *she* standing there when Susan's locked up?"

"She gave herself up, I couldn't stop her, I'm sorry."

"I didn't ask anyone to come get me!"

"We know that, but Susan made the choice."

"You must have *made* her – forced her to give in!"

Clara held the girl's hand gently. It was hot with agitation, but Clara's touch helped to calm her.

"You know, Mina. You know that's not what happened. Susan cares about you, deeply. And she knew – in the end – that she had the best chance to secure your release."

"But I didn't ask her to!" Mina dissolved and Clara held her in an embrace.

"It's what family do for each other. You've been braver than any of us could have expected, and Susan still knows we're behind her."

"But it was my fault," Mina looked up at her, the tears streaked down her face. "It was all my fault."

"No," Clara insisted and cupped the girl's face in her hand and caught some of the stray tears, "it's not your fault. It's about truth and lies, and propaganda. You're a victim, just like Susan."

Jennifer moved closer, gingerly, fearful of Mina. She gave her space like she would an angry cat.

"Susan told me what it was that seems to drive Evening. She and Susan have a shared past. This all goes back to before you were born. Susan knew that Evening Primrose wanted her in custody – that it was personal. We might never know what passed between them."

Mina looked at her, bitterly, but too exhausted and cornered by the facts to say anything.

"You've been through hell," Jennifer attempted to get closer to her. "This isn't the end, though. We'll get her back – I promise you. I'll go out and start by pulling in my contacts at the studio. There *will* be a way out."

Mina did not snap back this time.

Clara stayed silent. She left it at that, convinced that it would soon be their most dangerous undertaking yet and in complete ignorance as to the fate of her friend.

Mina

Mina sat with Adie and Aidan. Cece had set up a screened-off bedroom area for them in the flat. She could keep an eye on them that way. Their clothes were mended, Mina noticed, and their little faces glowed with washing. Their hair was neat, and they were well-nourished. Adie's little fingers touched the bruises on his sister's face.

"What happened to you?"

"Some people got angry with me," she hugged him tightly.

Aidan sat next to her.

Both boys had become calmer and more sociable, thanks to Miss Cece. How could she ever repay her for what she had done for her family? Then she remembered Clara's words about family and sacrifice. She thought about Susan again and tears stung her eyes.

"Does it hurt?" Adie asked.

"Not really, not anymore. Clara treated it for me."

"Whoever hurt you, I want to hurt them back," his defiant little body tensed.

She put an arm around his shoulder, "I know, little bruv, I know."

Once the boys were asleep, Mina slipped out. She was disturbed, anxious, and could not settle even though she was relieved that her brothers had some peace. The summer was well underway which meant that the heat was stifling and the insects loud. Tonight, she had been forced to face some truths. She still blamed herself, and Jennifer, for what she thought of as the entrapment of Susan; but she could not argue with the strategy. If Susan was Evening Primrose's target, then it seemed obvious that she would sacrifice herself, especially for Mina. Her brothers needed her; her mother might never be released. Susan would have thought about all of that. But would it not also mean that Evening Primrose was coming for the rest of them? Someone like that would not stop.

Mina hastily scurried down the fire escape as these thoughts ran through her mind. She landed in the alley behind the Emporium. Clara was still upstairs with Cece, so she knew that Gunnar would be alone in the shop, or going by the gloom of the interior, completely absent. She was fed up so decided to do what she had done many times now and 'borrow' some magazines from Gunnar's dusty collections. This was according to Susan's advice. 'Bury yourself in a good book,' that's what Susan said. Mina was too impatient for books though. The stock of magazines from a bygone age gave her an outlet and a window into other worlds.

She paused and waited at the outside door. There was, now she was near enough, a soft light coming from deep inside. That meant nothing, though, because she only needed to sneak into the storeroom behind the kitchen. She was in and crouching down to rifle through a stack of magazines. She found some titles that appealed to her, yellowing and crumbly. *National Geographic* and *Radio Times* were among her favourites. She liked to read the 'TV listings' from the early twenty-first century: 'Sunday, 22nd February, 2004. 16.35 News, 17.00 Songs of Praise with Choirgirl of the Year, Lucy Rhodes, 17.35 Tracy Beaker, 18.45 Antiques Roadshow from RHS Garden Wisley, 19.30 Ground Force with Charlie Dimmock and Tommy Walsh, 20.00 Down to Earth: Frankie has to make the biggest decision in her life. Tony's future hangs in the balance. 21.00 Polking Christmas: a special Drunk and Dangerous. The results of excessive alcohol intake during the festive season are the focus as police and paramedics cope with revellers in Plymouth, Swansea, and Hartlepool.'

Mina was absorbed in this slice of history, and it sounded so fascinating – the names and places, the jobs, and titles. She felt strange and sad as she read on. People back then seemed to love singing, drinking, gardening, cooking, and crime. They would love it round here now, she thought, especially the gardeners. The sound of voices from within disturbed her; they were coming from Gunnar's kitchen. Clara was not there, so who was he talking to? His voice sounded close, and the other voice was metallic and distant. A woman's voice, with something familiar about it.

"They are folding, that's good news. So, well done to you. I would have preferred it if there had been less of their agitation put out there – but at least this crackdown is quiet and discrete. We're not getting any fallout or resistance to it. The Cabinet is as pleased as they can be."

She heard Gunnar reply, "Because she gave herself up, the woman behind it, we've cut off the snake at the head. And no one knows who she is. The ghost woman."

"You've done good work, my friend."

Mina's eyes were wide as she crept along the passageway to the kitchen and tried to take this in. She passed the stacks of old news and artefacts of an old century. She peered through one of the small, cracked panes into Gunnar's kitchen. He stood, long arms folded and faced the Skyscreen. It was his interaction with the screen that made her drop down in shock. Her heart thumped. Evening Primrose was on screen, and she was *talking* to Gunnar. Mina's brain was in a flurry. How was this possible? The screen allowed Gunnar to talk back to Evening Primrose. *He* was her spy? Fuck! Fuck him! Gunnar was a Fed and had been all along – building a trap around them whilst he pretended to help. Every time they had met – it was in *his* kitchen, or he was *there*. *And* he had been fucking Clara all this time – but he didn't give a *shit* about her!

Mina looked around for a weapon. She would get him and teach him a lesson!

"But I will carry on here for as long as possible," she heard Gunnar still speaking and stopped. She held her breath to listen to their exchange. "They are all completely duped." His English seemed sharper and snappier, his tone firmer and pronunciation more precise. He was not the laid-back shopkeeper at all. He was one of *them*, he was a fucking Fed!

He continued in clipped tones. "All of them, down to the insurgent elements of veterans and activists, *and* the filthy abortionist who even thinks I care for her. We can get them all, silently and efficiently."

"Good, good, I'll rely on you, and have the troopers do the visible, rough stuff of rounding people up. We'll let them keep thinking that they are one step ahead of us."

Gunnar flicked the screen back to the regular Sky-stream. He walked into the back of the shop, towards Mina's hiding place.

Empty. No sign she had been there.

Mina ducked into the shadows beneath the fire escape in the narrow alley. Gunnar's face appeared briefly in the window, he looked around and then disappeared. Mina watched and waited before she re-emerged. You've been very cunning, Gunnar – but I can be cunning too.

Susan

Susan felt the cold tiles against her back. She wished she had brought a cardigan. But, then again, she had not really pre-planned her surrender. The cell in which she sat felt as though it was partly underground but not comfortably cool like her basement. She hoped that someone would think to check in on Ellery. It had been forty-eight hours since her arrest, she speculated. Time dragged in the Loyal Hospital with no clocks, and with isolation, and artificial light. She counted the tiles and wrote a story in her head. She had no fear at this stage of the isolation. She knew that there was worse to come. The interrogations, the mental torture, confinement, starvation. She did not know what to prepare for, so she saved her energy. It was no good trying to work out how she would hold out. She knew how to survive on a frugal diet, but that could be used against her. The simple promise of good food can make people desperate. She had seen that in action with the riots and the frantic behaviour at the Hubs.

Sounds reached her from within the building complex. When she was marched along the narrow corridors, she had heard the echoes of movement, boots stamping, cries of pain. Evening had not spoken a word to her. She had simply watched as Susan was led into the building with a smug expression on her face. At least, Susan hoped, Mina and Jennifer had walked away. Now, sitting in this cell on her own, she tried to keep track of time, unsuccessfully as far as she could tell. At intervals some food was pushed through the slot in the door. Mushy vegetables swollen from rehydration arranged on a tray alongside some squares of bread. Each time, an incongruous addition rested next to the foodstuffs, a small bottle of Duchy Natural Springwater with a landscape on the label. Filtered in the Cutswold Hills. The cap was sealed, but once opened, she sniffed at it. Although, why Evening would try and poison her now in custody, she was not sure, but had to be cautious. Everyone, everywhere in here was a threat. The words from another one of the novels of her youth rang in her head. Mary Shelley, '… the companions of our childhood always possess a certain power over our minds which hardly any later friend can obtain …'. Patricia cannot get over me.

A clank and a thud sounded, and the cell door swung open. A COF trooper stood, baton in hand.

"Come on," he wore a helmet, so he was anonymous. Large and out of shape – a thug. A typical example of the foot soldiers, not a trained officer. His baseline requisite skill was simply to be capable of brutality. She knew she had to comply, no resistance was possible or worth trying. He would just lay into her, otherwise. Beside Susan sat her shopping trolley. After searching through it, the troopers had allowed her to keep it. She took the handle and trundled it out of the door.

"Where are we going, please?"

The trooper's helmet turned to her. She could only see his mouth.

"Next secure holding cell."

"Thank you," maintain dignity and humanity, she thought. She shuffled along the corridor. She noticed that the guard kept his distance and was almost decorous in his behaviour. She smiled to herself in the knowledge that she still had the ability to disconcert with her manner.

Susan was led down some stairs, one, two flights. She had to lift her trolley up until they arrived at another series of passages with flagged floors. Down and down, through a dank, subterranean labyrinth and into a giant undercroft, with a wide vaulted crypt ceiling. Rising above her was a system of cages, with gantries and entrance points, stretching the length of the vast space.

"In here," her escort opened the door to an empty cage at ground level and locked the door behind her. She was dressed in her patched, salvaged fabric dress, her worn-out sandals, with loose, grey straggly hair but she stood with a defiant posture. The trooper retreated, and Susan examined her surroundings. There was a wooden bench on one side, a bucket in the corner, and a thin mattress on the floor. Above her and on two sides were more cages, stacked tier upon tier, row upon row.

Susan sat down on the bench.

"Hey, get off!"

She looked around and saw a pile of rags in the next cage roll over. It had been pressed against the metal latticed partition beside her bench and she had inadvertently sat on the strands that poked through.

"I'm sorry," she stood up and peered into the cage beside hers. The floors were slimy and the low energy lights were not very helpful.

The cluster of rags moved again, and a head emerged. Bald on top with a straggly circle of hair, male, with a scraggy beard. A filthy paw-like hand gripped one of the bars and heaved the heap into a more upright position in the adjoining cage. The heap settled itself and then grunted.

"Hello," Susan was determined to be civilised and cordial. "My name is Susan, who are you?"

Little eyes under heavy brows above a small, snub nose blinked in her direction, with a bloodshot bewilderment. She leaned in a little. "What's your name?"

A husky, dirty voice replied. "Derrick. Derrick Smallman." Those last words were said with a cough and a flourish. Once, this voice had been used to being obeyed.

"Why are you here, Derrick?"

The anguished face, strained and worn, looked out at her from within its ragged garments, like a scabrous and rough hermit monk. Derrick's expression twisted into a derisory laugh, whilst his eyes remained blank.

"Why am I here?" he coughed. "I'm a public servant. I tried to effect change – and they locked me up!" Those last three words were said in a dark, hoarse way.

"I'm sorry to hear that. I've been here for about two days, at least. How long for you?"

The rags called Derrick shrugged and grunted again. "Years, probably. I don't know."

"Is it Evening – Evening Primrose? Did she put you here?"

He looked at her with more interest and turned his pile of rags towards her.

"She put *you* here?"

Susan nodded.

"Well, then," he said with a sneer, "you must have committed a crime."

"Hmmm," she shook her head, "she and I go a long way back. There was a time when she liked me, even admired me."

Derrick held his face up to the bars, "You knew her too? Same here. Mirror images." He turned away again, "But you must have done something. She maintains the order, so she doesn't put you away without good reason."

"I see." Susan considered this. He seemed to be planted squarely in a particular field to defend the hierarchy.

She tried a different tack. "Of course, back then, she was Patricia. That's how I knew her."

"You knew Patricia?" Derrick gave her a probing look.

"Yes, before she reinvented herself to become a celebrity. She was my student and now she's an influencer. Look," she went to her trolley and retrieved the old, heavily-taped copy of Emily Dickinson's poems, and passed it through the bars to Derrick. He took it and turned it over, examining it with his dead eyes.

Susan explained, "She gave that to me when she was Patricia and a dedicated student. She was passionate and earnest. When the college closed, she was so upset that she protested, and gave me this as a parting gift. She even signed it."

Derrick flicked open the front cover and read, "To the best tutor, Susan. You opened my eyes and changed my life, I will be forever grateful, Patricia." He closed it, and after a pause laughed, then handed it back to her. "So, we both have history with her?"

"What's yours?"

He gave another laugh, "We slept together. She used to hang on every word I said – until she accused me of letting her down."

"She does *not* like it when she thinks people have let her down. How did you meet?"

The rags stood up and shuffled across the cell to plop down on the thin mattress in the corner. Derrick looked away as he spoke.

"She was strong and determined," a sense of profound misery could be heard in his tone. "When we first met, she was innocent and keen – it was amazing. She wanted to be a big part of the project." He was a shrivelled, sorry man sitting on a dank mattress in a cage.

"What project?"

"They called it the Smallman Project. After me. *They* came to call it that – I didn't use my own name!" He smiled in a quiet, smug fashion.

"What was it for?"

"To recreate government systems. To make them scale back and allow business to take over and rebuild from the inside."

"Nothing new about that. It's been the story of capital and government since – the late twentieth century. What else did you have to offer?"

"Non-traditional outliers and mavens. I wanted to have people in government that had experience from elsewhere – to restore what was greatest from our past and pioneer what's best for our future."

Susan listened to this and after a short pause, said "Why do you do this?"

"Do what?"

"Feed this line, still. You're sitting in your own filth, wearing rags after being taken down and humiliated. We're both in the same boat now – be honest!"

Derrick Smallman looked down at his sleeve and tapped it thoughtfully. "People," he began, "don't understand systems properly. Clever people, many, still make mistakes – but in politics those get magnified. So, I want to minimise mistakes and make work more effective … that was the Project," he finished quietly.

"The Smallman Project."

"Uh huh," he warmed to his tale. "We will reform government, every operation to stop wasting money and be clever about how we function."

She noticed how he continued in the present tense.

"I tell people, to *know yourself* – and face up to your mistakes. You need to think operationally, work harder than those around you – be at your desk first and be the last to leave. Don't stick to the rules, I say, and know you must recognise if you're going *to be* or *to do*. Patricia is so keen. She agrees with all of that and is one of my most loyal supporters."

He looked a little wistful. "We need to be rid of the depressing spectacle of politicians who thrash around with no priorities and no ideas. Innovation. Strategy."

Derrick started to sound tired. "We need more than gimmicks. We need innovation. Strategy. We have to dismantle the institutionalised dysfunction, the ineffective bureaucracy, and do more than just trash our opponents."

Signs of light and enthusiasm glinted in his face as he spoke. Susan could see how infectious his manner could be, and how it must have seemed to Patricia. But his moods shifted, and his emotional states fluctuated. Some of the old firebrand spirit was in evidence in the prison-worn figure. She understood how a young woman might be drawn in. The argument for streamlining and efficiency was attractive.

"Yes," Susan agreed, "people do hate wastefulness."

"So, you agree with me? I want to restore the greatness of England and go back to a time when we could achieve anything! Did you know that the Spitfire – that won *the* War of the twentieth century for us – was developed by having scientific competitions and challenges presented to the public? If we put our minds to it, we can be more effective and less wasteful. We can be innovative. Innovation. Strategy." Derrick grew a little wheezy. The damp conditions, Susan could feel it too, made too much talk and fast breathing difficult.

"Yes," she spoke whilst he paused for breath, "I can see how this is a useful attitude to adopt. What was your motto? 'To be or to do'?"

"No," he fretted back at her, irritated. "It was a propositional thesis – a motto is a childish thing!"

"I see," she was conciliatory.

"I was a disrupter, a cynic, a maverick!" He grew more agitated.

"I understand," Susan spoke calmly. He reminded her of Patricia and her other students. There was an urgency to pronounce on things and to tell an audience what was wrong. "Doing, not just being. That's good advice."

"Always, always." He looked exhausted. She felt some sympathy for him. "Innovation. Strategy." He repeated this and then fell silent.

Susan and Derrick, the architect of the present system, sat in the gloom of the undercroft full of cages, cages on cages. She could hear sounds throughout the building. Echoing thuds and occasional shouts.

"And so here we both are," she said quietly, "doers – not beings."

Clara

Clara looped her locks up into a tight head wrap. She knew what was in store this time. In the Pivvy she coordinated Mina and Edgar with tools and backpacks.

"Ready to go?" she asked them in hushed tones.

The two youngsters nodded.

"So, when we get down there it will be quite cool. Cooler than you're probably used to. And be prepared for a fight. There are people – well – that are strange and savage."

"The Russellers? Yeah, you warned us plenty," Mina sounded worldly and bored.

"Yes, the Russellers. Don't underestimate what we'll find there. They come from the deepest tunnels, so we have to hope that they won't emerge when we're there."

"I just want to go in," Mina twitched impatiently.

Ever since Mina's release and seeing Susan take her place, Clara had noticed that Mina was antsy and on edge. She just wanted to be out there in action.

"And we will. We'll be in and make contact with Philomel and get out."

"And we need the Lunders to help us?"

"Yes – I only got so far with my knowledge when I was there, and I know that Philomel can do more for us. Now that the challenge is so much bigger than before, we need help."

The evening across the Square once they emerged from the Wilderness was punctuated by the roosting flight of finches. The light from the setting sun was dazzling and cast long, stretched shadows. The team of three kept to these shadows and the quiet places along the way. Clara retraced her steps back to Russell Square. The stairway down to the ticket hall was cluttered and smoke-stained. They entered, carefully, stepping over detritus. Clara noticed that there must have been a camp in there since her escape. The stench and the scorch marks on the walls gave this away.

"Be careful," Mina whispered, "there might be sleepers still here."

At the entrance to the long, winding, exhausting stairway each one wound their rechargeable torches before setting off.

"Point them down," Clara cautioned, "and step gently. Noise rouses them. If one of them hears us, we'll be trapped – and we can only double back and climb as fast as we can. OK?"

Mina and Edgar nodded, mutely. Hearts thumped as they began their descent.

Clara recalled the experience, but this time she felt more prepared and calmer. By torchlight things looked intimidating and grim, however. She risked flicking the light around the walls and steeled herself when she saw scratch-marks, deep and long into the tiled walls, from weapons – or claws? She was not sure. They kept close to the wall and tried to hold the handrail whenever possible. Another unfortunate side-effect of having a torch meant that Clara now saw evidence of the Russellers this time. Rusty blood-stains and smears. Underfoot, they felt and heard the crackle of brittle, dead vegetation – at least, that's what she hoped it was. Just vegetation.

As Clara predicted, the temperature cooled, so that the atmosphere, whilst oppressive was not too suffocating. They reached the platform, finally. Mina and Edgar sat down to recover a little. They could cope with the temperature change, but their ears had to pop.

"It's the depth. The air pressure changes and, also, sounds get exaggerated too. Beware of that."

Once they were recovered, Clara moved them on. They had to wade the tunnels. Clara led the way. Each one toted their back-pack high and slid into the water. Their progress in the waist-deep water was accompanied by gentle plopping and swooshing sounds. They placed their feet carefully along the floor of the tunnel where the ghosts of the old tracks lay. They worked steadily along; their faces glowed in the eerie light of the bioluminescent life. Slight gasps and noises emitted from Mina and Edgar behind Clara that told her when they encountered the strange blind fish and the skittering crustacea.

After hours of this, Clara eventually paused and held up a hand to the others.

"Wait," she whispered, and taking extra care with her footing she moved to the opening at the end of the tunnel. The mist nets in place were clear indicators, she knew, that they were close to the Lunders' base at Goode Street. Clara lay in wait near the tunnel entrance from where she could see the platform. A pair of Warrener fisherfolk moved boxes in their diligent, focused fashion. She hung back in the tepid water, with occasional chilly currents swirling around her thighs. After a few minutes, with great relief, Philomel came into view. Clara gestured to Edgar and Mina to stay in the shadows, lit by the bioluminescent light, whilst she set out to attract her friend's attention.

"Hey, hey," she tried a husky whisper to make enough noise and let Philomel know she was there in the tunnel.

Wide eyes, framed with a dark, heavy fringe registered Clara from the platform. She saw Philomel check that the coast was clear and slide into the water to wade softly to where she waited. They embraced each other, and Philomel expressed her surprise to see her return to the Lunderworld. Within a few minutes, Edgar, Mina, and Clara were established on the platform and bringing back some warmth and circulation to their legs. Philomel gave them a hot, sweet drink that seemed to do the trick in stimulating blood flow. As they dried off, Clara made the introductions and Philomel nodded and smiled at the newcomers. Mina was uncharacteristically quiet, perhaps the impact of the Lunderworld was too much, even for her to comment. Edgar was observant.

Philomel listened intently as Clara described their predicament. "So, we need you," she said, "we need your help, there's a desperate situation on the surface."

Philomel nodded and with this encouragement, Clara continued, "We want to cripple our opponents." Philomel smiled in a sly fashion. "It means we need you to come to the surface with us. Do you think you can come to the surface? Just for a little while?"

Philomel shrugged and nodded.

"Good," Clara smiled gratefully.

Susan

Susan sat in the corner of her cell. Bored and in pain. She tried to think herself out of the boredom and distract herself from the pain. The hard surfaces of concrete, stone, and metal made the edges of her joints throb and burn. No matter what position she adopted she could not relieve the pressure. She looked up at the high, vaulted ceiling above the cages, some of which contained slight, crouched figures. This prison was not at capacity, but that did not mean that there weren't other cells throughout the whole complex of the Loyal. She had the impression that this place rambled off into a labyrinth and was probably full of forgotten souls in hidden corners.

Derrick Smallman sat curled up in the corner on his mattress. He had grown tired and hoarse with talking. As he snoozed, Susan had time to think. She considered his words and the account he had given. Throughout, he maintained a position of self-righteousness as the aggrieved protagonist of his own narrative. She had listened patiently to his bitter reflections and personal angst and issues. She did not buy into his story. What had made sense to her was the interaction – romantic, sexual, and emotional – between the young Patricia and Derrick. Patricia, absent of a father, had latched onto a strong personality, and been fully invested in his schemes. The more devoted she was, the more let down she would then feel when it all fell apart. Susan looked at the sleeping Smallman. That had been Patricia's anchor. This is

England. This is warfare. Derrick liked to describe things in a combative fashion. He stirred and started muttering. Even in sleep he did not let up with his monologue.

With a banging and a scraping, the door into the undercroft opened. Two guards came into the cell complex dragging a docile, unresisting figure. Her dark, matted hair obscured her face, and she had an agonisingly thin frame and wore a ragged dress. Susan looked at her and saw the future of incarceration. Wordlessly, the guards dumped the woman into the cage next to Susan. She hit the floor like loose bones in a sack.

Once the guards left, Susan shifted close to the bars and reached through to touch the woman's arm. At her touch, the woman flinched violently. Susan saw the bruises on her exposed skin.

"Sorry," she pulled back as the woman skittered away across her cell in fear. Susan crouched down and spoke softly. "My name is Susan. What's your name? I have some water left. Here." She passed the little bottle of Duchy water through the bars.

Cautiously, fearfully, the woman looked at it. She scurried over and grabbed it. The water vanished down her throat. She wiped her mouth and looked at Susan with dark, pained eyes.

"Thank you," her voice was very quiet. "I am Jacinda."

Susan reacted to this and scrutinised her with a two-fold recognition. "Jacinda. It was *you*. You were taken that day at the Hub." She now understood. Despite the faded, strained, thin frame, her face was still identifiable as that of the woman in the posters created by Mina and Charlie.

"Jacinda, you're Mina's mother?"

Something like an electric shock seemed to pass through the brittle body. "Mina? You know my Mina?"

"Yes," Susan looked around at the sleeping Derrick Smallman, "shhh! Yes, I know Mina."

"How is she? Where is she? And my boys, what about my boys?"

Susan moved in closer now she had her trust. "Yes, they are well." She omitted the information that she had exchanged herself as a forfeit for Mina. "She's with your sons. When I left them, they were safe. Cecilia is looking after them at her place."

Jacinda fell back against the bars, relief flooded her face. Her eyes did not fill with tears. Susan realised she was too spent and dehydrated to cry anymore.

A curt voice came from behind her.

"What are you doing there? What are you talking about?"

Derrick Smallman was awake.

"Are you talking about me? You *are*. You're talking about me, I know it."

Susan turned to him, and spoke slowly, "No, Derrick. You can go back to sleep. We're not discussing you."

He sat up sulkily in the corner of his cell. "Well, I can't. Not now you've woken me up with your chattering." He peered past her at Jacinda. She looked like a wild woman in her cell. "Who's *that*?"

Susan sighed. Petulance, it seemed, was the order of the day for these waking hours. Was that what she had in store? She did not know if she preferred this version of Derrick to the chatty, vain version.

"Is that your friend, then?" he asked. "She looks skanky," he sneered.

She looked him up and down, "You're one to talk."

This was like dealing with a difficult teenager. It reminded her of teaching new students and having to overcome the obstacles of their know-it-all reticence at the start of a course. This made sense. It did not jar at all. Derrick Smallman, the architect of their present times, sat there behaving like a brat, in the prison cell next to her. It made perfect sense. Their world was chaotic, spiteful, and run by self-serving, over-privileged, vainglorious grifters. Susan asked herself – if a frustrated, resentful imp had to construct a society then what would it come up with? This. It surrounded her. On one side, a war widow close to starvation, and on the other the bitter, little man, the originator of the project. He was no use to them now. He held no influence. Patricia was done with him, and even if she knew he was here, she was willing to let him rot.

Jacinda started to hum a wordless tune. She was oblivious to Derrick. Susan saw that she had now entered a sort of fugue state. There had been a flicker of reality when she had heard how her children were accounted for, and this seemed to result in her switching off. What had been a slight glimmer left in her dark, haunted eyes was now gone.

"Oh, will you shut up?" Derrick snapped across at Jacinda. She did not register him. He hated to be ignored. Susan intervened.

"Just leave her alone," she scolded him. This seemed to work in the moment as he pouted and sat back.

"It's because of you, you know? She's a result of what *you've* done. Your legacy."

"What are you talking about?" he sounded exasperated by her.

"She's a war widow. Her husband was blown up in the Ardennes in one of your European wars. She's had to manage on her own with three children."

"That's what the vouchers and academy system are for. Food allowance and education can be anyone's who deserves it."

"Deserving. I see. And who decides who deserves what?"

"Society doesn't owe any of us a living," Smallman said with a grunt. "I had to pull myself up by my bootstraps."

"Liar," Susan snapped directly at him. "You're doing it again!"

"Don't call me a liar, you old bitch!"

She looked at him and laughed, "Is *that* all you've got? I know that's the hype you've sold over the years to everyone but," and she leaned towards the bars, "do yourself a favour and cut the bullshit. Quit, and try honesty here, just this once." She looked around, "It's not as if you have anything more to lose."

"Fuck you! Fuck both of you." He turned away from her.

Jacinda continued with her little crooning song, adding lyrics this time. "Liar, liar, pants on fire."

MINA

Mina tucked her hair behind her ears and shucked another small oyster as she squatted on the Goode Street platform.

Philomel smiled in her direction as she noticed Mina's technique and nodded in approval. Over the days and nights with the Lunders, Mina had taken to the lifestyle. She loved the cool temperature down here unlike anything she had experienced. Plus, the food – the sheer abundance of proteins. She found she did not miss the daylight as long as there was a supply of shrimp and molluscs. Whilst she had celebrated this bounty and, frankly, been gorging herself, much to Philomel's amusement, Clara and Edgar had been busy with their own project.

Under Phil's direction they had harvested some different varieties of fungi. Dun-coloured and speckled mushrooms, frilly fungi that clung to the timber partitions on the platform, and the humble little grey-green deathcap. They sliced them finely, laid them out to dry, and then set about rendering them down into powders and tinctures. All this took place in secret, so that none of the Lunders knew of their presence. Philomel kept her visitors hidden. Fortunately for them, some festivities were fixed to take place, creating a distraction for the community.

On what felt to Mina like a night-time, Philomel took her on a jaunt. First, she handed Mina a decorated half-mask. It was painted hessian and secured with ribbon ties.

The eyes were cut-out with cat-like styling. Excitement built for her as Philomel led her along corridors and down flights of stairs and along the tunnels to the Bakers' celebration. Before they reached it, the sounds of music and the flickering light of lanterns beckoned them in.

The wide platforms and archways of the Bakers' station were separated by a faster flowing stream. At first, Mina and Philomel kept close to the walls in the leaping shadows. A fresh breeze blew along the tunnel as she looked about. The Bakers played music on makeshift instruments, with plaintive, melodic tunes. Generous with their talents, they hosted many other groups at their festivals and with the ingredients brought to them created generous feasts. Mina edged her way discretely to a table where things the Lunders called 'cookies' were laid out on wooden boards. She tasted one and it melted in her mouth. She turned around and found herself mask-to-mask with a tall wolf.

The man behind the wolf mask spoke, "Hello, little kitty-cat, I've not seen you around here before. Do I know you?"

"You must! But we're all in masks tonight!" And she squeezed past another group to avoid any further conversation.

The bricks that formed the walls and arches of the Bakers' station were slick with moisture and the stream gurgled and slopped past the platform. Fights broke out now and then as people jostled for the food and drink, but nothing serious. Mina managed to avoid any of the fracas, and with a handful of the cookies made her way back to a vantage point that Philomel had found. The two of them looked down on the platform from just below an archway in the roof where they could sit on a little gantry and munch on their snacks. Philomel gestured to her with 'Are you enjoying this?'

Mina nodded. She found the whole situation intriguing and attractive as the flickering lights lit the masked faces of the revellers. They danced and waded in the water. At intervals around the walls she noticed there was a motif painted on the bricks. A face in profile with a large, pointed nose, a domed hat, and a curved stick with a bulb on the end coming out of the mouth. She wondered who it was supposed to be but before she could think to ask anything there was a distraction at the end of the platform.

At first it seemed as though there were people celebrating loudly. A cracking sound went off; some flames flared out. A wave of water rushed out of the tunnel, knocking some of the Bakers into the stream. They were washed into the next tunnel. Then she saw them. Pale figures covered in grimy, cracked armour. Their mouths were dark, their heads bald, and their skin creamy and fleshy. Philomel was on her feet and darted about to look for a weapon.

"What is it? What's going on?"

Philomel looked at her desperately, and then she articulated some hoarse words. Mina had never heard her voice and did not even know she *could* speak. But in this moment, when their lives were at stake, she spoke.

"Russellers," she half-mouthed, in a husky way. "Run." She grabbed a large piece of wood and gestured to Mina to follow her. They moved swiftly in the half-light of the brick tunnel but had to head back to the Bakers' platform in order to access any kind of escape route.

The two young women had to plunge into the crowd that had started to panic and run. They were pushed against a wall and watched as the desperate partygoers now fled in disarray. Philomel reached for Mina's hand, so they did not lose one another. Brandishing the piece of wood like a club, she created a path for the two of them through the Bakers fleeing from the gibbering, scampering Russellers.

"They're coming, they're coming," a woman screamed near Mina's face.

In a frozen moment, Mina turned and looked down the platform. The stream was stained red. A chilling sight met her eyes. A Russeller, clawing and ripping at the arm of a Baker, stood in the stream. Its dark eyes met hers and its mouth gaped open as it dropped a piece of disembodied flesh into the water and black blood dripped down its chin. It stood in the water wearing its makeshift armour of grimy ceramic tiles wired together with metal threads. A battle-ready, subterranean creature. Its fellows flooded onto the platforms and headed in her direction. Philomel was by her side and shielded her, then pulled her into a side tunnel.

The two clutched each other as they ducked in the darkness. The frantic Bakers stumbled and fell as they scrambled along the station with the Russellers clawing and shredding at their limbs. Mina cowered back as a Russeller held onto the back of the man in the wolf mask and plunged sharpened teeth into his shoulder. Blood sprayed onto the tiles and the platform. Using the wooden club as a battering ram, Philomel barged open a doorway in the passage for them. It led nowhere. A cupboard with a firm door, at least that they could wedge shut with the timber. They ducked inside and held the door whilst the maelstrom continued. Mina flinched in the dark when blood sprayed through the slatted opening in the door. Philomel put a finger to her lips and they both remained silent as the horror unfolded outside.

Breathing hard, after what seemed like an eternity, Mina watched as Philomel edged the door open a crack. She looked out and shuddered. Mina sobbed slightly as she asked, "What – what's out there?"

Philomel looked back at her in the dim light of their hideout and gestured for her to stay put. She eased the door open a fraction and looked out, then back at Mina and shook her head with a look of sickness and revulsion. They slid the door open, and it moved on a pool of blood. Mina and Philomel stepped into the passage.

Mina covered her mouth in shock. Fires burned on the platform from where torches had dropped. Bodies floated in the stream and bobbed away down the tunnels. The Russellers had left no survivors. There was nothing that they could do except make their way carefully among the blood and wreckage. As far as Mina could tell it was not looting or theft that compelled the Russellers, just violence. They had ripped through the Bakers at their festival and moved on. She did not know what this meant, she just knew that the Russellers could never be allowed to make it to the surface.

Evening

"So, so ugly," Evening tutted as she looked down at Susan's hands spread palms-down on the table. Stubby, grubby fingers, with grime in every corner and bitten nubs. "You never took pride in your appearance. That's something your lot always reckoned was beneath them, wasn't it?"

Susan did not reply.

"You academics and writers. It was supposed to be a sign of how clever you are; that you didn't have time to run a brush through your hair or use deodorant. You're a fucking mess now, aren't you?"

She circled Susan in the concrete, windowless room. "We need to re-train you, I think. That might be the way to go," she mused. She stopped in front of her, arms folded. On the table in front of Susan sat the ragged volume of poems. With one of her fabulous pink manicured fingernails, Evening slid the book nearer to Susan. She bent down to look her former college tutor in the eye.

"Why did you bring this with you? Did you think it would nudge my conscience?"

"I hoped, I suppose. It might have awakened something nostalgic in you."

Evening laughed in a mocking, derisory way. On the outside she managed to exhibit this tone, but internally she was wracked. Her feelings of inferiority and inadequacy still burned her, aggressively revisiting her psyche in a way that made her feel sick. She tried to bury them, unsuccessfully, and so turned on Susan.

"We might just offer you a forced re-training phase!"

"I was beside Derrick in the holding cells," Susan spoke softly to her, "and he told me about your affair. He calls you Patricia too."

Evening was jolted by this, "What?" she felt the power she had in the room ebbing away, and now rage began to build. She lunged forward to Susan and pinched the woman's cheeks with her rich talons. "My name is *not* Patricia *and* get it in your head – I'm in charge and you speak when I tell you!" She threw Susan's head back, leaving scratches and red weals on her face. Susan gently rubbed at these marks.

"I'll have you beaten if you say the wrong things. And I'll have you beaten if you don't answer my questions. Be very careful."

She noticed Susan risk eye contact with her. Evening fumed about the whole situation, still angry at the news about Eliot imparted to her by the bitch Jennifer on the night of Susan's arrest. He was so, so stupid, a liability! She had been planning his removal, anyway, and then along came the bombshell. Impregnating her assistant, leaving evidence! Fuck that upper-middle idiot. His days were numbered. She would get rid of him and reinvent herself as a single mother. But for now, she had to deal with the problem of Susan.

"So, you think that you have a place to speak out? You think people want to hear your messaging?"

"Honestly, I don't know. I have nothing to push, no propaganda."

"What do you mean?" Evening's frustration mounted, but she exhibited coolness.

"I don't know if people want to hear my message, or even if I have one."

"So, you admit, you don't have the answers," Evening felt triumphant. Simultaneously, she experienced a shift back in time. She was Patricia confronting her tutor, angrily, in her office. Anxious and impatient for what she thought should be happening and was at every turn thwarted and disrupted by inaction.

"Do any of us ever have the answers?" Susan continued.

"That's the line they sold me. A dud – smoke and mirrors – that was all. Followed by death and disappointment. I was lied to."

Susan just returned her fury with sad eyes.

A few days later, Evening sat in her office in the Loyal Hospital. She took regular sips of fine Scotch. She hardly set foot in the Sky-stream studios nowadays and she slept in her suite at the Loyal. Things bothered her, but she squashed them. She knew, deep down, that there was nowhere to go and nothing to learn, but she had to make an example of saboteurs and dissidents. The Cabinet's directive had been clear, so she had to hand things over to Dr Helkiah Crooke. Susan's fate now lay in his twisted little hands, she thought. The incarceration had been long and drawn out, and ultimately too messy. She had to make a decision. A trial was out of the question and Susan was simply uncooperative. Some more names would have been useful, so that Gunnar could stay undercover, but now action had to be taken. It was out of her hands. Persuasion from the Doctor was the order of the day. She justified everything in her mind.

Susan

Susan focused on the pain. She tracked it, inch by inch, through her body, accompanied by intense nausea. From her stomach, it worked its way around to her kidneys and spine and sent stabbing sensations all the way down her back and across her scalp. The ordeal at the hands of Dr Crooke had been exhausting and came back to her in intermittent flashes if she closed her eyes, so she tried not to. She had vomited on herself more than once – mostly bile and liquid – so she stank even more. But she felt inured to the grime, filth, and stench of the Loyal now, and her place in it.

The repulsive, cracked, withered little man – Helkiah Crooke – had taken a positive delight in torturing her. The infliction of pain on her ravaged body had given him a visible reaction of pleasure and she shuddered at the recollection.

"I used to be a big fan of your books," he sniggered and wheezed at her, "especially the erotic ones."

There was nothing more to be done. She had no information to give him, and so she endured what he did to her without crying out too much. She knew she would be put on show as a broken, repentant dissident. An enemy of society and a betrayer of her fellow criminals. Not with a show *trial*, however. Just a show.

The next day, two visitors came to her cell. They introduced themselves as members of Evening's team from the Sky-stream studio. They were there to do her hair, make-up, and supply her with a new set of clothes. One cut the mats out of her hair, washed it, and gently combed it through with a serum that smelled wonderful. Susan got to bathe in warm water and then they cleaned and trimmed her toenails and fingernails with delicate little tools. She wept quietly whilst this happened. To be touched by kind hands and feel contact without aggression was too much. She was groomed and dressed in a way she had never known in her life. Simply, humbly, with a suitable look for a repentant rebel, but none-theless she appreciated the sensations in the moment.

They fed her too. Mashed potatoes and actual fibrous meat, which she vomited up almost immediately. Her stomach just could not tolerate the rich protein. From then on, they gave her rice and thick soup, lots of it. She knew she was being fattened up. She was to be an example, to show the world how she had become a fat, turncoat collaborator. If she refused and tried to hunger strike, then the threat of Dr Crooke hung over her. She was unresisting, but not because of the possibility of more torture. The pain had been almost unbearable, of course, but she felt that she had only one way out and she had to face the conclusion to her ordeal. The final act was coming, and she had to muster all the courage she could, so she needed her strength.

Susan's time in the Loyal dragged on, over days, possibly a week or more. She could not tell. The meals continued, and she filled out. In the panel of hammered steel riveted above the sink in her cell, the face of a stranger looked back. Her cheeks had filled out and she had developed a small double chin. A well-fed, groomed 'have' with a confession to offer and redemption to be sought. Your story isn't done yet, Susan, she thought, but who will write the end?

Jennifer

Jennifer was playing a risky game. She was back at the Sky-stream HQ but kept a low profile. She had slipped back into her job with no questions asked. No one seemed to want to challenge her, so she just assumed her tasks and maintained a presence. In the past week, she had carried on as though back off leave. Evening Primrose was not there, so as her erstwhile assistant, people took it for granted that she must have been reinstated. Evening's actions could not be questioned or explained. Jennifer could take advantage of her boss's legendary reputation for control and total unaccountability. When she crossed Rothermere Square on the first morning of her return, she had half expected her ID card to be flagged and the guards to pounce. She moved through the security barriers with ease. With no Evening Primrose in residence, Eliot Charming had tried to take charge, and the staff at the Sky-stream were relieved to see Jennifer.

When she arrived at the office suite, she found her desk undisturbed, and she set about some meaningless 'busy' work. She took her device from its charging cradle and reactivated it with her thumb print. The Sky-stream feed came to life. She had not seen it in a long time.

'STAY TUNED,' it shouted at her, 'Dissident admits crimes – LIVE on The Evening Primrose Hour – coming this week'.

This was something new. Evening was tampering with the schedules. She was ousting Eliot. What's going on? She had to get word to Clara. Who else could the 'Dissident' be except Susan? Jennifer was distracted with her thoughts, when she looked up to see Eliot barrelling towards her desk.

"Have you seen this??" he held up his device in a desperate, panicky way. "What's going on? And where is she? I haven't seen her in weeks, and I have no idea where the children are!"

Jennifer controlled her reaction to seeing Eliot again. He had never usually known the whereabouts of his children as she recollected. She stood up quickly, as if on task.

"Stay right here," she said decisively to waylay him. "I will go and find her and get to the bottom of this!" She knew that taking this sort of tone with him would work.

She quickly left the mezzanine floor and found a secluded spot from where she could contact Clara.

'No sign of Mrs Harris,' she used the codename that Susan had bestowed upon Evening. It was, she had said, the name of a character in a story by Charles Dickens. A woman who is talked about but never seen.

A reply popped up from Clara. 'Can you carry out the plan on Colonel Mustard?' The origin of the codename for Eliot eluded Jennifer, but she felt it suited him. The message continued: 'While the cat's away ...'.

She read Clara's words with an expressionless face.

A few minutes later, and Jennifer joined the milling crowd of Sky-stream employees as they departed the building. She needed to move on and faced no obstacles or impediments as she walked out onto Rothermere Square. Up ahead, towards the centre of the Square between the statues and oases of landscaped shrubs, some construction was under way. She took the chance to pause, briefly, under the pretext of checking her bag, straightening the strap of her shoe. Brief, busy actions, just seconds so as not to raise suspicion, but long enough to take in what was going on. A wooden frame, a platform, created by a construction crew. Alongside, more timber was standing by as carpenters swarmed around in a flurry of hammering and drilling.

So, something was afoot, something that had not yet travelled as far as the Sky-stream feed. This was the most worrying feature of these activities, of deep concern to Jennifer. Disarray and confusion surrounded Eliot in the studio, but out here in the Square, plans were taking shape that had Evening's fingerprints all over them. She moved on to the tram stop and once there, sent an urgent message to Clara.

'If we're both going to strike, we have to do it soon.'

Evening

Evening recollected how often men had told her to calm down. She had been, as a girl, quick to feel distress. Life with Aurora was unpredictable and went off the rails regularly. Something of a wild, chaotic ride with her mother. After that experience she tried to control things as an adult. Trying to be independent, at work and at her studies she took shelter in her opinions and behind walls in which she only reluctantly allowed cracks and chinks to develop.

Now, standing in Rothermere Square at night, after her construction crew had departed, she could survey the results of her work. A product of her anxiety and a desire for control? Perhaps. Too late to back out, though. She had to plough forward. Power, she was lately realising, was about commitment. She had to see things through because any crack or hesitancy would just look like weakness and indecision. All of the rhetoric, the crack-downs, the broadcasts, they all had to lead somewhere. Otherwise, what was the point? If authority was not backed-up with action, why bother?

For the first time in weeks, Evening re-entered the Skystream studios. The night-time skeleton staff were on duty and had not been expecting her.

The guard at the barrier was flustered and surprised at her approach on foot to the gates.

"Welcome back, ma'am."

"Thank you," she nodded graciously. "Can you put in a call to the COF? I want a squad mobilised to protect the studios."

"Yes, ma'am," the guard responded with some bewilderment, and immediately followed her order.

She arrived in her office. Much to her approval, it had been kept dusted and in order. She passed by a cleaner vacuuming the expanse of the plush carpet and smiled at her. Evening liked to see people performing their function and kept in their place. She waved a hand, and the opaque walls became transparent. After her sojourn in the more bleak, traditional surroundings of the Loyal she was glad to be back in the sleek offices of her rightful place. She took a turn about the mezzanine and then stood to overlook the lobby. The COF squad had arrived as required. Shaw waited below at their head. With a smile on her face, but not in her eyes, Evening gestured to her. Shaw at once mobilised and waved the troop out and into position. The circle was closing in.

CLARA

I've heard it in the chillest land – And on the strangest Sea – Yet – never – in Extremity, it asked a crumb – of me.

"But whatever you ask of me, I give willingly," Clara now said to herself out loud. She had been reciting the verses of 'Hope' in her head. She had learned them so thoroughly from Susan that they had become her mantra as she carried out everyday tasks. Her present task, however, was a little more out of the ordinary. In the kitchen of the Emporium, she brewed some tea with a special added ingredient.

Earlier that evening, after exchanging messages with Jennifer, Clara had arrived at the Emporium. She had planned a reunion with Gunnar, after her time away with the Lunders. He was pleased to see her. His hands slithered down her bare arms as he said, "You grow more lovely every time I see you. Like a succulent wine."

She turned to him and laughed softly, "Wine? What's that?"

He took her hand, "Come," and he led the way up the wooden steps on one side of the kitchen. This took them to his bedroom, and they landed softly on his bed.

Clara took in the smells and sensations as she had sex with him. He was great at it, she thought, well-schooled and committed all the way as his lips worshipped each of her breasts and he expertly helped her to climax. Surrounding them on the low bed were the musty stacks of books and magazines. You thought this through, didn't you? She mused as he pulled off his clothes, his excitement mounting. You knew exactly how to draw me in with the promise of old knowledge in abundance. She rolled on her back, willingly, and allowed the spider to fuck her – one last time – in his web.

When Mina had come to her with the information on Gunnar, Clara had not known what to think at first. She felt sick and betrayed. Everything that had passed between them was a lie. This cut her as it sank in. He had been an agent and an instigator. He had enveloped them in a space where he acted as a buffer and a safety net, giving them reassurances and sanctuary, and all the while gathering information and luring them with falsehoods. She needed to recruit Philomel to help her and maintain a front.

As Gunnar lay, slightly buzzed, Clara followed her usual ritual. Wrapped in an antique silk kimono, she padded softly to the kitchen to make the tea. As the kettle boiled, she scooped some dark, smoky leaves into the pot before adding the water. She opened a little paper packet and sprinkled in some of Philomel's special dried mushroom powder. Clara, the robe loose and floating around her beautiful body, returned to Gunnar in bed, carrying the tea tray. Small ceramic cups clinked next to the green teapot. She placed it carefully down on the bed and Gunnar pulled her in for a long kiss. He offered her the joint and she took a draw.

"This is nice," she said. "It's one of the things I will miss. Excellent weed."

He poured some tea. She watched him.

"Miss it? Why? Where are you going? You've only just come back."

"Not far, not far. And not for long," she smiled at him. "I'm missing Susan ever since her arrest. She was such a great influence. I used to be so happy in her company." Tears welled in Clara's eyes.

"My darling – she *is* such a great influence," he insisted, and reached for her hand. "She will be back." And he swigged his tea.

Clara smiled, satisfied, and poured him another cup. She felt such a deep loathing for him at that point that she knew she would have no problem with what was to come.

"Hope," she said. "Hope – yes."

"We do have hope. And each other." He smiled his broad, wrinkly smile and she admired his lean body and large hands that cradled the little cup. He took another sip. "You seem sad tonight, my baby. It makes me sad to see you like this."

His fake accent, she pondered, I wonder what his real voice sounds like. Mina had told her everything. How much of an act he put on and sustained.

"Sad? I suppose so, a little," she took another draw on the joint. He had not noticed that she had not touched her tea. She stood up and moved gracefully around his bedroom.

"Hope," she recited, "is the thing with feathers – That perches in the soul – And sings the tune without the words – And never stops – at all …"

"How lovely," he spoke softly in reply. "You speak so delightfully."

She paused and turned to him. "Do you know that I found out about the mycelium web here, in your Emporium, among your magazines?" She moved back to the bed and topped up his tea.

"The what?" he looked curious.

"The mycelium web," she crossed her legs and settled in, warming to her subject. "It's a system that connects plants, trees, and fungi underground. I've seen it myself."

Gunnar listened quietly.

As she spoke, he began to develop a strange expression. She carried on and smiled and talked enthusiastically but always kept him under scrutiny.

"It's an incredible phenomenon, really it is. Chemical and organic. Trees can give each other warnings of harm."

"Uh," he tried to stand, but had to quickly sit down on the bed, doubled over. He had a confused look on his face.

He opened his mouth, to plead possibly, but no words came out.

"You're going to be OK," and she eased his head back onto the pillow and removed the tea tray. "I added some hallucinogens to the mix, so it might be quite a pleasant transition. The fungi I have discovered are so versatile, and my fascination with it started here, in your place, as I learned about the web."

"Uh," was all he could manage as a response, but he tried to lean forwards. With the gentlest of pressure, however, she pushed him back in his weakness.

"I made sure it's not going to be harsh or as painful as it *might* have been," she stroked his forehead. "I want you to relax. You'll sleep soon and then there will be some pain – just some – unavoidable before the end. No more than eight hours or so. It was the best that I could do for you, but it will be very, very bad. Agony, in fact."

He managed to swallow some breath and speak, "What? What are you talking about? I can't see you properly, your voice is strange. What did you do to me?"

Clara pulled on her clothes as he spoke. He tried to claw at her, but his efforts were futile as the toxins flooded his system. When she was dressed, she sat on the edge of the bed and spoke.

"I betrayed you, Gunnar. After everything we've been through and all we've shared – emotionally, sexually, spiritually – I betrayed you." She pulled a thin blanket over him. "You know those others that you've betrayed? The ones beaten, tortured, and raped?"

He breathed in a fast, stertorous fashion, beginning to panic.

"I'll tell them that you suffered for hours before you died."

Susan

Susan smiled slightly as the gentle hairdresser fluffed and fussed around her. The chair in the make-up room at the Sky-stream studios was comfortable, luxuriously so, so that she was loath to leave it. She was getting used to this sort of treatment and no longer cringed at seeing her features in the mirror. She had begun to fascinate herself. The young man with the clipboard and headset poked his head around the door.

"We're ready for you in five minutes."

Reality was slightly skewed for her since arriving at the Sky-stream HQ. She could even imagine, amongst the delicious beverages and sumptuous buffet servings, that she was a person of note, and this was somehow normal. A monitor mounted on the wall in the corner of the room showed the live Sky-stream broadcast. Susan watched as the camera cut from Evening – Patricia's – face, strained and concerned, to that of Susan's recent fellow inmate, Derrick Smallman. He, too, looked different from when they were in the holding cells in the undercroft together. His hair was cut and tidy now, not wiry and unkempt around his ears. His face, like hers, was fuller. Bald and fleshy, Derrick spoke quietly and clearly.

"There was a plan among the Cabinet members to compel change through starvation and forcing people into desperate measures."

Evening's voice was clear and bell-like as she questioned him. When the camera turned to her, she was dressed soberly and conservatively. Her hair was wrapped in a neat chignon and her nails were a dull colour to match her muted lipstick.

"And so, you're saying, that our government, who we have in place to protect us and uphold the law, was deliberately withholding rations from its own people, in order to exercise more controls?"

"Yes," Derrick's voice was firm and confident. "They were not acting in the best interests of the populace, far from it. The ministers, and especially the Premier, discussed the food crisis as a means to 'thin the herd'."

"And those were their very words?"

"Oh yes, the very words," Derrick Smallman had a dead sort of look in his eyes as he spoke with the ghost of a smirk around his mouth. "Let the bodies pile high."

Evening turned to look directly into the camera. "There you have it. Straight from the special advisor to the Premier. They want you – and your parents, and your old folk – to die."

A chime of background music, incongruous and foreboding, surged as she finished her link, "We'll be right back."

Susan looked down at her hands on her lap in the make-up chair. Her nails were grimy and stubby no longer. Groomed and neat, part of Evening's engineering for success, she pondered. In order to align herself with the Cabinet in the beginning, Evening had fostered propaganda and organised trust in the hierarchy so as to be indispensable to the government. Now, Susan realised, she had turned on her masters. It was really quite brilliant. She had coerced the originator, Smallman, back into her web, and got him in on the betrayal. Brava, Susan had to concede that.

Smallman would admit to anything now. Susan looked up at the screen again when she heard his complaining voice. His admissions, live on air (albeit with a thirty second delay just to be on the safe side) accused and implicated the Cabinet and the political class. Evening looked down the camera.

"Don't be afraid," she reassured the viewer. "We will look after you." She rose and the camera followed her as she walked across the studio to a large screen. Below the screen ran the legend, 'LIVE = raids carried out by COF squads'. "Your Civil Order Forces are out there, protecting *you* – the ordinary subject. As I speak, they are on their way to round up the enemies of the state – the enemies of *you*, the people."

Susan looked on, as Evening announced the tactics. This was it, she thought, ad hoc law. Open defiance. A coup d'etat. The camera cut to Derrick Smallman with captions running along the screen, 'The law of the land will be upheld. We will make society safe and bring back control'.

"We're ready for you now," the engineer looked around the door once again, "this way, Miss Jenkins."

Susan shuffled along the corridor to the studio floor of the Sky-stream. The music played them into another break as the lights came down. Derrick Smallman was led from the sofa and headed towards her. He paused in his slow, faltering walk, his gait still affected by months of atrophy in a cell.

"Hello," he greeted her. "We struggle on, comrade," and smiled at her.

Susan looked him up and down. He was neat, in an expensive tailored suit.

"Fuck you," and she carried on walking.

MINA

In Cece's flat, Mina chewed on her fingernails and the corner of her mouth. She was reminded of her mother's habit of chewing on her stained fingers and immediately stopped and spat out the cuticle skin shreds.

On the Sky-stream were shots of the Cabinet leaders and ministers of state. Their suits no longer neatly pressed. COF troops unloaded them from the vans where they had become dishevelled. Their faces were on show as they were jerked to their feet, the sound on mute. Some tried to appeal to the camera, but their protests were dumb. Instead, the ticker-tape feed scrolled across the screen cataloguing their crimes. Evening Primrose's commentary dominated every corner of the media.

"The grifts, the disasters, the corruption – we're putting an end to that for you. This group have caused you enough suffering. They are not your friends. They are not your protectors."

The stream intercut faces of the Cabinet members looking outraged and fearful with footage from food riots, floods in the Eastern wetlands, and the Moorland fires in the Northern Shires.

"We will right the wrongs. There will be a new beginning," Evening's voice sounded passionate, with a slight emotional crack behind it, over the images of suffering and destruction, and retribution against the authorities. Next, she appeared on screen. She was dressed in a bright but sober outfit. Spring-like colours and behind her a background of blossoms on softly waving branches. This was another evocation of nostalgia and times gone by. Springtime in England had long since departed this pastoral manifestation. She spoke warmly and confidently.

"We will lead you forward to a brighter future. Where there is destruction, we will re-build. Where there are wounds, we will heal. Where there is sickness, we will provide the cure. And when there is greater stability, when order is restored, I promise you, there will be free and fair elections."

The Sky-stream cut to a scene from a Suburban Hub. Workers on the back of trucks hurled packs to the waiting subjects. "We are, right now, distributing free rations." People scrambled for the hand-out. "The lean times will soon be over. We will revive your communities. Greater fellowship is on the horizon."

The stream cut back to the pack of government ministers now lined up in the courtyard of the Loyal Hospital. They blinked in the lights of the COF vans. A couple stood rigid and stoic, clearly determined not to be intimidated. They had that look of privilege that said 'All this nonsense will soon be sorted out. Do you realise who I am?' Another shouted and protested, his outrage palpable and becoming apoplectic. Most, however, remained confused and quiet, looking around fearfully. It looked to Mina as though the reality of the situation had not yet dawned on most of them. Soon, she thought, they will break you. She had been there. At the end of the line, one man, a high-ranking minister by the quality of his suit, perhaps even the Premier, it was hard to tell these days, wept quietly. A wet urine stain spread down his trouser leg.

"He gets it," she said drily.

Then, another cut to Evening Primrose's lovely face. Filters made her look achingly beautiful. She smiled beneficently. "We deserve peace, and freedom, and fellowship."

Music swelled in the background. Triumphant, glorious music. A choir began to sing, quietly at first, and then rising slowly.

> "Albion, sweet Albion,
> Your days of darkness now are gone.
> From every Shire and every Town
> We come together
> And Glory crown."

The lyrics scrolled across the screen and the music and voices reached a crescendo as images of the Capital and the countryside were displayed on screen.

> "Albion, dear Albion,
> The Greatness that was so hard won
> Has once again returned anew

To shining shores,
And hearts so true.

Now, England, our Dear Albion,
Shall smite her foes
And traitors doom."

At this point in the anthem, figures were seen, lined up in shadow. Mina recognised the exterior of the Sky-stream studios and Rothermere Square. Evening was lit in a moment, standing atop a platform near the gates. She was flushed with success. The platform was swathed in decoration – blood-red crosses on white background, with blue rosettes formed of eucalyptus leaves and wreathes of willow branches. She was bathed in a delicate shade of lilac light. A mic stood in front of her. Something was coming, Mina felt it in her gut. She held her breath. COF troops moved into position around the platform. The music played out and faded slowly. The camera cut between panoramic shots of the Square and dramatic low-angle shots of Evening. Silence reigned.

Cece murmured, "Lord, that woman is possessed." She moved closer to Mina and instinctively took the girl's hand.

"People of the Capital, and beloved Subjects of Albion," Evening's voice echoed out across Rothermere Square. A small crowd of the populace were shepherded into place around the platform, within a cordon of COF troops but not close enough to have any interaction with Evening on the platform. "Welcome, to the new order. To Progress and Prosperity."

Mina's spine tingled. She had a sense of something stirring – melancholy mingled with tension. She realised that the mounting excitement could lead to fear and dread – or exultation. Disturbing and unnatural. She was stewing in this and clasping Cece's hand, hard, as Evening carried on talking.

"Have you got enough? Have you even got sufficient? Or do you struggle every day to make it through? We understand, and we're going to do something about it. I've rounded up those who called themselves your leaders. They will be dealt with in due course. They will have their day in court." The assembled crowd let out a cheer. It had an echoey, eerie quality with something artificial about it. But, nonetheless, it was impactful.

"And, tonight," Evening's speech continued, "we will clean house." She looked directly into the camera as it swerved around to meet her, "And you will all bear witness to how dissidents are dealt with."

Mina and Cece held each other as a series of cuffed prisoners were led into the Square. The camera remained static as one by one they shuffled past. First, a bald man in a good suit, with little piggy eyes, and large ears. He was followed by a couple more people, eyes downcast and visible bruises. They, in turn, to the horror of the watchers on Cece's sofa, were followed by the frail form of Susan. In shock, Mina burst out, "Susan – no!" And as the figure of Jacinda came into view behind her, "Mum," she said quietly. Cece held onto her tightly.

CLARA

Clara moved as swiftly as she could. She stood on the tram, sweaty and agitated, all the way to Rothermere Square. The sultry summer night took hold. Everything, every part of her body, was in a state of tension. When the tram pulled in, she leapt out and onto the pavement as soon as the doors opened. Anger and outrage spurred her on. She kept going, pulse racing, and ran on to Rothermere Square. Cece had messaged her as soon as the broadcast dropped, and the pieces fell into place. Evening Primrose's plan was in motion, and amongst its primary victims were to be Mina's mother and alongside her, Susan.

The sweat poured off Clara as she sent a flock of birds scattering up to roost in a high, wide ash tree. Her breathing came heavy as she pounded the route across the Media Quarter. She rounded a corner, panting hard, and saw the beginnings of the ritual taking shape outside the Sky-stream HQ. Above, drones flitted and hovered above the small crowd and the ranks of troopers. The new structures erected around the Square included Evening's platform and, flanked by braziers that sent sparks whirling into the night sky, an execution scaffold. A gibbet stood with a row of six nooses looped up in preparation.

"No, no, no," Clara sobbed and ran towards the edge of the crowd. She battled her way through the gathered crowd as far forward as she could, as far forward as she dared. If she could not prevent what was to happen, at least she could bear witness. She stifled further sobs as she shielded herself in the crowd, out of sight of the troopers. A thrump-thrump-thrump of a military drum sounded as the prisoners were marched towards the scaffold. There was a pause as they were edged into place. Over loudspeakers dotted about the Square the charges and sentences were called out for each person in line. Behind the stentorian tones of the martial voice played the lilting melody of the New Albion anthem. Each charge and sentence were the same.

"Derrick Smallman – guilty of dissidence and treason – sentence – death. Jacinda Suresh – guilty of dissidence and treason – sentence – death. Susan Jenkins – guilty of dissidence and treason – sentence – death."

The condemned were to be dispatched in groups. The first were moved into position. This contained Derrick, the bald-headed man, and two others. They mounted the scaffold, and the troopers placed a noose around the neck of each one. They were left unhooded. Clara watched with dread. As a woman trained in anatomy and medicine, she knew what was coming and steeled herself for the violence of the end. With a sickening jerk the bodies dropped, and the moment before it happened, the bald man tried to shout something, but it was incoherent. The people around Clara gasped audibly. There was a snap, creaking, and the bodies swayed and struggled. One died immediately thanks to the snap. But that was as far as the mercy went. The bald man and the other choked slowly over the next several minutes.

The troopers gathered around grew more and more distressed. But had to look on, helpless. They had no means of dispatching them any quicker; the rope had to do its work.

One female trooper, clearly the Commander, hurried over to Evening who stood impassively fixed beside her mic. She covered it with one hand as the officer engaged in a quiet and urgent conversation. All the while, the two men jerked and strained at the end of the ropes. Red, white, and blue. Evening waved the officer away with an irritated expression.

The bodies were finally cut down.

The next group of prisoners were brought forward. This time, Susan and Jacinda were in their number. Paralysed with dread and grief, Clara could only look on.

Susan

Susan looked up at Evening as she walked below the platform, a camera in her face. The drones buzzed overhead, and the crowd filed into the Square in an obedient, controlled manner led by the troopers. Evening looked away and above their heads. Susan knew that Patricia could not look in her direction.

A missile hit Jacinda on the side of the face. Susan saw her cower. She looked around for the culprit. The crowd contained members who had been armed with small rocks and stinking vegetables. These, they hurled liberally into the faces of the prisoners, with added insults and spittle. Up ahead, Derrick Smallman swore and retaliated with his own profanities.

Once they had been made to run the gauntlet, rivulets of blood trickling from hairlines and down temples, the troopers brought them into line. They were arranged on show beside the scaffold. Jacinda tried to move behind Susan, breathing hard. Fear emanated from the innocent, harmless woman so that it was almost tangible. Susan turned slightly, and with her bound hands touched Jacinda's.

"What will they do to us?" she whispered to Susan, trembling violently.

Susan decided on reality. "This is the end." She took a deep breath. "It will all be over soon."

Derrick and his fellow prisoners were led to the scaffold. She heard Derrick jostle the trooper and try to shout something. He was clouted on the side of the head. This is Evening's show, she thought, no one can be allowed to upstage her. There will be no time for words and less time for farewells.

"Look at me," Susan turned to Jacinda, "keep your eyes on me." She summoned up a smile. And as the bodies of the men shuddered and twitched, she focused on the ashen, gaunt face of Mina's mother. I might be of some comfort to her, and she is certainly a comfort to me. She could see the daughter in the mother's eyes.

Susan, with a hard swallow, made her way up the stairs and looked directly at the noose. She turned to face the crowd, now silent and aghast after the first batch of bodies had been removed. It was just as the rope was put around her neck that she saw her. Clara was there in the crowd. Her beautiful, anguished face scorched with tears looked up at her. She had come at the end, to bid farewell. They locked their gaze and Susan, again, smiled. Jacinda sobbed to one side with long heaving breaths.

The troopers were preoccupied. This time, Susan realised, they would give them a hood. She had time. So, she spoke.

"Hope is the thing with feathers – that perches in the soul," she knew the cameras were on her and even muted, people would know that she spoke. And the troopers, and the crowd – and Clara especially. Dearest, loveliest, bravest Clara.

"And sings the tune without the words – And never stops at all," another voice joined in. It was Clara, "And sweetest – in the Gale – is heard – And sore must be the storm – That could abash the little Bird that kept so many warm."

Darkness. The hood was pulled over Susan's head, but she carried on. And this time, still more voices joined. The people in the crowd knew the words!

"I've heard it in the chillest land – And on the strangest Sea – Yet – never – in Extremity, It asked a crumb – of me."

Susan heard the gasp of horror and cries in the crowd at precisely the moment she heard the creak of the trapdoor as it opened beneath her feet.

JENNIFER

The disappearances had increased. People were scared. Every day more and more vanished and tension ramped up on the streets. The days of order and prosperity were, it seemed, a long way off. Jennifer's star, however, was on the rise. She hovered in a zone of relative safety. She had, after all, been on hand when Evening returned to the Sky-stream studios and been integral to the composition of the New Albion anthem, at very short notice. Eliot had gushed at how helpful and invaluable she had been, so as to cover how much he had foundered in her absence. Jennifer had smiled bleakly, because she knew what absolute nonsense it was, and felt that whatever befell her now, she would maintain a steady course. Everything was now focused on her end game.

Jennifer stood and watched the stream of new interns make their way up to the mezzanine. She ticked them off on her clipboard. Lambs to the slaughter. Making a pretence of doing her work, she was able to eye Evening in her office. Her boss paced up and down. Jennifer had inveigled her way back in because she was efficient and because she had proven to Evening that she could be devious but also keep her mouth shut. A killer combination. Evening valued deviousness. But Jennifer knew it was all easily destroyed. She was on borrowed time, so she had to work fast and be two, or three, steps ahead at all times.

Jennifer coasted along for the rest of the day and observed Evening in celebratory mood. She even allowed Eliot in on it. He had earned a reprieve from Evening. Of sorts. Or so Jennifer supposed. But her heart was still and cold. She looked on and awaited her opportunity.

Once the interns had completed their induction, framed by Evening's addresses to them about the 'Sky-stream Way,' Jennifer wrapped things up. The foyer was silent, and the long summer day still lit the Square and gleamed in through the glass walls and skylights. She stood for a little in the silence of the building. This really is a beautiful space, she thought, and what a creative sanctuary it could have been in different hands. She looked out to the Square. Rothermere Square, where less than two weeks ago the first of the executions had taken place. Among them, Susan. Jennifer chewed on her lip to stifle the sadness. Since then, each day, the triumphant sound of the New Albion anthem, followed by more death. She walked slowly upstairs to the kitchen in Evening's suite. The twins, Peach and Plum, were back in residence. To offer up, she supposed, that family atmosphere. She passed their playroom, which housed a lavish children's wonderland. Peach Primrose, the little girl, sat on the floor listlessly playing with a wooden truck. On a pile of cushions on the other side of the room, Evening's son, Plum, slept. His thumb firmly in his mouth. Their nanny stood against the wall, stuck to her device, scrolling, scrolling. Jennifer thought about Adie and Aidan, and the hooded corpse of their dead mother.

Jennifer entered the kitchen and took a platter of hors d'oeuvres out of the fridge. There was a pate with mushrooms on toast points, pickles and a tomato salad on bruschetta, and some mini salmon puffs with dill. She laid them on two plates and then casually removed the sachet of dried mushroom concentrate from her bag. She opened it gingerly and sprinkled it carefully onto the servings. Dried, flaked Inkcaps. She washed her hands thoroughly after handling.

"Here you are, Chef left these ready for you." Jennifer placed napkins and plates down on the glass-topped table of Evening's office. "Is there anything else I can do for you this evening? Evening?" she turned to her boss, and then to the other person sat across the room. "Doctor, anything you need?" she asked Helkiah Crooke.

The medic's crabbed hand took several of the hors d'oeuvres, like a claw in a fairground game. He snaffled them down. Jennifer hid her satisfaction at the sight of one of her enemies swallowing the toxic garnish. She glanced at Evening out of the corner of her eye. She was standing behind her desk and looked too busy to eat. Jennifer's mind raced at one hundred miles an hour. Would she even take a nibble of just one bite-size snack? Jennifer agonised internally. How could she interest Evening in eating without appearing too obvious? Her boss yawned and made her way around to the easy chairs. She took a seat opposite Helkiah with a sigh and turned to Jennifer.

"You can make me a drink. Doctor?"

"Oh, yes indeed," Helkiah replied between bites. "I would love a glass of one of your delicious Kentish vintages – perhaps a Churchills or a Howletts?"

The timing was all off. Jennifer had to have them both ingest the dried Inkcap and imbibe alcohol within half an hour in order for the toxins to take effect. It couldn't just be Helkiah that succumbed. She had to get them both. Jennifer moved in a deliberate fashion to pour the drinks. With each breath, she tried to find a delaying tactic – any delaying tactic. She searched for the glasses. A deep cut-glass tumbler for Evening's regular Scotch. A generous red-wine long-stemmed bowl for Helkiah's Kentish wine. She tapped her fingers on the door of the drinks cabinet as she searched out the bottles, uncorked the wine, and let it breathe. She watched Evening in the reflection of the glass door. She showed no sign of taking a single mouthful from the plate.

Jennifer lifted the lid off the ice bucket. She made a noise and started out of the office.

"Where are you going?"

"We're run out of ice. I'll just get some from the kitchen."

"Oh, don't worry – I'll take it neat," Evening waved a hand, then turned back to Helkiah.

"It's no trouble," and Jennifer was out of the door. She cast a quick backward glance and almost jumped for joy. Evening leaned forward and took something from the plate. Jennifer momentarily dawdled to ensure that the bite of foie gras was deposited in her carefully lipsticked mouth without a smudge. Evening frowned as she began to chew. Jennifer hurried with her errand.

When she returned with the ice, she poured the drinks with trembling hands but by the time she had turned to serve them she calmed. She put them on the table and paused.

"Oh dear," she spoke carefully, casually, "did you not like it?" and indicated the hors d'oeuvre spat out into a napkin.

"That?" Evening looked at it in disgust. "It was tainted." And she took a healthy swallow of whisky.

Was that enough? Jennifer's thoughts went into a tailspin. Had Evening had enough of the Inkcap? She examined what was left in the napkin under the pretext of removing it discretely and efficiently. The almost intact toast triangle with a blob of foie gras still in place. She thought she could detect some of the Inkcap sprinkles – soggy and soaked into the surface. Evening must have just held it in her mouth and then spat the whole thing out. At least, she took a look at Helkiah as he guzzled his wine, it would work with the Doctor.

Jennifer was about to pack up and leave when she turned back to Evening, a little hope in her voice, and asked, "Since that wasn't to your liking, can I get you anything else?" She felt the crushing disappointment and fear.

Evening replied with a throwaway, careless tone, "I'm not that hungry. And, anyway, I had a couple of those salmon things."

Jennifer's heart soared in triumph. She held in her reaction. She could hardly believe her luck. Or, perhaps, she had misheard? She looked down at the half-empty plate in front of Evening, with its sprinkle of crumbs. She watched as her boss polished off the Scotch.

That's it, she thought, I've done it.

She spoke quietly, "I'll be off for tonight, then?"

"Before you go."

"Yes?"

"I'll have another," Evening waggled her tumbler in Jennifer's direction and clinked the melting ice cube.

"Of course, Mizz Primrose."

CLARA

The purges were under way. Blood on the streets.

Once the body of Helkiah Crooke was discovered, poisoned, and lying in a cramped foetal position where he died mid-spasm, the COF troopers were everywhere and out for blood. Evening Primrose lay in the Intensive Care Unit of the Cheltsea Hospital. Tubes and wires kept her sustained, but the unspoken fact was that she was probably already gone. Clara thought how they were keeping her going as a kind of ghoulish propaganda. Every day there was an update. Would she recover? Would her signs improve? Clara and Cece knew that the indicators were not good. It was a body, with leads and connectors, monitors and drip-feeds, but no future. No life.

Once Jennifer had reported back to Clara, she was convinced that the whole 'keep Evening alive' project was fake. Just a charade. Evening could not have survived the toxins and must be brain-dead. Kept alive on a ventilator. Eliot Charming had already appeared on the Sky-screen with the air of a grieving widower. The COF Commander Shaw, Mandy Shaw, who was the overseer at the executions, appeared to have seized control with Eliot's support. There was an ad hoc structure of martial law in operation. Shaw singled out a couple of the former Cabinet ministers, granted them a reprieve and they had stepped in to manage things. Shaw was not a natural bureaucrat. Clara discovered that Shaw had a command out of an HQ at the

Loyal and the adjoining Barracks. The government, what there was of it, was now comprised of Capital officials, COF command, and some civilian ministers, backed by force and punishment.

Clara met with Charlie.

"They're waging a dirty war against their own people," was Charlie's opinion, and she could not disagree. With the power vacuum brought on by deaths among the elite there had come a new force. A new, deranged form of regime.

Clara checked over the van with Charlie. She wanted everything to be set up and prepped for the journey ahead. They had to travel further afield from the Capital. Things were breaking down, so escape was the only solution.

Jacinda – gone.

Susan – gone.

She had spoken to Mina. All the girl wanted was revenge and that was understandable.

If Hope was to survive then they all needed to move on.

Clara was with Charlie looking over all the kit and supplies they needed. She wanted everything ready for the journey ahead. The chaos in the Capital was too much now.

Water, bedding, rations, batteries.

Charlie helped her to gather everything.

She would leave, with Edgar and Grammere, Mina, Adie, and Aidan. Perhaps North to the Shires? But there were the fires. Maybe, they could travel to the West – the Duchy and the Principality? There was employment to be had on the Prince Swainsea Archipelago for fisherfolk and refinery workers.

In the narrow alleyway near the Square, they tied bundles of kit together. It would be a cramped arrangement, but Clara was confident that they could make it. They could find somewhere to lie low and avoid the tyranny of the Capital. They might be able to build a proper community.

"I came past Gunnar's old place," Charlie muttered. "It's all shut up. He's not been seen in a while."

"I know," she was subdued. She did not want to admit anything that might hurt the people she cherished. "But it's better not to ask too many questions," she replied quietly. "You know – people vanish, you shouldn't get involved." Clara forced the dreadful thoughts from her mind. Nothing had been done and no one had reacted in the weeks since Gunnar. She had enough to fill her days, now, and more than enough to deal with in preparation for the journey. Edgar and Cece rounded the corner into the alley, leading Adie and Aidan. Each boy carried a solo bag of belongings. Clara looked at the children, moved at the pathetic sight. She knew she had to make it work. This decision to travel onwards had to be the right one. People depended on her. Carry on and find a way. But, without Susan? She felt a lump in her throat and the tears rising. Hope, she said to herself, Hope is the thing with feathers that perches in the soul. A mantra to help her through.

"Grammere," she kissed Cece.

"This looks," Cece frowned, "small." She inspected the cab and the rear of the van.

"I know," Clara was apologetic, "but it's all we have."

Charlie looked at her and smiled ruefully, "Sorry, Duchess."

"Oh no," Cece's tender heart could not bear being misunderstood. "It's wonderful."

Charlie laughed, "Not a problem. We'll make it work."

Clara looked past her brother, "So, where is she?"

"She told me that we should meet her around the corner in the square at the Wilderness. Just by," he paused, "Susan's place."

"Why would we do that? What *is* she up to? Oh, never mind," Clara felt worn out. She could no longer second guess Mina. "When?" she asked Edgar.

"About an hour from now," he looked worried. "She said she'd be ready, and we just had to meet her."

Clara walked to the end of the alleyway. OK, she thought, but you need to *be* there, Mina. They had to evacuate. There was no future in the Capital. Move on, Mina, move on. In grief, in anger. But move on.

Clara had offered Jennifer the chance to leave, but she had refused. She told Clara that her future was in the Capital. The people she had grown up with and worked with – they were her world.

"I'll work out what's right for me. I have blood on my hands. I have to lie low and work out a future."

Clara had spoken to her at the Pivvy. They secured and protected the printing press.

"It has a future," Jennifer reassured her, "I'll protect it. And one day – you'll come back here and we'll re-open this and use it again, but for now get the young ones away."

Clara looked out into the road. Time was pressing. The light was fading, and the birds were drawn together in their flocks, humming and swarming back to their roosts. She mopped her brow with her sleeve and swore quietly.

"Come on. You need to get here, Mina."

Mina

Mina strapped her boots on and buckled up the stab vest she had from her imprisonment in the Loyal. She was about to embark on the sort of mission that typically Edgar would have joined. He would be willing to get roped in. He was her right hand, and non-judgmental. But, she had prepped everything she could, and from here on it was down to chance, and she had to do this alone.

The dawn had broken. Mina positioned herself at the gateway of the Loyal. She pulled the cord that sounded the bell.

COF troopers quickly appeared.

"I want to speak to Commander Shaw," she faced up to them, hoping that they did not detect her nervousness and body armour. She tried her best to look like a surly teen. Let them judge me, please, let them judge me.

The guard looked her up and down, and eventually, "This way," with a jerk of the head. They clanked the gateway open.

She was led along the tiled corridors and through more creaking security gates. Her escort showed her into the inner sanctum of the Commanders. The door behind her thudded shut. Mina walked forwards, cautiously, into the office with vaulted ceiling and flagged floors. There was a mess-room atmosphere around the Loyal now, according to what Mina could see. As she walked past open doorways, laughter was funnelled towards her, raucous and spiteful. Heat and vape smoke fogged the air. Sweat and boots. The orderly manicured world of Evening Primrose had savagely declined in a short span of time.

Feet up on the mahogany desk, Commander Shaw picked at her fingernails with the blade of a paring knife. She did not speak until Mina had gained some distance into the room. Shaw stood up, slowly, and walked around the desk. Mina could tell, from her gait, that the Commander was rather the worse for wear. This she knew from her mother's behaviour over the years. Mina had counted on the fact that Shaw and her troops would have discovered and helped themselves to the ample cellar at the Barracks.

"OK, girlie, what you got for me?" Shaw steadied herself against the desk. She was a heavy woman, uncomfortable in her surroundings. Burly and thuggish. There was a degree of grace to her form, however, a wrestler's strength and a ruddy complexion.

"Be my friend," she pointed a stubby finger at Mina, "and I'll be yours."

"I can show you where they are, where they're hiding out."

Shaw made a whistling noise as she breathed in and out of her nose. She looked at Mina with folded arms and a sideways, matey kind of a smile. She patted Mina on the shoulder and appraised her physically.

"You know what? Have you ever thought about joining us here, at the COF? I think you've got what it takes. You're scrappy, sure of yourself, and strong. We could use a recruit like you."

Mina stiffened, unconsciously, as though standing to attention with a proud tilt of her head.

"Thank you, Ma'am. I'd like that."

"Good, good. I see a bright future for you."

Mina realised that Shaw either did not recognise her from when she was locked up there, or only loosely connected her with past events. So, she was not dealing with a bright spark here, and anyway she was used to white people who were unable to distinguish her brown face from any other.

"So, kid, what you got for me?" Shaw poured some more liquor.

"You'll need to bring enough people. A large squad. They aren't armed, but there's lots of them."

"I see. Artsy-fartsy types who don't believe in a hard day's work or a fair fight? I get you."

"Yeah, that's right."

"I see it. We'll bring some weapons, show of strength and all that, but we're not in any danger from them!" She snorted with laughter and pressed a button on the intercom.

"Tell the squad to suit up. And … Collins' team can also get their gear on – lightweight all-round."

Twenty minutes later, after the scramble, Mina stood alongside Commander Shaw in the Loyal Courtyard. The Commander treated her as though she was already a member of the brigade. She was kitted out in some COF issue gear that was slightly too large.

"Mina here," she addressed the assembled troops, "has intel for us on the whereabouts of the Ghostwriters. The murderers of our leaders and comrades. She's going to lead us to their base, and we can make more arrests and wipe them out once and for all. The murders of the brave Commander Gunnar Hanson, who risked his life for us deep undercover, and Dr Crooke, and the poisoning of our leader – Mizz Primrose – will now be avenged. They want to attack us with these filthy tactics? Well, we'll take the fight to them."

The troop cheered.

"Mina's gonna be up front with me in the lead van. Collins will follow and be point man in the second crew. Let's move out!"

Mina could not help but enjoy that ride across the Capital. She was excited and impressed by the skill it took to navigate the streets at the wheel of the van and how people leaped out of the way to avoid getting clipped or mown down. There was a part of her character that was tempted by the trooper's life. She watched how it was done.

They pulled into the Square, and the squads piled out of their transport to congregate along the edge of the Wilderness. Mina maintained a business-like expression and kept her face serious. She knew how close the COF squads were to the Pivvy. Just a short ramble into the Wilderness. If they decided to explore, they would discover everything. She could picture where sat the printing press, the boxes of type, the reams and rolls of yellowing paper. Probably all covered in bird guano and lizard shit by now, she thought and sighed internally. But still, geno-trackers would quickly establish the identity of *all* the Ghostwriters. Dare me, Shaw, dare me, and I'll show you something that will truly shock you.

"This way," Mina took off.

"Stay on her," Shaw directed the troops, "let's move out."

Down a side road, away from the Wilderness, she led them. Mina moved fast and skilfully. This forced the squad to keep up with her at least with a jog-trot. She knew this would be too much for most of the vapers and the drinkers very quickly, even with light armour and non-lethal weapons. She wanted them tired and at a disadvantage. However, to her dismay, Shaw could keep up with her. The woman was like a bristly terrier at her heels. She might huff and puff and turn bright red, but she seemed unstoppable.

'Rats,' thought Mina. But they were almost there. The entrance to Russell Square station.

Shaw paused, "OK, let's check on our kit here."

Mina peered into the ticket hall through the dark entrance. There had been more fires lit there since last her last visit.

"In here," she beckoned to Shaw and Collins. Her boots crunched on the brittle vegetation and burnt debris. She threaded her way carefully. The COF troopers behind her were less careful. They thudded and slid about clumsily, most of them talking and swearing loudly as they went.

"What the fuck is this dump?"

"Fuck me – it stinks. It smells like all the fucking pikeys in the Capital just took a massive shit in here!"

Their hostility and disgust played out blatantly behind Mina.

"Come on, this way!" she spoke with enthusiasm, excited by her mission.

"Belt up," Shaw reprimanded her team loudly, "and follow the kid."

Mina felt jubilant. Not only were they following her without question, but they were doing so in the noisiest way possible. Noise was needed. Keep going, she plotted quietly, keep going. She ran a personal risk, of course, but it was worth it, and she knew what to expect. She had her cunning. Mina was willing to take that risk, after what she had seen played out on the Sky-screen. Witnessing the executions of her mother and Susan had caused something to break inside.

As she neared the lift shafts and the stairs, she made more noise. Her coughs echoed down into the depths of the underground and she tapped the walls. She tried as many casual noisy acts as possible to create a lure.

"This is it," she called to troopers, "down here. You'll find them down here." She pointed to the dark stairwell. "This is where they hide out and there's no exit – you'll have them trapped."

"Come on," Shaw moved the troopers into position. They shambled and shuffled into the confined space. "Let's prep." She turned to Mina, "Lead the way, ready when you are," and she flicked open her telescopic baton with a flourish, "I'm right behind you."

Mina's mind plummeted down the stairs for a moment. She had to reach for an excuse.

"I'm not a trooper – yet!" she laughed and stepped towards Shaw in a confidential fashion. "This is *your* moment," she gestured to the rest of the troop, "you don't want any of them to undermine you and say stuff like you had a kid take over. I've come as far as I can. The glory has to be yours."

Shaw looked down at Mina, with emotion, and then lunged towards her with a hearty hug, slapping her on the back. The Commander was still a little bit drunk. The air was knocked out of Mina's lungs. "You're a diamond, kid. I'll never forget what you've done for me."

"Thank you," Mina coughed. She stood to attention with a smart salute. "And I look forward to serving under you in the future, ma'am."

Shaw returned the salute, "I'll see to it, Suresh, I'll see to it." She turned to the squad with a gesture to wave them on to the stairs, "Let's move out. Double time." She smiled at Mina as the line of COF troopers headed down the stairs.

Mina ducked out of the way and stepped back as she watched one after another disappear down the stairs, into the darkness of Russell Square. She felt a miniscule twinge of guilt. It was death for them – for sure. She had, however, taken up her position in the whole scheme of things. An avenging angel. She continued to back away, discretely, towards the lift shafts. She turned and listened hard. There it was, small but distinct, the scuttling, scratching noise of the Russellers.

Her job was done.

Enough noise to lure them out.

The troopers continued to file down to the deepest part of the Underground. You'll meet the monsters now, she thought, and you have no idea how terrifying they are. You wanted to find an enemy, and you created one. But she was just an old woman with a pet cat and wrote down poems and slogans, you pieces of shit. You wanted an enemy, and you created one. But she had a dead husband and hungry children and out-of-date ration vouchers. So, to help you out, I've found you a real enemy. But you'll be sorry I did. The Russellers can't be controlled, and they will shred you.

Mina shuddered at the thought, but she had to steel herself and get away. They were on the move. Shaw gave her a final wave and a wink as she entered the stairwell.

Off you go, Mina smiled.

As soon as the last troopers had vanished, she was off. She scampered for the entrance and back into the Square and the light and air as fast as she could. There would be carnage. Lightly armoured troopers did not stand a chance. She moved swiftly with visions of Russellers snapping at her heels. When she reached the entrance to the station she paused and listened, but no sound could be heard from within, from down there. There would be a log jam and a crush of bodies on the stairs. Down, down – one hundred, two hundred – and they would get you. She turned to leave.

Outside in the clear air she waited cautiously, watching and listening, before she started her run back to the Wilderness. She had things to do and places to be, and she left the Russellers to do their work.

CLARA

It was not as if she did not expect something dramatic, but this time Mina certainly did manage to surprise her.

A black COF van hove into view.

"What's going on?" Clara called out to Edgar and Charlie and backed into the alley.

The black van jumped, shuddered, and jerked to a halt. Whoever was driving this was not a trooper or was very new to it. She watched warily from down the alley as the door opened. Mina clambered down to the road. She was a little wobbly and held Ellery under her arm.

"Come on," she beckoned to them, "we can use this to get out of here!"

"What the hell?" was all Clara could manage. She gaped at her young friend, shod in boots and wearing a stab vest, looking for all the world like a mini COF trooper.

Mina marched towards her, "We can load up people and supplies in this – *and* no one's gonna try and stop us leaving the Capital."

So, with two modes of transport, the battery-powered van driven by Cece and Charlie, who now agreed to flee with them, behind the wheel of the bio-fuel trooper van, their little convoy could leave the city. Adie and Aidan sat in the spacious rear of the COF van with Mina and the scraggy, annoyed, rather recalcitrant Ellery. Mina had stopped by Susan's basement. The idea of this caused Clara to feel a stab of grief and her tears flowed as she listened to the tale on their journey Northwards. Ellery had remained close to home in the weeks that Susan was gone. Mina had discovered him curled up on the crocheted bedspread – she brought that too to keep him happy. He had evidently been coming and going through a broken windowpane and lived off birds and lizards, according to the evidence of tiny remains and debris scattered about.

Mina had also carried out another salvage task which made Clara's emotions spike again, and her heart soar. In the back of the van, the forbidding, blacked out van, were most of Susan's books. Granted, Mina had stowed them unceremoniously by grabbing them in piles as she made a break for it, but they were there. Intact. Precious.

CLARA

Clara looped back her grey locks and tied them in a head-wrap. Her slim, careful hands were a little wrinkled and she moved a little slower these days. Her fine, arched brows framed her eyes with their long lashes. None of her beauty had diminished with age, however. She pulled Susan's crochet blanket around her shoulders a little tighter. Over the years spent up in the Northern Shires, she had grown more accustomed to the slightly lower temperatures. Instead of the sweltering, year-round conditions it was mostly balmy. The unexpected, unpredictable storms still battered their homestead at intervals, but at least they did not have to put up with the lies about the weather over the Sky-stream. Here, they were out of range of the broadcasts and had not heard the high-level propaganda in years. News filtered out of the Capital, inevitably, but the air was free of a lot of things, especially now the Moorland fires had burned out.

Clara was still a lover of open windows and outdoor adventures. There were many fine Wildernesses in their locality where she could get lost as she searched for supplies and medicinal ingredients. Their sheltered homestead comprised of an old set of farm buildings ringed with a drystone wall and ancient trees bent double by the winds that used to blow at this altitude, but now the air was mostly still and warm, they were wizened relics of an older climate.

Charlie, Aidan and Adie, Edgar, Mina, Grammere, and Ellery had fled that night and driven as long and as far as the little van lasted. After that they towed it behind the COF van on the quiet roads, the cracked and broken highways of England. Smoke and lights in the distance suggested communities from time to time, but they did not stop until evidence of any dense populations was left behind. Years ago, they had passed the sign that stated in grimy and worn lettering that they had entered 'Yorkshire'. The limit of the Northern Shires, from what Clara knew, before the Borderlands. Far enough.

Far enough away from their history in the Capital. Here, the reach of the Cabinet regime was weak. Charlie and she made a life there. He had always loved her, he said, and so they decided to settle together in the farmhouse. Cece had approved, warmly. Gunnar had been reduced to a bad memory. Now, Grammere was buried out on the hillside where she had loved to roam. Clara was grateful that her grandmother's strength and wisdom all her life had been rewarded with a quiet, peaceful final phase. Their family was not characterised only by loss, however. Mina and Edgar's daughter, little Susie, played outside with her uncle Aidan. A gentle boy had become a gentle man and thrived in the peace and quiet. Adie, restless and more adventurous, like his sister, had recently headed North to the Borderlands to make contact with other communities. They had known for some time, thanks to their radio, that others had survived the Capital purges, had taken to the road and found a sanctuary in the Regions. Now and then, messages reached them from Jennifer. The former Sky-stream assistant was a pamphleteer and constantly on the move for her safety, but canny and determined, and writing, always writing.

Clara stroked the aged Ellery who was curled up on a cushion beside her. He was her limpet still as he had been ever since the escape from the Capital that night, long ago. He was probably a teenager in cat years at the time, so he must be the oldest surviving feline ever known by now. Still, he kept her company as she worked. She noted everything down as often as possible. People needed to know. In fine script, she told the story of the Ghostwriters. Whether anyone would ever read it, she did not know. Whether anyone would share it, she did not know. But still she wrote and hoped for the future.

Acknowledgements

Many thanks to Paul March-Russell, Una McCormack, Susan Kelly, Ellen Parnavelas and all the team at Gold SF; Kate Mattacks, Kristin Arnorsdottir-Edwards, Yvonne Grace for their support, and to Antony and Alexander Malcolm for story ideas.